The GameKeepers

Also by J.B. Manheim:

FICTION

The Deadball Files

Book 1: This Never Happened:
The Mystery Behind the Death of Christy Mathewson

Book 3: Doubleday Doubletake:
One Ball, Three Strikes, One Man Out

Book 4: The Federal Case

SELECTED NONFICTION

Strategy in Information and Influence Campaigns:
How Policy Advocates, Social Movements, Insurgent Groups,
Corporations, Governments and Others Get What They Want

Strategic Public Diplomacy and American Foreign Policy

All of the People, All the Time:
Strategic Communication and American Politics

The
GameKeepers

Whitewash, Blackmail, and Baseball's Darkest Secrets

BOOK TWO of The Deadball Files

a novel by
J. B. Manheim

MILFORD
HOUSE
an imprint of Sunbury Press, Inc.
Mechanicsburg, PA USA

MILFORD HOUSE

an imprint of Sunbury Press, Inc.
Mechanicsburg, PA USA

For information about special discounts for bulk purchases, please contact Sunbury Press Orders Dept. at (855) 338-8359 or orders@sunburypress.com.

To request one of our authors for speaking engagements or book signings, please contact Sunbury Press Publicity Dept. at publicity@sunburypress.com.

FIRST MILFORD HOUSE PRESS EDITION: July 2023

Set in Adobe Garamond Pro | Interior design by Crystal Devine | Cover by Lawrence Knorr | Edited by Sarah Peachey.

Publisher's Cataloging-in-Publication Data
Names: Manheim, J.B., author.
Title: The gamekeepers : whitewash, blackmail, and baseball's darkest secrets / J.B. Manheim.
Description: First trade paperback edition. | Mechanicsburg, PA : Milford House Press, 2023.
Summary: A National Pastime subject to recurring scandals and embarrassments. A secret society of Baseball elders dedicated to protecting the Game. A secret repository. Failsafe security. It worked perfectly for nearly a century. But then . . . Enter Liz Fairchild and baseball sleuth Adam Wallace, with the fate of the game in their hands.
Identifiers: ISBN : 979-8-88819-116-3 (paperback) | ISBN : 979-8-88819-117-0 (ePub).
Subjects: FICTION / Sports | FICTION / Mystery & Detective / Historical | SPORTS & RECREATION / Baseball / History.

Product of the United States of America
0 1 1 2 3 5 8 13 21 34 55

For the Love of Books!

For Harv, Marv, and Papa Doc
Who taught me to love The Game
And Norma, Ellen, and Edythe B.
For tolerating the same

The Lineup Card

The Box Score

Author's Note

The GameKeepers is the second volume in The Deadball Files. The book includes some of the characters from and extends the story developed in the first book in this collection, *This Never Happened: The Mystery Behind the Death of Christy Mathewson.*

Some readers may be tempted to view this book as a puzzle to be solved, one built on the shadows of real people and deeds. To the author, those shadows, if they exist at all, lie in a different, parallel universe, where their comings and goings may seem familiar but where they are unconstrained by anything we might regard as reality. Thus, any similarity between the characters or actions portrayed in this book and any presumed "real-world" counterparts is imagined. It matters not by whom. This is a work of fiction, and, with the exception of documented or widely known statements or events, the resemblance of any characters or actions represented here to any person, living or dead, or to any seemingly similar occurrences, is strictly coincidental. Any actions attributed or motives ascribed to Major League Baseball, its officials, owners, clubs, or players, including any dialogue, that are not publicly known or documented, are entirely fictitious. There is a line somewhere with fact on one side and fiction on the other. When in doubt, jump to the left. Whichever that is.

Warmup Pitches

When General John J. Pershing, widely known as "Blackjack," arrived in France in June 1917 to lead the American Expeditionary Force, the point of the sword for the country's entry into the Great War, among his immediate needs was that for actionable intelligence. Effective command and control of a force that would eventually number more than a million men required near real-time knowledge of conditions in the field to a depth of several miles behind enemy lines, as well as information on the intelligence capabilities and activities of the other side.

Once the United States' engagement in the war in Europe began in earnest, the intelligence problem was addressed systematically at two levels. In Washington, Colonel Ralph Van Deman lobbied the Secretary of War, Newton Baker, to establish a Military Intelligence Section in the department under his leadership, which he did in May 1917. Military intelligence evolved over a short time into a function of the General Staff, operating such programs as the collection of foreign intelligence, code-breaking, and rooting out subversion in the Army. None of those capabilities, however, was positioned to provide field-level intelligence when Pershing landed in France. For that, the general had to create his own operation on the fly.

He assigned that task to Colonel Dennis Nolan, who, after studying the British and French approaches to the challenge, crafted a two-tiered system that came to be known as G2/S2. S2 referred to operations at ground level, where battalions and regiments were responsible for gathering information along the front lines. Scouts or other observers were embedded with patrols as they advanced against the enemy, gathering information about the terrain and the opposing forces as they went and sending that up the intelligence chain of command. G2, which never comprised more than a few hundred officers and men, was organized in progressively broader stages to receive, process, and interpret this flow of data. The skills at both levels improved over time, as did the flow of information to and through the resulting system. By mid-October 1918, a month before the Armistice, the combined G2/S2 capability allowed the Army to build an accurate picture of the disposition of the German forces, the locations of observation posts, and the strongest points of resistance.

At war's end, the veterans of this service returned to civilian life—some of them to professional baseball—bringing with them the experience, skills, and perspectives of their intelligence work.

"We did not choose to be the guardians of the gate, but there is no one else."

—Lyndon Johnson
Press Conference, July 28, 1965

Batter Up!

Max Tomhoff looked out over the room with a wary eye. All of his years as the Marbury House Auction Master had hardly prepared him for this. There was a buzz in the room, but not the normal buzz. There was a crowd in the room, but not the kind of crowd he was accustomed to facing. The focus was again sports memorabilia—*baseball* memorabilia—but there were no rowdies in the room this time, nor even anyone speaking too loudly. Their places were taken by important people, familiar people, people at once known and unknowable. The men in the room were all dressed in suits and ties, the women in comparable business attire. Only the television crews around the perimeter were the exception. They were dressed as one might expect, in jeans and branded or captioned T-shirts, many with their heads topped by logoed baseball caps proclaiming their identities, their loyalties, wearing their disrespect as a badge of honor, trolls merging into the black forest of cameras. If anything, the tension in the room seemed wound more tightly than the last time he had dealt with such materials. Everything seemed more reserved, more serious this time.

The room was different now as well, different from the one he remembered from three years ago. It was older by far and more ornate, yet more closely focused, more attuned to its purpose. Three years ago, the last-minute challenge had been to have everything in place for the sale. But the furnishings in the room today were fixed; there was no scramble to arrange chairs for the attendees or to organize the front of the room. The lighting and sound equipment had long been deployed, seats reserved and labeled where necessary, security precautions set in place. The degree of preparation reflected the workings of an experienced staff. They had done this before.

Once again, it had been quite a week—quite a month, really—as he and his colleague Frederick Marchant, the House's Director of Acquisitions, had completed their research and other preparations. Things would be different this time, of course, with altogether different procedures because of the circumstances. Not by any means your traditional auction setting. The objects of all of this attention would not be on display today, at least not in the customary way. No lighted mahogany cabinets, no special mounts, no acid-free fabric liners. But there would be many questions raised about them, and to answer those, Max and Frederick needed to fill their memory banks with everything they could learn about the items in question. This was not a day to look foolish or uninformed.

Frederick was quite nervous. He was a smart fellow and very good at his job, but he was, in the end, a typical back-office man unaccustomed to occupying the forefront of a public event. In fact, Max could not remember a single time in all the years they had worked together when Frederick had so much as ventured into the room during an auction, even to stand anonymously off to one side as the action commenced. It was one thing to sweet talk a seller in the confines of one's office, and quite another, he supposed, to face that seller if perchance reality did not come up to the expectations he had sold. Frederick simply did not have the temperament for it.

Max was different. Max lived for the spotlight, for the full attention of the crowd. He thrived on the pulse of energy that went through a room as he took his place. As an auctioneer, he was a natural, an artist, the orchestrator of a performance. He owned his time at the podium. He reveled in it. That, he had always thought, was Max Time.

And now, here he was. In *this* room. In *this* moment. Before *this* audience. The lights came on. The microphones went hot. The audience hushed. The LEDs on the cameras glowed red.

Once again it was Max Time, though today he, too, faced it with some trepidation. Today, the gavel was in another's hand.

"The committee will come to order. The witnesses will be sworn."

There are women in this world, adventurous women, amorous women, who are attracted to public men. Is it the closeness to power they seek? To the glamour? To the lights and the attention? Are they living vicariously by acting out sexual fantasies? Is it about imagined love, about lust, or about mere bragging rights? Even sociologists and psychologists offer no single explanation, no definitive reason. But these women do exist. Politicians have their acolytes. Rock stars have their groupies. Professional baseball players have their Annies. And successful book authors have their . . . what, their bookies? Probably not. But whatever the term, these thoughts raced through his mind as Adam Wallace could not help but notice the woman who kept eyeing him from the far corner of the room where he sat autographing copies of his latest book, *The Contemporaneous Journal of Jocko Drumm*.

Adam, in his fifties and showing it, though surely no mirror-breaker, did not think of himself as an alpha male who would attract such attention. He had heard stories of such women from some of his younger writer friends, but he had discounted those as hollow boasts or, if true, as mere reflections of changing generational norms. Sexual mores had evolved greatly since what he thought of as his prime years.

Born in DeKalb Falls in far Upstate New York, Adam had been a good student in a not-so-good school, always successful but, though he didn't realize it at the time, never challenged. It wasn't until his first year at the university—itself an institution of modest reputation and capabilities—that he came to appreciate just how underprepared for life he was. That realization, in turn, led him to two decisions. First, he would meet the academic challenge before him through hard work, hard work, and more hard work. Second, he would never go home again—at least not to stay.

The first decision was made easier in his second semester when Adam enrolled in a required course in the English Department, Creative Writing. He found that he really enjoyed even the most rudimentary of exercises in the class, and toward the middle of the semester, the professor, an older woman who was probably nearing retirement, began to make encouraging comments on his work. A friend had once told Adam that the key to a successful life was to find something you really enjoyed doing, something you didn't think of as work, then con somebody into paying you to do that thing as a career. It was from that supposed insight and these transitory moments of praise that writing became his life. *Ah*, he would say of that characterization if he stumbled into a reflective mood today, *the naivete of youth. Nothing is that easy.* But from the vantage point of a college freshman, all things were possible. He had found his path.

Once he overcame the guilt that naturally followed from it, the second decision was easy as well. He kept his intentions to himself for years, until graduation neared, but by the time he had worked up his courage to tell his parents of his plan to leave, he found, to *his* surprise, that they were not in the least surprised. His mother told him he'd been telegraphing his intentions for years. After college he went back to The Falls, as the town was known to the locals, collected some of his things, and struck out for New York City, determined to become a writer.

Two years in a roach-infested basement apartment and a variety of dead-end, low-skill jobs gave him what he kept telling himself was the "life experience" writers supposedly need if they were to thrive in their craft. But his days as a famous novelist never quite came around. False start followed false start, one a failure of imagination, the next a failure of concentration. The excuses piled up like so many crumpled pages until, at last, he began to feel their weight. Like the multitude of would-be Hemingways or Clancys before him, he was just about to give up hope when he landed a job as a night copy editor at a failing industrial magazine. In the barrel of literary employments, that was about as close to the bottom as one could get. At the same time, though, it was as close to the top of that particular barrel as Adam had ever been. At last, he could convert his love of words and phrases into cash. Unfortunately, they were someone else's words and phrases. He was, he knew, little more than a glorified grammar cop.

That is when his life took its real turn for the better. Precisely because the publication was on its last legs, its writers began to depart for better opportunities. Though it would not have been fair or accurate to describe any one of them as gifted, most could be described as sufficiently capable of finding more stable and promising employment elsewhere within their profession. So they did. In their absence, the magazine was still in business, still on at least a few newsstands and C-suite coffee tables. It simply wouldn't do to send out nothing but white space and advertising. The editor, desperate to fill his pages, scoured the remaining staff for talent, and that led him to read once again Adam's exceptionally brief resume.

"Hey, kid. You studied writing in college. Is that right?" he said one evening as he was leaving work and encountered Adam just coming in.

"Yes, sir. I did that."

"English major, eh?" replied the editor, greatly appreciating a private joke of some sort. "Were you any good?"

"Well, I thought so," came the modest reply. "Of course, it was a small school."

"So you're doing what, copy editing for us?"

"Yes, sir."

"At least you're not driving a cab. That shows some kind of dedication, I guess . . . How'd you like to work days for a change?"

"That'd be great, if it happened. Honestly, it's hard being single in the City when you're working the midnight shift. But I thought all the copy editing here was done at night."

"It is. I'm talking about a different job. We have a couple of new openings for feature writers. You want to try your luck at that?"

Needless to say, Adam had jumped at the chance. It wasn't the great American novel he'd be writing—just some puff pieces on people, deals, and new technologies in a dying corner of the American industrial complex. But it was a real writing job, one that came with real publication credits, albeit modest ones, growing visibility, and, as it happened, other opportunities as editors elsewhere began to recognize his abilities. Soon enough, the magazine failed. But by then, Adam had established the basis for his future career success.

All of that, of course, was now fading toward the vanishing point in the rearview mirror of history, along with typewriters, pay phones, thirteen-channel TVs, the leftovers of big American cars with fins, and all the other keystones of his vaguely remembered earlier years. It wasn't, he thought dryly, only sexual mores that had evolved so greatly since he had passed what he considered his prime.

Yet each time he glanced up from his task, there she remained, not exactly staring, but watching all the same. Longish sandy brown hair, nice face, librarian's glasses, a little taller than average. Maybe mid-thirties, he guessed. It was hard to be sure just from the few glances he stole. Wouldn't do to risk locking eyes. He could see she clutched a copy of his book, yet she never joined the line of those seeking his autograph. *Clearly*, he thought, *I have misread the situation. I have believed all that bullshit I've heard more than I was willing to admit. Just maybe this is my own fantasy, my own overactive imagination at work, probably because this book fair is being held not at a bookstore but in a hotel meeting room. Next thing you know, she'll sidle over and slip me her room key. Come on, Adam, get your head together! There are just some shy people in this world, and if one of them wants to buy your book and keep to herself, who are you to complain?* Satisfied with this explanation, he returned his full focus to the task at hand.

That working hypothesis lasted for about twenty minutes. After the line of signature seekers wound down, Adam slipped off to the hotel bar for a beer before heading home. He settled onto a stool and reached to his left for the pretzels. When he turned back, he was surprised to see that the stool just to his right was now occupied by She Who Is Too Shy, whom he had clearly misjudged yet again.

"Mr. Wallace, would you mind if I join you for a few moments?"

"Uh, sure. Okay." Just then, Adam's beer arrived. "Beer?" he asked.

"Love one. Thank you." Then she began, "Mr. Wallace—"

"Adam. Just call me Adam."

"Adam. I'm Liz. Liz Fairchild. I'd really like to ask you some things about your book. I've read it through twice now, and my head is full of questions."

"Okay."

"For starters, how much of this really happened? You wrote it as fiction. That's clear. But I can't help but feel that there is more to it than that, and I am having a hard time finding the line between fact and fiction.

For example, all those letters and papers and notebooks and things. Was all that real, or did you make it up? I know JT Willett wasn't a real person—I checked. But was that just an alias you created to cover up a real sportswriter? And the journal pages. Was there really a guy named Jocko Drumm who wrote them? You see what I'm trying to get at, right?"

"You told me your name. Liz. But you didn't tell me anything about yourself. Are you a reporter of some kind? A reviewer or a lit critic?"

"No."

"Lawyer of some sort, or working for a lawyer? Maybe an investigator?"

"No. None of those, and nothing else you might think of as nefarious. I have a special interest in all of this, but it's not one you could guess or one you should worry about. Honestly, I'm not quite ready to share that with you just yet, and I can't promise at this moment that I ever will be. First, I need to know that I can trust you. Then I might tell you something you'll find really, really interesting.

"So, let's just start with the suitcase full of papers. The pay roster and logbook from that Army unit with all of those baseball players who later were inducted into the Hall of Fame, the letters from Ty Cobb and Jane Mathewson and Branch Rickey, the claims by those old veterans that something untoward happened that involved Cobb and Mathewson. Was that real? I mean, you obviously don't have any of those papers. Did you make all of that up? Or do they really exist?"

Adam began to answer, then stopped. Who was this woman and what was she after? Then he heard himself speak. "Look. I don't have the papers. I cannot prove to you that they exist. What I can tell you straight out is that they do exist, or did as of a couple of years ago. I saw them with my own eyes, and I read them. Every word. You probably saw the write-up from the auction, and maybe even the catalog listing from that auction house, what was it . . . Marbury House, here in the City. Neither one did justice to the actual contents of those papers. They were very detailed and, to me, at least, very convincing. And they actually were stolen by some people who were then able to convince the auction place that they had the right to sell them. I'm not sure how good the due diligence at Marbury House was, but knowing what I know, I can understand how they came to that conclusion."

"And you and your friend Jason, if that's his real name, actually tried to get the Hall of Fame to chase down the sellers and sue the auction house for the proceeds?"

"Well, I won't comment on whether Jason Drumm is a real person or a *nom de guerre*. But yes. We became convinced that the Hall of Fame was the rightful owner of the papers. And I wouldn't say that we tried to get them to chase down anybody—that got a little complicated—or even to sue Marbury House. That would not have been our call. But Jason really wanted them to know the facts, or as many of them as we had. And if you read the book, you will know that Jason"—he said the name with air quotes—"felt more than a little guilty about some related things, like his whole life on that farm, and you'll know why. He really wanted to offer to help them if they wanted him to."

"Which," she said, "gets us to the journal. In your book, you said that Jason, or whoever he was, signed the ownership of the journal over to the Hall of Fame. And he gave them the actual journal as well. But in your book, you reproduced what you said were the actual pages of the journal. Heck, you named your book after that journal. Was that real? If you didn't have the journal, how could you do that?"

"Now we get to why I asked you if you were a reporter or a lawyer. Want to change your answer before I go on?"

"No. Same answer. Please continue."

"Okay. It's true that the Hall has the actual, physical journal, at least as far as I know. That's the last place I saw it. And it's true that Jason signed over his rights to them. But if you remember from my book, before he did that, I had made a copy of the journal and given it to my Columbia professor friend for translation. When the professor sent me her report to pass along to Jason, she also returned the copy of the journal. I used that copy, already in my possession, to write my book."

"But in your book, you said that you and 'Jason'"—she added air quotes this time—"confirmed that there were no other copies of anything, so far as you knew, and that aside from the auction display, nobody had seen the papers. Was that a lie?"

"No, what we both said was true. I don't remember whether it was the lawyer or one of the other folks, but they already had Jocko's journal in their hands. And what they asked us, very specifically, was whether we had shown the papers from the suitcase to anyone else. We had not. They never asked about the journal, and they seemed to have forgotten that we had told them about the Columbia report. Or they didn't really care."

"But couldn't the Hall argue that by the time you wrote it or by the time it was published, they owned all of the rights to the journal—what you call *Jocko's Journal*? Couldn't they sue you for publishing it?"

"Yes, I guess they could. But they haven't, and even though I asked you about being a lawyer or investigator, I don't think they will. I think they'd be very happy if everyone believed that my book and everything in it is a fiction, something I made up. And I am pretty comfortable with that. People who read the book seem to enjoy toying with that boundary between what's real and what's not, but honestly, you are the first one who's ever asked me such detailed questions. Must mean you liked the book." Adam smiled, and Liz smiled back.

"We'll get to that," she said matter-of-factly. "But doesn't all of this raise a big question? Who do you think actually has the papers? Where do *you* think they are?"

"Honestly, I don't know the answer to that. And as you can guess, I have given it a lot of thought. I don't know, but I have my suspicions."

"You think the Hall of Fame has them, don't you? You think they were the anonymous buyers, probably after they tried to arrange a private purchase as soon as they got a first look at what was there. And you think they have chosen to bury the evidence of what might have happened back a hundred years ago. Am I right?"

"Like I said, I have my suspicions. And you can read between the lines of my book as well as anyone . . . based on this conversation, probably better than most."

"Well, yes, I can. But what if I'm here to tell you that your suspicions are quite possibly wrong? What if I'm here to tell you that you—we—might be able to prove it?"

"Okay," replied Adam after a moment. "You have my attention. Who are you?"

"Would you be Corporal Fairchild?"

"Yes, sir," replied the tow-headed man of perhaps twenty as he jumped down from his perch on the rear bed of the Class-B Liberty Truck, stood to attention, and flashed a sharp salute to the approaching officer. *Jeez*, he speculated. *This guy doesn't look a whole lot older than I am.*

"At ease, Corporal. Let's get ourselves squared away. I've just been seconded over to G2 from artillery for this mission, so I'm still learning the people and procedures over here. It appears that we will be spending a lot of time together over the next couple of weeks. Are you checked out on this truck?"

"Yes, sir. I know engines pretty good from before the war, and I did some training on this beast when I was assigned as a driver. It ain't new, and it ain't beautiful, but it should get us where we're going. Wherever that is, sir."

"I'll explain that to you in a minute. But first, are we provisioned for two weeks? Do we have enough fuel? Can't count on rations or gasoline where we're headed."

"Yes, sir, Captain. We have tools and a jack, tenting gear, a dozen jerrycans of gasoline and some oil, a full set of spares, several canteens of water, and eats. Even managed a few treats from a guy I know who owed me a favor—some of those new Lorna Doone cookies, couple boxes of Cracker Jacks, and some Juicy Fruit. But the one thing we don't have is arms. I got my sidearm, and there's one rifle and a few rounds in the truck. But if we get into some deep trouble, well, sir, the only other thing we have to dig us out of it is literally a shovel, and, begging the captain's pardon, we only got one of those."

Cheeky bastard, the Captain thought to himself as he flashed a quick smile. *This might be an interesting couple of weeks.*

"Mount up, Corporal, and stick a spur in this old warhorse. Let's get out of here. I have all the maps we'll need, and I'll explain the mission as we go. You're smart enough to be assigned to G2, so you'd figure it out pretty soon anyway."

With that, the pair climbed into the cab of the Class-B, Fairchild turned over the engine and pushed in the choke, and, once they had a smooth idle, they were off.

"Take this left," instructed the Captain once they had cleared the gate of the compound.

———⋙ ⋘———

"How'd you end up driving guys like me around France, Corporal? You sell automobiles for a living or something?"

"No, sir. I used to be infantry, sir. A real mud sucker. And then one day, I guess I just got lucky and I got reassigned to G2 and made into a driver. It's the Army, sir. Don't have to make sense. They point, and you go. At least for guys like me, sir."

"Corporal, they don't put just anybody in G2. If you're going to do this kind of work, intelligence, even if your only job is to drive a truck, then you've got to have that very thing, intelligence. And somebody somewhere has to have concluded that you're a patriotic son of a bitch who knows how to keep his mouth shut."

"Yes, sir. If you say so, sir. But that's about a mile above my pay grade."

"Okay, Fairchild. Enough of this horseshit. I'm a captain assigned to military intelligence, I'm on a critical and time-sensitive mission on the personal orders of General Pershing himself, and my immediate boss, Colonel Nolan, hand-picked you to drive me around and assist in other ways as needed. Do you think for one minute that I did not take a close, hard look at your personnel file?"

"No, sir," replied Fairchild. "I guess you would have done that."

"Indeed I did. And you know what I found out? You did start out in infantry, just like you said. And you probably sucked some mud in the trenches. But there came a day not that long ago when your company was surrounded by the Huns and cut off, and those bastards were pouring fire onto your position, and there wasn't any help in sight for one simple reason. Nobody knew you guys were there. And who was it that managed to sneak out of that trench hauling a sack of grenades and a Browning M1918, get around behind that German bunch, and take out every last one of them? Why, that would be Private Fairchild, wouldn't it?"

"Well, yes, sir."

"And who was it that helped the last two survivors of that company limp and drag their way back to the American lines, even though he'd been hit pretty good himself? Would that also be that same Corporal Fairchild?"

Silence.

"Look, Corporal. I appreciate that you didn't really want to talk about that, or brag about it. That's a real sign of character. But I know. And I want you to know that I know and that I respect you for that. And you should also know that General Pershing himself was the one who made sure you were properly looked after in that field hospital, promoted to corporal, and assigned to a unit where he could keep an eye on you. He and Nolan both told me I could trust you with my life, which is just what I'm about to do. And Soldier, that's saying something.

"So here's the deal. For the next couple of weeks, you and I will be on the road almost constantly. We're going to eat together, we're going to tent together, we're going to shit in the same pit. Only difference is, you get to dig it. I want you to keep your eyes and ears open, and if you see or hear something you think is important, I want to know about it. Right away. Can you do that, Corporal?"

"Yes, sir. I can do that, sir. At least now I know why we have that shovel." Fairchild took the chance, got away with it. Even earned a smile. "But can the captain tell me where it is we're headed, sir?"

<hr>

"My great-granddad, Jake was his name, he was a soldier back in World War I. I'm not real sure what he did before the war. Couldn't have been very long out of school. As the stories have come down through the family, he volunteered for the infantry and spent a lot of time in the trenches. Made corporal somewhere along the way, and there are some old medals that I remember seeing when I was a kid. Not sure what's become of them since. But he was some kind of big war hero.

"Well, when he came back, of course, the whole country was a mess. I don't know if you've ever read anything about that time right after the war—around 1919 and 1920—but there was a lot of stuff going down. Jobs were tight because all the returning soldiers wanted their old jobs back, or new ones, and there just weren't enough jobs to go around because the economy was scaling back after the big wartime push. And a lot of those veterans were walking wounded, physically or mentally, so public drunkenness was rampant. That led right to the temperance amendment, which turned out to be its own curse. There were race riots all over the country and even an oil shortage. The whole society was in the process of transitioning from horses to automobiles, and all of a sudden, the oil was running out. Or so they thought.

"For some reason, there was still a part of the American Army over in Russia fighting against the Bolsheviks, and that really set off the anarchists back home. There were bombings on Wall Street and even bombs sent through the mail—to judges and senators. Somebody mailed a bomb to the attorney general at his home. And to top it off, even though the pandemic seemed to have passed, people were still incredibly nervous about the Spanish flu and thought it might come back any time. Eventually things leveled out, if you can call the Roaring Twenties level, but it took a lot of living through to get there.

"Now, according to my dad, who used to tell us the old family stories, when Grampa Jake came back home around the end of 1918, he tried to settle down and get work as a mechanic of some sort. He found a job at a garage in Brooklyn, and he met and married my great-grandmother, Mary Lynne Bell, her name was, that next year. But apparently, one day my great-grandmother was shopping or visiting or something in lower Manhattan and she got caught up in some kind of riot. There was an explosion, and then a rush of people through the streets, and a bunch of cops on horses chasing after them, swinging their clubs. Mary Lynne was in a rush to get out of the way and tripped on a sidewalk. She fell against a building and cut her head and hurt her arm. The way my dad told it, when she was finally able to get back home to their little apartment in Brooklyn, Grampa Jake took one look at her and, well, he went crazy. And the very next day, he quit his job and packed up everything they had and moved to the middle of nowhere in Upstate New York, up in Otsego County. Must have been where they ran out of gas, or something, because there was nothing there. Of course maximizing the nothingness could have been the whole reason for stopping there. Anyway, not long after that, they borrowed some money, bought a local farm, and started growing feed crops and raising cattle. They had a dairy operation, and I think they must have done some butchering, too. Over the years, that became the family homestead. Beautiful area but really remote. And they started a commercial landscaping business, which was a natural, I guess, if you were a farmer and wanted something steadier. We still have that company. Do a lot of groundskeeping for the nearest town and some of the businesses up there."

By now, the beers, as well as their replacements, had been drained. "I don't want to interrupt," Adam inserted, "because I suspect we are getting to the point here. But, can I buy you dinner? I know a great Greek place not far from here."

<hr>

"Otsego County. That sounds vaguely familiar. What's up there?" Adam asked as they started on the dolmades appetizer.

"It's off to the west of Albany, and it's pretty rural," Liz replied. "The biggest town is Oneonta. Not exactly a tourist magnet. But it's probably the other town that's rattling around in your memory. Otsego County is the location of Cooperstown."

"So what you're telling me is that your family is from somewhere near Cooperstown?"

"Quick study," she said with a touch of sarcasm in her voice.

"You continue to have my full attention."

"That's good, because I'll need it to walk you through the rest of this story."

Just then the waiter arrived with their entrees. Adam scarcely noticed.

"So there they were, my great-grandparents, up there in nowhere New York, farming and doing a little dairying. Happy enough, I guess, and it sure did get them away from all the chaos in the City, and then, of course, most of the excitement of the twenties that followed. And soon enough they had a baby, my granddad. Named him Charlie. Not Charles, but Charlie. Aunt Rose came along a couple of years later, then Uncle Sid after that. Three kids in all. Then, of course, times turned hard and they were scratching to get by. I don't think they were in danger of losing the farm like some folks, and that meant they wouldn't go hungry. But it couldn't have been easy all the same. And that's about when this thing happened.

"According to the story my dad told, Grampa Jake was out on the tractor one day around 1934 or 1935 when this fancy car comes driving along the road, slows down, and takes a turn up the dirt drive to the farmhouse. Well, naturally Jake was curious, so he finished his row, pulled up the tines, and headed the tractor over that way. And when he got close, the door of that car opened and out steps this man in a suit, and he waves to Grampa like he knows him, and he's smiling. And it takes Grampa a minute or two to place the guy, because he hadn't seen him since the war. Turns out it's his old captain, or something like that. And the two of them shake hands, all formal-like, and then they just smile and embrace like they were best of friends.

"And the guy says something like, 'Jake! Corporal! I'm glad you remember me. It's been a long time, and I wasn't sure if you would.'

"'Damn right I remember. That was the scariest two weeks of my life—not so much what we were doing, but just wondering if you'd find a way to get yourself killed out there and I'd have to explain to a bunch of generals how I'd come to lose a captain.'

"'Well, you almost did, as you remember very well, I'm sure.'

"'Come on into the house and meet my wife and kids.'

"So they went inside and had a grand reunion, if you can have a reunion where only two of the six people there have ever met each other. Mary Lynne made the invitation, and the Captain agreed to stay for lunch, especially when the youngest boy, that would have been Sid, was dispatched to the garden to pick some fresh sweet corn. Over that and some greens, along with homemade butter and bread and some cold beef, the two men traded war stories, and the visitor told the children something they'd never heard from their father—that he was a genuine war hero, twice over. The visitor even explained the old German rifle that was displayed over the fireplace in the main room, something Grampa Jake himself had been reticent about whenever asked. And when lunch was over, the Captain asked Jake if they might take a little walk outside."

———

"Pull over up there in that wide spot off to the side, and I'll show you what we are doing."

Fairchild pulled off the road and killed the engine. Neither man had realized how noisy that beast of a truck was, or how much it vibrated, until blessed silence descended and the shaking subsided. They could even hear birds chirping away in the nearby trees. *Probably in French*, thought Fairchild, who did not fancy himself as much of a bird watcher.

"Corporal, a couple of days ago, Headquarters G2 was able to put together a fairly comprehensive map of all of the German deployments facing the First and Second Armies. That whole sector of the front. I got the sense the French and the others were doing the same in their own areas, and this was just the AEF's part of something bigger. Liggett and Bullard, the sector commanders, were both there with Pershing, and they both signed off on it. You were at Saint-Mihiel; you know how difficult and dangerous it must have been for those poor S2s to move around out there enough to map the entire line, but that's what they did. There must be something in the works, because our mission is to confirm their work, all of it, and we have only two weeks to get it done."

"Crap, sir. Begging the captain's pardon."

"Crap is right, Corporal. Now, the good news is that we don't actually have to push up to the line, let alone over it. The brass are willing to trust the judgment of the guys who gathered the intel. But that took a while to do, and they want to make sure it's still current. So our job is to start as far up to the northwest in the First Army sector near the French Fourth as we can get given the roads and the conditions of battle, and then more or less trace the line south and east into and across the Second Army sector until we get to the French Eighth. I am to confer with whatever S2s and unit commanders we can find to confirm that things are still pretty much as they were when the first probes were made. Your job is to get me there and back to Pershing as quickly as possible, and along the way, to see if you pick up anything from the grunts or supply sergeants or anyone else you end up talking with. I don't have to tell you that their information can sometimes be better than what the officers want the top brass to know. Your other job is to keep your damn mouth shut. If you need to trade gossip for gossip, make sure whatever you say is total bullshit. Am I clear?"

"Yes, sir, crystal clear, sir. I am ordered to be a bullshitter, sir."

"Think you're qualified for that duty, Corporal?"

"Shit yes, sir."

"Good. And for the record, I am coming to believe you're right. So, crank it up, Corporal. We have a long, hard, and I guess loud ride ahead of us. And once we get past Auberville, things could get harder. The roads up there are bad. If we get in a fix with our own guys at any point, I have letters from Liggett and Bullard that should answer any questions. If we run into the other guys, well, like you said, we have that shovel. Let's get going."

—————

By day three of their trek, they had something of a routine—up at dawn, eat and break camp, try to be on their way within thirty minutes or so. Then it was a tedious process of following the badly marked French dirt roads, poor in the first place and rendered nearly impassable by the years of warfare, making what sense they could of the terrain and road maps the Captain had brought along for navigation, turning toward the sound if they heard big guns in the distance, and otherwise inquiring of those they passed as to the current location of the local command centers. Neither the roads nor the command centers were nearly as structured or even as readily identifiable as one might have expected, but through good navigation, gut instinct, pure determination, dumb luck, and the occasional flash of their pass from a general officer, they worked their way southward and eastward close to the line of battle, though not perilously close.

Or so they thought.

On the afternoon of that third day, for a brief moment, all of that regularity went out the window. They were making their way along what passed for a main road and in search of the dirt track they were supposed to follow to the left when Jake suddenly slammed on the brake and jerked the truck to a halt.

"Sir! Get out and get down!" he yelled, and he moved to do the same. Just then, a bullet zipped through the window opening on the Captain's side of the truck, hissing past the very point where his head had been just a few milliseconds before. Fortunately for him, he was already under the truck and rolling toward the other side. But Jake was nowhere to be seen, and the Captain worried he'd been hit by the single shot. He pulled his sidearm from its holster, tried to make himself small behind a tire, and waited for the inevitable attack by the German scouting patrol he was sure they had stumbled upon.

Two or three minutes passed that must have seemed to him like two or three hours. Suddenly, there was a single shot somewhere ahead and off to the right. Then . . . nothing. A moment later there was a thrashing sound in the woods in that direction and a familiar voice shouted, "Captain, don't shoot. It's just me. And we finally have us some firepower—a genuine Gewehr 98 sniper rifle and a mess of rounds."

"Jesus Christ that was close! How on Earth did you know to stop?"

"Captain, you sit in those trenches long enough, peeking over the top, and you learn to pick up the littlest of movements. Just becomes second nature, not something you even think about. And this guy was careless. I saw a little flash of light, like a reflection off a mirror, off to the side and up ahead there. Probably the light hitting his sniper scope. And I was just starting to process that in my head when I saw some leaves move, and the rest was just instinct. I will say you moved pretty quick for an officer, though. That guy was a pretty good marksman, judging from this hole in the cab."

That's when the Captain looked over and up and realized just how close he had come to being in the proverbial wrong place at the wrong time.

"Damn, Jake. Pershing and Nolan were right. You straight out did save my life."

The corporal said nothing in response. He just took a quick tour of the vehicle, making sure the tires were intact and the engine and gasoline tank were undamaged. Satisfied, he climbed back up into the cab.

"Any time you're ready, sir. We have a deadline." And he smiled.

———

The pair wandered down a dirt path and reached a nearby barn before the visitor was ready to speak. He pointed to a pair of hay bales.

"Settle in, Jake. I have a long story to tell you, and then something to ask you. I have spent the last two months trying to track you down, and now that I found you, I want to make the most of it. The men I work for need someone they can depend on for something they regard as very important, and I told them I think you're the guy.

"You know, I was a lawyer before the war. Had myself a job with a big Chicago law firm. But when I came home, I didn't want to go back to that—the Chicago part. So I set up a little law practice over in Ohio. Moved the wife and kids. Even bought into some businesses there, automobiles and such.

"When I was back in law school, I got to know a particular fellow pretty well. I don't want to say his name. But he was some sort of big something-or-other in big-league baseball. Now, he was older than me, maybe eight or ten years, and he was actually over in France right there at the end of the war, same time as us. Being older and connected and all, he was a major, so he wasn't up at the front or anything, but he was there. 'Course I didn't find that out until later.

"Anyway, three or four years ago, the local ball club where I live got into trouble, what with the Depression and all, and some local businessmen took it over. And they asked me if I'd run it. Not on the field, of course, 'cause I didn't know anything about that, but the business end. And I said sure, why not. So I got into doing that, and one of the things I wanted to do was connect that club with a big league feeder system. Figured we'd get some better players and hopefully even draw more fans that way. And looking around, there were three or four possibilities, and I decided to try for one of the National League teams. And when I got in touch with them, who do you think I ended up talking to, but my old law school buddy, the Major. And we worked it out.

"Now, I won't say we always got along after that. In fact, a couple of years later, the son-of-a-bitch hired me himself, then by damn if he didn't fire me. But by then I had my own contacts, and I caught on with that downstate team, and that's where I am right now."

"Well, Captain," Jake inserted, "I follow that game a little, and I know that team you're with needs a new shortstop pretty badly. But I have to tell you, I can't hit for a damn. So I'm thinking you're not here to offer me a contract."

The Captain smiled. "No, Jake, I'm not here to offer you a contract. But I am here to offer you something else, or really to see if I can talk you into taking something on.

"Jake, baseball's in trouble. You remember how there was so much public complaining back during the war about how baseball players thought they were better than everybody else and for a long time they didn't have to join up. And then, when the government broadened out the draft, a lot of them just went and worked for defense industries, but all they were really doing was playing ball in commercial leagues. Meantime, the major league game itself was being played by kids and old men. And then everybody came back, and things got back to normal, and what happens? Damned if the White Sox don't take a dive in the World Series the very next year. And the year after that, there was this Cobb and Speaker thing—gambling again, or at least that was how it looked. That one they kept pretty quiet, so I don't know if you even heard about it. And then along comes Babe Ruth, and he starts breaking contracts and flaunting the rules and just basically putting his thumb in his nose toward anybody who tries to exercise a little authority and keep the game on the up-and-up. But he's Babe Ruth, and what can you do? Toss him out of the game, break up Murderers' Row, and you'd have a real riot in New York.

"Truth is, even though I've been in the game for a little while now, it wasn't something I had thought very much about. I have enough trouble just getting my guys out on the field and keeping them there. But one day not too long ago the Major showed up at my office, and he said to me, let's take a walk. Matter of fact, just like I said to you."

<hr />

"Gentlemen," began the most senior of the three, with his customary stiff formality, after providing his guests with some rather good cigars and some better brandy, "thank you for making the time and for traveling here to meet with me. I have chosen the two of you because I know of your integrity, your deep respect for the game we all hold dear, and your discretion. I am going to ask each of you to join me in a special initiative. But prefatory to that, I must ask that, whether or not you decide to participate in the activity I am about to describe, you each give me your express personal commitment that you will keep this conversation and its subject matter secret unto your respective graves. Do I have your assurance?"

He looked from one to the other, received nods of assent, and was satisfied.

"Excellent. Both of you have already done more than your share to advance the interests of baseball, and yet, we continue to confront challenges—serious challenges—to the progress we have made in earning back the public trust after that debacle of a World Series, progress that has, not coincidentally, allowed us to make the sport profitable for all parties. We have all done what we can toward those ends consistent with the positions that we hold, and yet we are all limited by the responsibilities that attend to those same positions. There are things that must be done, but that we simply cannot do. Or at least, we cannot be seen to be doing. And that is the key.

"So, gentlemen, what I propose is that the three of us form a self-perpetuating alliance to work outside of the public eye to defend our beloved game from those who would bring it down—from the gamblers, the lowlifes, the greediest owners, the malaprops, the cheaters, and the charlatans. Let us marshal our resources—and I am sure you'll agree, among us they are ample—and take on those who would work against the interests of baseball. Let us step in informally but as forcefully as circumstances require, to do what must be done to protect the game when we are unable to accomplish that through formal means. I propose to you that we serve together on our own initiative as the protectors, the keepers of baseball for the good of the game, that we become, in effect, the GameKeepers of our sport." He left the words hanging in the air.

"Sir," said one of his listeners, filling the void after a brief, respectful silence had passed. "Sir, I hear what you are saying, and I certainly share in the underlying sentiment. But I am having a hard time visualizing just how we might go about doing this. Among us we have a certain—how shall I say it—a certain prominence, enough such that anything we do is likely to attract public attention. How on Earth would we be able to do anything meaningful behind the scenes?"

"Yes, you're quite correct," came the reply from the host. "Our first challenge is to decide what must be done to remedy any particular situation that may arise, and *that* we are well positioned to do. But the implementation of those decisions is the key. It must be targeted, it must be swift, and it must never be connected in any way to us. I have given this a great deal of thought.

"What I propose is that we reserve all ultimate decision-making to ourselves, act only when we are in complete agreement as to both the problem and the solution, explain ourselves to no one outside this circle, and that we retain the services of an intermediary, a worthy adjutant who is in charge of carrying out our decisions and proposed course of action once we have settled upon them. One of us should serve as a liaison to this individual, and that would be the only one of our number who might be at risk of discovery. If we find the right person to act for us, someone of character, perhaps we can minimize that risk. But that person would also be charged with ferreting out critical information without being discovered and with undertaking, or at least organizing, what could be some fairly nasty business from time to time, perhaps even with bending or ignoring the rules of normal civilized behavior. So it must be a man with an edge to him, a man who is not afraid to dirty his hands. It is an odd combination we need, a man who is at once trustworthy and capable of pressing the limits. For this, I am at a loss. Do either of you by chance know such a man?"

"I may," said the other listener. "The fellow I am thinking of has his flaws, but he has integrity, and, importantly, he's not afraid to mix it up. He does have a dark side, but I think we can trust his word. And he knows the game." He offered a name that was familiar to all three, and his companions nodded their approval of the suggestion.

"Well, if we are all in agreement here today, then I will ask you to sound him out. Offer him whatever inducements you must. Once that's done and he's on board, we'll need him to arrange a small group of functionaries—probably some sort of investigator, perhaps a strong-arm type or two, though let's be cautious about that. It will depend in large part on what he can take on himself.

"Now, one of the things that's driving me forward on this is that I find myself with a great amount of information—call it files, evidence, complaints, or what you will—that I profoundly wish to place out of harm's way. Permanently. Over the last few years, I have made it a point to collect and, insofar as I could, take out of circulation all kinds of material detrimental to baseball. I suspect you both may have been collecting as well. There's a lot from the 1919 problem as you can guess, and some from the thing with Speaker and Cobb and Dutch Leonard right after that. But it seems there is a good deal more dirt to be shoveled. People just seem to think I'll want this material, and they keep sending it to me. We'll need a place to store all of this information that we already have and whatever comes our way in the future, anything at all that we do not want made public. Sadly, I expect there will be quite a lot of it over the years. So more than anything, we need a repository of some sort, someplace no one would ever suspect or happen upon by chance, and we need someone we can count on to keep watch over it.

"I'm sure we'll have other needs as well, but it will be important to keep this circle very small and very discreet going forward. It is in our personal interests to do so, of course. But it is also the case that to act otherwise and to be discovered would do at least as much damage to the game as the actions we will be seeking to obscure, mitigate or deter."

"So, Jake," the Captain began. "Let me tell you what the deal is. But first, I need you to swear to me that nobody will ever know what I'm about to tell you. Whether you decide to do what I ask or not, absolutely nobody can know this was more than a conversation about the old days between a couple of wartime buddies. Will you promise me that?"

"Of course I will."

"Excellent. And I know your word is good as gold. So here it is.

"There's this group of very influential people—real small group with, I have the impression, lots of money—that has decided to be not exactly a bunch of coat and tie vigilantes but sort of the unofficial keepers of the true game of baseball. As I understand it, their idea is to protect the reputation of professional baseball by whatever means they think are necessary. Very hush-hush. They've got code names and everything. Truth is, I don't even know who they really are. I get instructions from the Major—he's probably one of them, but he could be some kind of operative, just like me—and I carry them out. I don't have any idea how many others like me there are, though I wouldn't think very many.

"Now here's the thing, and here's where you come in. At least, I hope so. They expect that in the course of doing whatever it is they plan to do, they are going to come across a great deal of pretty sensitive information. Just what it is, I couldn't tell you. But they seem to be very concerned that no one ever finds the information itself or figures out that they have it. And to keep that information secure, they are doing a little construction project, building a kind of repository out in the middle of nowhere. And I have to say, when I finally tracked you down and saw where you're living, I was really pleased. Because they are building that thing very close by, up in Cooperstown, and I was afraid I'd have to persuade you to move out here. But here you are already. Must be fate.

"Anyway, they need someone to watch over this repository, or vault, or whatever it is. Not to go into it, mind you, or have anything to do with the stuff they keep there. But just to keep an eye out just in case and also, very importantly, to hold onto the only set of keys to the place and to give them to me or to one of them, whoever, when it's time to add to or access the material. And I am asking you to commit to doing that job for us—not just you, Jake, and this is important, but I am also asking you to commit your family. Because the way they have this set up is that they want to hold down the number of people who know what's going on. As I understand it, their little group is set up so when one of them drops out or dies, the others pick somebody they trust to join up. And for guys like me, us, who are carrying out their wishes, it's supposed to be a family affair. So I agreed to tell my oldest boy—I've got two now and a girl, you know—about what I do when he turns twenty-one, and to get him to step in for me when the time comes, and so on going forward. Sort of a hereditary deal. And I would ask you to do the same, to bring your own oldest boy in when he's twenty-one, and for him to bring his oldest boy in, and so on down through the generations. Make it a kind of family business, but one that's no one else's business—even wives and other kids besides the oldest sons.

"There is no pay for what I'm asking you to do, and I know that, unlike me, you're not 'in the game,' so to speak. I'm not even sure how much of a fan you are. But the group will find ways to help you in return for your services, and that will also go down the line. All I can say is that they are powerful friends to have. You might find a new piece of farm equipment outside your barn one day, or a new market for your . . . whatever it is you're growing out here. One thing you will find is steady work. Because here's what we'd like you to do.

"Since you live so close to town, you don't need to move to Cooperstown. In fact, it's better if you don't. But you need to start a business there doing landscaping. You're going to call it the A. Holt Greenstick Company. Sounds like a landscaper. If anybody asks, just tell them you named it in honor of a close buddy named Holt, who died in the war. We'll build you an office and equipment storage building in the middle of town, and, if you're of a mind, you can use some of the land you have out here for the rest. We can guarantee you contracts with the town, including basic maintenance at the ballpark they are renovating up there, and with the county, and with a big hotel in town, and that's for starters. That should give you some idea of just how influential these guys are. We'll set you up with tools and a truck or two—whatever you need—and you are free to hire workers and grow the business as much as you want and keep any profits you earn. It's a pretty darn good deal. But the important thing is that being a major landscaping contractor, you'll be able to move around to lots of places in town pretty freely and nobody will ever ask any questions.

"One of the places you'll be working, and I won't say which yet, will also be the place where the repository will be. It'll be made to look like something else. All I can tell you for now is that the whole thing will be out of sight, and nobody will notice it being built because it'll get lost in the clutter of a much bigger project. But you would be the one person who knows where the entrance is and has the key that opens it. And you'd have a couple of other keys, but we'll get to that when the time comes.

"Now this is important. You will *not* be the one going into that special area. *Ever.* Your job will be to keep the keys, hand them over to me or someone else who's authorized to go in, and get them back when they leave. There'll only be one way in and one way out, so it's just a matter of finding some excuse to hang around near the entrance while you wait. Think of it as a safety deposit box at the bank, and you're the banker. The security of the box is your business but not what's in it."

"Well, that's all well and good, but if it's not you that comes up here, how do I know who's authorized to get the keys? You said you don't even know who these guys are."

"Excellent question. In addition to keeping the keys, we want you to keep a roster of sorts—a list of the members of the core group, because any one of them would have the right to access the repository. But you can't know their real names, so what you'd have is their code names, and each time there's a change, you would be notified to update your list. And you'd also be responsible for keeping a log of every time that someone asks for the keys, me included. That's as much to protect you as anything else. Again, it's like a safety deposit box."

"So some stranger shows up at my house or at work and says, 'I'm secret agent number one,' and I hand over the keys?"

"Not quite. We've thought of that, too. So we've worked out a little sign and countersign exchange. I know. It sounds a little S2 to me, as well. But if you think about it, it makes pretty good sense. It allows for the access process to continue years into the future when you and I are long gone, and that's the idea—a process for protecting the game that perpetuates itself through generations. We all just teach our kids the signs and the countersigns when the time comes. So, what do you think? Are you in?"

***

"So, the way I understand it, this captain, whoever he really was, tells Grampa Jake that there's this small group of people who want to set him up in the landscaping business. No idea why. I always assumed, and I think we all did, that it had something to do with his wartime service, and that's why they sent his old commanding officer to make the offer. So he'd know it was legit.

"Well, Grampa Jake must have said yes, because pretty soon he opened up this landscaping company in Cooperstown. We think he named it after some friend he knew over in France, maybe one of the guys he served with. Must not have made it back. And over the years, it was pretty darn successful. Lots of commercial-type work, even when everything else was slow. It meant we could enjoy life on the farm, but we weren't dependent on it like so many of our neighbors. We figured the old boy was a heck of a businessman, and he passed it down through the family to my grandfather, Charlie, then my dad. My brother would have been next in line."

"Would have been?"

"Yes. Eddie was learning all about the business as he was growing up, though I have to say, kind of reluctantly. His head was always somewhere else. But around the time he turned twenty-one, he seemed to get really interested. Dad must have laid out a path for him to take on a bigger role. But then, Eddie's best friend decided to enlist in the Army, and somehow, he convinced Eddie that he should join up as well. Be all he could be, and all that. And don't you know, he did that. Maybe he was remembering Grampa Jake. Anyway, you can guess the rest of the story—went through some kind of training down at Fort Polk in Louisiana, shipped out to we don't know where, and sure enough, about four months later we got the visit nobody wants to get. We were all heartbroken, of course, but it really seemed to hit my dad the hardest, like not only had he lost his only son, but he just didn't know what to do.

"This all happened about ten years ago, and eventually things got back to a sort of normal. Dad kept running the business, and I tried to help out with the office part when I could. I always knew I wasn't Eddie, but that was probably as much or more me than it was Dad.

"Well, about this time last year, Dad took me aside and he said he had something really important to talk with me about when I could find the time. And we agreed that we'd drive over to Oneonta that Sunday for a nice dinner, and we'd have a talk. That was on a Tuesday. On Wednesday, I got a call from one of the guys at the company saying Dad had had a stroke and the paramedics had taken him to the hospital in town. By the time I could get there, he was gone."

"Liz, I'm so sorry to hear about all of this. You have my sympathies."

"Thanks, but it's been long enough now that everything has more or less sunk in, except on the bad days. But it gets me to the reason I'm here."

—————

"My mom was listed in his will as my dad's executor, but she wasn't really up to it, so I stepped in and took care of as many of the details as I could. I'd just give her the papers from the lawyer, or whatever, and she'd sign them to make them official. You wouldn't believe how much paperwork there is, and how many rules, when somebody dies. So, I got started on getting death certificates and changing all kinds of accounts and deeds and leases and things into my mom's name—all of the personal stuff. That came first, because I had to make sure she was all set day to day.

"It was about six weeks ago, more or less, that I finally had a chance to start sorting out the business. After my brother died, my dad had made me a partner, so I had a head start there. And a couple of weeks before he himself passed, he'd apparently arranged for me to have control of the company when the time came. I figured that was what he had wanted to talk with me about that last week. So I made sure all the books were in order, and I signed some papers of my own. After a while, I finally had a chance to look around the building we have in town, and it was a mess. That's what happens, I guess, when you have three generations of men in charge of someplace."

At that last remark, she glanced up at Adam with the hint of a smile and was rewarded with a distinctly male gesture, also accompanied by his own hint of a smile.

"So I started in cleaning out the desk my dad had used all those years. It's one of those great big old oak ones, about three feet deep, or maybe four, like the doctors and lawyers used to use a hundred years ago. Must have been pretty nice when it was new, but it was pretty well beat up by the time I got to it. And it was full of pretty much what you'd expect: old bills, seed catalogs from last century, a couple of computer manuals from the nineties, gasoline receipts from around the 1950s, and an assortment of burger bags, chewing gum wrappers, candy wrappers, and old matchbook covers. Like I said, typical.

"As I was working my way into one of the lower drawers, I noticed that the drawer seemed a little shorter than the others, and the back of the drawer seemed flimsier. And when I looked a little closer, it almost looked like there was a false back on the drawer. So I pulled that drawer all the way out, and sure enough, there was this section way at the back. And in that section, there was a metal box with a combination padlock on it.

"I didn't remember seeing any notes with combinations on them, and I wasn't going to waste a lot of time trying to figure it out. So I walked over to the shop and grabbed a bolt cutter. When you need a tool, it pays to be in the landscaping business. And I just cut that thing off and opened the box. This is what I found."

And with that, she reached into her oversized purse, which had rested all this time on the floor, hard against the leg of her chair, pulled out two large manila envelopes, and laid them on the table, cleared by now of dishes but for a pair of coffee mugs long since gone cold.

———⚓ ⚓———

The three men drove out Chestnut Street, took the right to cross Grove, and zigzagged their way to the very top of the hill just to the south and west of the Village. The corn was weeks short of full height, so at this time of year, the Village of Cooperstown lay before them in its full splendor. In the middle distance, they could see the rustic baseball field, once known as Phinney's Lot, with its 250-seat wooden grandstand that would soon be expanded and transformed into a 10,000-seat ballpark complete with baseline bleachers, a six-foot outfield fence, a new scoreboard, and a painted sign denoting "Doubleday Field, Birthplace of Baseball." The ballpark would be modern in many ways, even though the use of reclaimed materials from the recent demolition of the grandstand at the fairgrounds gave it a distinctly retro appearance. On the parking lot to the northeast of the field sat the bandstand Ambrose Clark had recently moved to the site, also from the fairgrounds, which added to the old-timey feel of the place. They could see the additional land on the Pioneer Street side of left field that the Village was acquiring from the Phinney family and other neighbors, and the start of the new extensions of Church Street, separately from Pioneer and Chestnut, that would never quite meet. The upgrades combined with the throwback feel of the place provided what the trio concluded would be a perfect setting for the festivities to come, the 1939 celebration of the centennial of The Game, which, the mythology held, had been invented by Abner Doubleday on this very spot.

Beyond that lay the two-block-long commercial center on Main Street. At this distance they could not see the decay that had set in by the fifth year of hard times, but they all knew it was there. Soon, the more distant of these buildings on the south side of Main would be replaced by the First Church of Baseball, the National Baseball Hall of Fame and

Museum, though at this point that could only be seen in the mind's eye, and only the eye of a knowing mind at that, since the plan had yet to be announced to the public. Across Fair Street, they could just make out the end column in front of the YMCA building which, but for a half-dozen houses, marked the eastern edge of town. The river beyond made that official. To the north lay the impressive building and manicured grounds of the resort where they had dined last night and would again this evening. The hotel was surviving, but as one of their number glumly noted, it could do with some serious renovation and a good painting. It's first quarter of a century had seen its share of pestilence, hard living, and hard times. Bounding the hotel grounds on the north, the lake shimmered in the breezy sunshine. The steamer *Natty Bumpo* lay at anchor at the foot of Fair Street, while smaller craft plied the Coburn and Cooper landings just to the foreground.

"There," said the senior member of the group, pointing down and toward the east. "We are going to put it right there. And that spot just to the right, where that yellow truck is, that's where we'll put the repository. There will be a sign. Nothing obvious and nothing that would draw attention. But you'll know it when you see it. And we have a fellow I am persuaded is quite trustworthy who will help you with the logistics. Name is Fairchild, if you ever need it. Jake Fairchild. But remember, he will only know you by your code name, so stick with that. It goes without saying, of course, that it will be better to work through our own man whenever possible." He turned to one of his companions and added, "You might want to be especially careful about that."

"Of course," came the reply.

One envelope looked much older than the other. The paper was rougher, and the envelope itself was held closed by a red string that wound several times around small metal posts in a sort of figure eight and was kept in place by two well-worn small circles of lightweight red cardboard. It was this envelope that Liz opened first. She unspooled the string to release the flap, then turned the envelope on end and a set of keys tumbled onto the table with a minor thud.

Adam studied the keys for a moment, then yielded to his curiosity. "Okay, and these are keys to what, exactly?"

"I have no idea," Liz replied. "All I know is that they have a kind of a tired look to them and they were in this envelope and locked in that box. Also, they seem kind of oversized . . . bigger than you'd probably have for your front door. I guess I'd call them industrial-sized, for want of a better term."

"Look at the shapes of them," Adam offered. "They almost look a little bit, what, art deco?"

"Well, that's an interesting observation," she said, "because this was also in the envelope." At that, Liz again tipped the envelope toward the table, and out slid a small journal of the type college students might use for making notes in class, and a small, irregular piece of paper that showed both age and wear. Liz opened the journal, which bore no label or title. Mostly it was blank, but on two facing pages in the middle of the book, a record of some sort had been maintained. It seemed to cover a period of perhaps eighty-five or ninety years beginning in 1935.

"What the heck is this?" Adam wondered aloud.

"Again, I don't really know. But it obviously has something to do with the keys, partly because they were all together in the same envelope, and also because, as you see, there are key symbols drawn in for some of the entries.

"My guess is that this is a log of some sort, maybe keeping track of who is using these keys and when. Why anybody would want to do that I don't know, but it appears that Grampa Jake must have started this thing back in the 1930s, and then I'm guessing that my granddad took over in the seventies. See how the handwriting changed? Plus, Grampa Jake died in 1975. And I'm sure that the last set of handwriting is my dad's. Going over all of his papers, I have gotten to know that hand very well. And then there's the date. My granddad died in 2008, but I remember he was sick for a long time before that, maybe ten years or so, and that seems to be about when it changed again. It's like they were passing this task, whatever it was, down from one generation of Fairchild men to the next. Maybe that had something to do with the way Dad acted after my brother was killed, and maybe that's what he wanted to talk to me about the week that he passed away. We'll never be sure."

1935 — Moss, Hall Monitor, Tree
— Successful
— Successful
1936 — Tree
1944 — Hall Monitor, Tree, Haircut
1951 — Successful
1957 — Successful
1960 — Tree, Haircut, Horse Lover
1965 — Haircut, Horse Lover, Starman
1967 — Successful
1970 — Successful
1971 — Successful
1972 — Successful
1973 — Successful
1974 — Successful
1978 — Haircut, Horse Lover, Blade
1984 — Haircut, Horse Lover, Olympian
1985 — Successor
1986 — Olympian, Successor
1987 — Successor, Olympian
1988 — Olympian
1989 — Haircut, Horse Lover, Renaissance Man
— Renaissance Man
— Haircut, Horse Lover, Lot Lizard
— Lot Lizard, Bargain Hunter, Straight Arrow
1992 — Successor
1996 — Straight Arrow
1999 — Successor
2001 — Successor
2003 — Successor
2005 — Bargain Hunter

2007 — Successor
2012 — Lot Lizard, Straight Arrow, First Fan
2013 — Tres
2018 — Tres
2019 — Tres
2021 — Lot Lizard

"I wonder what these entries in the last column mean," observed Adam as he examined the notebook more closely. "I mean, 'Tree,' 'Success,' 'Haircut,' 'Renaissance Man.' There doesn't seem to be any rhyme or reason to them, no pattern at all. But there are never more than three on one line, they change over time—sometimes a long time and sometimes not—and there's never more than one word on the same line with one of those key symbols. You didn't find any kind of code list or anything like that?"

"No. Nothing at all," Liz confirmed.

"That would make it too easy, I guess," said Adam. "Could be any-thing, I suppose. Things. Events . . . I'd be taking a wild-ass guess here, but I think these words stand for different people, some kind of a small group that changes its members over the years. I don't know how you'd go about figuring out who they were or what they were up to."

"Or what it had to do with my family!"

"Yeah, that, too. But, what's this other thing?"

They turned their attention to the small scrap of paper that still sat where it had fluttered to the table. On inspection, they noted that it was written in yet a different hand, apparently using a pair of fountain pens, with lines alternating between black and blue ink, both colors beginning to fade badly. It had a very formal look to it, like someone had taken their time with it.

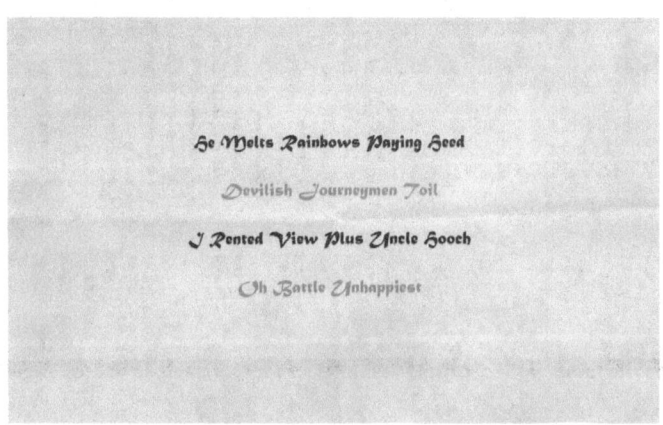

So Melts Rainbows Paying Feed

Devilish Journeymen Toil

J Rented View Plus Uncle Hooch

Oh Battle Unhappiest

"He Melts Rainbows Paying Heed?" Adam read the line as a question, indicative of his own confusion. "What the hell does that mean? What does any of this mean?"

———

"Captain! It's been a long time since you've been up here," Jake said as his friend walked into the small restaurant where they were meeting for lunch. "We've got the workshop all set up, we've laid in a bunch of supplies, and I've got more out on the farm, and we're getting started on all our contracts. I've hired on about six guys so far. Not sure how many more I'll need, but they're all grateful to have the work with the way things are. Makes me a pretty popular fellow."

"Jake, it's good to see you, too. I'm glad to know that everything seems to be going according to the plan. But now it's time that we get to work on our little project. Time to pay the piper. So once we are done, I want to show you where the door is that we're going to be interested in using, and I want to give you some keys."

With that, both ordered a bowl of the beef stew, one of the three choices on the menu. Jake opted for a glass of tea over ice chipped off the block he could see through the curtained doorway to the kitchen. His companion settled for hot coffee, then immediately regretted the choice.

"How's that boy of yours doing?" queried one of the other. It didn't matter which, because they both had the same question, and that answered, twice, they made small talk until each had finished his stew and the small stack of saltines that came with it. The captain paid for both lunches, then turned to Jake.

"Let's take a walk."

It was not a long walk, perhaps the equivalent of two city blocks. And at the end of it, Jake clearly showed the surprise that he felt.

"Here?" he asked. "Here?"

"Yep. Watch this." With that, the captain performed a bit of mechanical magic, and the impediment swung aside to reveal a steel portal with a door handle and, embedded just above it, a large lock.

"We had a bit of a time explaining this to the guys we used to build it," he said with a smile, "but we came up with a story and they bought it. Besides, it was a small detail in a big job, the proverbial pimple on an elephant's ass, and I don't think they gave it a second thought. Besides, they were from out of town.

"Now pay attention. We might as well do this the right way from the start. You take the keys." He handed them over to Jake. "Now, here's a piece of paper. You can keep it. In fact, you need to keep it. Any time anybody wants to open this door, they will address you by name—except for me, you won't know theirs—and they will say this first line to you. The one in black. And you give 'em back the one in blue. Then you do the next pair, and if everything is right, you give 'em the keys. Then you back away and find some way to stay busy until they come back out that door and give you back the keys. You *always* get the keys back. And that's almost it. Except you never, ever, under any circumstances, go through that door. You do that, we'll know, and you're fired. I don't care if the place is burning, or flooded, or what. Understand?"

"I do. I get it. Seems kind of strange, but I get it."

"I'm counting on you. I'll be coming up here two or three times as we're getting started. Not sure whether anyone else will be coming or not. But after that, things should slow down. You could go a year or more without anybody coming up and asking for the keys.

"It goes without saying that you need to keep all of this safe and out of sight, someplace no one will have any reason to ask about it, and some place no one will come across it accidentally. But it needs to be someplace where you can get to it on very short notice, even at night or on a week-end. So probably not a bank vault or someplace like that."

"I have just the place. I have this big old wooden desk. The drawers must be about four feet long. I'll get a metal lockbox and stick it at the back of one of those drawers. That ought to do it."

"I like that. That should work. You can just keep everything together in there. One more thing. Here's that logbook I told you about." He passed a nondescript journal to Jake. "Now, in that logbook, they want you to keep two kinds of records year by year. First, you need to keep track of everybody who asks for the keys, including me. Second, you are to maintain a record of the members of the group who have the right to ask for those keys. There are three of them right now. Don't know if it will always be three, or more, or fewer. But somebody—me or somebody else—will always let you know who they are. Before you make any entries to that record, though, use the challenge code. Don't just take the word of any old fool who knocks on your door. Got it?"

"Sir, yes sir," Jake responded with a touch of irony.

"That reminds me. I have a code name, too, and that's the name you need to keep in the log. Now take the book here and write this down. The year is obviously 1935. And your first entry for the year is: Moses, Hall Monitor, Tree. Those are the code names of the guys we work for. Moses, Hall Monitor, Tree. No idea how they came up with those. But there you have it."

"And your code name?"

"Oh, yeah. Call me Successful."

Jake thought for a moment, then smiled. "The other kids used to give you a tough time, eh?"

The Captain returned the smile and nodded. "And some of the teachers, when I deserved it."

<hr />

"Okay," Adam continued, "so there's all these things we don't understand—the keys, the dates, the code names, this weird slip of paper. I get it. There's an interesting little mystery here. But what's that got to do with me or my book? And what's it got to do with Jocko Drumm or Jason or the old papers we had? For that matter, I don't see anything here that even makes a connection of any kind to baseball. I mean, maybe this captain you talk about was a communist agent back in the thirties and your family has been a sleeper cell for almost a century. Or a drug dealer or a rumrunner working for some kind of underworld kingpins You've got that lake up there, and you're pretty close to Canada. Maybe somebody's hiding stolen art or pre-Columbian artifacts. Or maybe they all worked for Coca-Cola or Colonel Sanders, and they buried the secret formula somewhere in Cooperstown. This could be literally anything. So what are you doing here?"

"You are right. You are absolutely right. And that's what gets me to the second envelope that I found. Have a look at this."

Liz carefully replaced all the items on the table, including the keys, back into the first envelope. Then she released the more contemporary metal clasp on the second one and slowly dumped its contents onto the surface. Out slid a stack of papers topped by what looked to be a page of notes that had been made on a yellow legal pad.

"I found this in the same metal lockbox with the first envelope. It was the only other thing in there, and it was obviously much newer. In fact, this page of notes is all in my dad's handwriting. So, based on the logbook we just looked at, that means it can't be older than around 1999, when the handwriting changed. Actually, it probably wouldn't have been before 2008, which is when my granddad passed away. Presumably my dad wouldn't have been poking around this stuff too much before that, just out of respect. But I'd say it's more recent than that.

"You can see that it's all done in pencil, so it's pretty clearly not meant to be a formal record of any sort. And I'm no handwriting expert, but it just looks to me like it was all done at the same time. Otherwise you'd probably see some smudges in the older notes, or some variation in the darkness of the entries on the list or of the hand itself. Those things do change as we age. And that leads me to think that the whole thing can be dated by the last item on the list, which has something to do with the year 2021. But that still doesn't answer your question. So let me turn this page around and let you have a look at the contents."

With that, she rotated the stack of papers on the table by 180 degrees, and Adam glanced down the list.

"Two things catch my attention right away," he said. "And they probably won't surprise you. Thing one is that this is a list of baseball scandals going back more than a hundred years. I'm not sure what some of these are, but I know enough about the game to see that all the big ones are here. The Black Sox, Pete Rose, some drug scandals, and of course the Astros relaying catchers' signs to their batters in the World Series. It's like a laundry list of events that have embarrassed professional baseball, including some that were downright illegal. I imagine if we looked up some of the more obscure ones—like wife swapping?—they'd probably fit the same pattern."

"You're spot on. And actually, it looks like my dad did just that."

With that, Liz slid the top page of the stack aside and spread out some of the pages below.

"These are all computer printouts of old news stories and the like about baseball scandals. There's one or more stories for every one of the items on Dad's list. And as you can see, he was a pretty thorough reader. Most of them have margin notes or yellow highlighter or some other kind of notation for whatever he thought were the important points. There are old stories from *Sports Illustrated* and the *San Francisco Chronicle*, there's a transcript from some old Ted Koppel program on ABC, there's even a printout of something called the *Mitchell Report*. If you look at them, they correspond with all of the events on his list, and they're either contemporaneous news accounts or some kind of later follow-up summary."

"Was your dad a writer? Maybe he was researching a book on baseball scandals. Judging from this list, there'd certainly be enough material for that."

"My dad was a farmer and a landscaper. That's all he ever was, and I cannot imagine him writing a book."

1919	Black Sox scandal
1926	Discovery of Cobb/Speaker gambling allegations
1957	Cincinnati ballot stuffing for ASG
1972	Yankees wife swapping scandal – Mike Kekitch - Fritz Peterson
1974	Beer Night riot in Cleveland
1985	Pirates drug trials
1986	Players union files Collusion 1 case
1987	Al Campanis race remarks - Ted Koppel transcript
1987	Players union files Collusion 2 case
1988	Players union files Collusion 3 case
1989	Pete Rose gambling scandal
1999	Cinci Reds - Marge Schott praises Hitler
2001	John Rocker insults everybody not named John Rocker
2003	Sammy Sosa corked bat
2004	Balco steroids/designer drug scandal - SF Chronicle (Victor Conte)
2005	Congressional Committee rebukes MLB
2007	Mitchell Report
2013	Biogenesis HGH scandal (Tony Bosch)
2013-2015	Cardinals hack Astros computers (Chris Correa)
2017 - 2018	Astros cheating scandal
2021	Cobb/Mathewson auction

Liz continued to spread the pages slowly to one side until she came to the last one in the stack. "Then," she said, "there is this. Recognize it?"

Auction of Baseball Memorabilia Sets New Record

By Aubrey Winston III
Special to *The Times*

Until yesterday, the highest price ever paid for an item of baseball memorabilia was $4.4 million for a New York Yankees jersey said to have been worn by Babe Ruth in 1920, his first season with the team. That record was shattered yesterday in a sale at Marbury House Auctioneers, where a collection highlighted by a personal 1925 letter from Ty Cobb to Jane Mathewson, widow of pitching great Christy Mathewson, expressing his condolences upon his friend's death, fetched $7.8 million.

The collection also included a letter from Branch Rickey to Mathewson asking him to assist in forming an Army unit for World War I comprised of prominent baseball players. Mathewson, it may be recalled, was exposed to mustard gas while serving in Flanders during the war, which was widely believed to have contributed to his death from tuberculosis a few years later. Also included were artifacts from a prominent early sportswriter, JT Willett, and some other documents.

Bidding opened at $3.7 million, and the Ruth jersey record was surpassed in less than a minute of spirited competition. The winning bid was submitted anonymously but is widely believed to have been entered by a well-known baseball enthusiast. The auction house declined to confirm the bidder's identity, and *The Times* has so far been unable to establish that independently. Calls to the suspected bidder have not been returned.

Christy Mathewson pitched for the New York Giants in the early years of the last century, and has been regarded as the best pitcher in the history of baseball. The value of the collection is presumed to lie primarily in the two letters, which bookend Mathewson's military service.

Mathewson, Cobb, and Rickey are all members of the Baseball Hall of Fame.

"Damn." Adam couldn't help himself. "That's why you're here."
"That's why I'm here."

Pinch Hitter

Jake heard the outside door of the office creak open, and looked up from his desk to see a visitor approaching.

"Captain! Is that you? I almost didn't recognize you. What's it been . . . almost ten years?"

"Jake, how are you? Yeah, it's been quite a long time since I was last up this way. I hope everybody is doing well."

"We're fine, and as you can see, business is booming. I got about a dozen guys out working on crews, and I have a couple of girls who work here in the office. They're both off having lunch somewhere in town. I have you to thank for all this, and believe me, I do, every day. How is your family doing?"

"Everybody's good. I have the two boys, and the girl, you know, and they keep popping out grandbabies. Well, not the boys exactly, but you know what I mean. We're getting to be quite a large group. But listen, I came up here for a reason. I trust everything is going all right with our little project? No problems or anything?"

"Far as I know, everything is just fine. In fact, there's only been one other person up here, some guy I didn't know. But he had the right code name—called himself Tree—and he knew the drill, so I let him in. But even that was maybe seven or eight years ago. Nothing since then."

"Well, that's good. And the people I report to will be happy to hear it. But here's the thing. There's been a little change at the top. The kind of thing they knew would happen. So I need you to make a new log entry showing the current makeup of the top guys. Moses is gone, and the new guy is calling himself Haircut. So the log entry should read 'Hall Monitor, Tree, Haircut,' and if Moses ever shows up in the future—and I will tell you with certainty that will never happen—but if somebody using that name shows up, you just play dumb. But if Haircut shows up, well, he's legit as long as he knows the ritual. Got that?"

"Got it. Let me make the change right now." As he spoke, Jake opened the deep lower drawer of his desk, pulling it beyond the false back that was part of the original design, removed a metal lockbox, opened it, took out the logbook, opened to the page he was using, and made the requisite entry. He then returned the book to the box, the box to the drawer, and the drawer to full stop. "Oops! Guess I should have asked if you needed the keys before I closed it up again. Do you?"

"Nah. I just came up to make the change. Figured I should do that in person. Say, how's that boy of yours? He must be twenty-one by now. Is he off in the service?"

"No. Charlie turned twenty-one a year or so back. You know, it's funny the things you wish for. Kid had a little bit of a wild streak. You never knew what he'd do next. Nothing that hurt people, mind you. Just, well, just a little toward the edge, if you know what I mean. When he was, what, sixteen, Charlie got the idea that he could be a daredevil bicycle rider. He had this old Montgomery Ward bike when he was a kid, and one day he found it stashed in a shed. So he pulled it out and started speeding around and doing stunts, or trying to. Well, to make a long story short, Charlie and the Monty Ward met a large rock and a big old oak tree and they had a little disagreement. The bike was a total loss, and Charlie didn't fare a lot better. Smashed his leg and his hip up real good. Doc had him in a cast for the better part of a year. And ever since it came off, he's been walking with a limp. Things didn't settle quite right.

"Now, that was hard on Charlie, just because he was Charlie. Didn't like being a gimp, not one bit. And he took it out on everybody around him for a long time. He still had that roguish streak to him, so he worked real hard at discovering his limitations. Finally grew into himself after a year or two, and I think he's pretty happy and settled now. Got himself a girlfriend and all. Nice girl. But still, as a parent, you wish that sort of thing had never happened to your kid.

45

"And that's the funny thing. Because now I thank God that it did. Because if that hadn't of happened, why, today Charlie would be off in France or Saipan or God knows where, doing just what you and I did back in the day, or laying stone cold dead and six feet under in some place we never heard of."

"That's quite a story. I've been lucky myself. My boys were too old by the time this war started, and my grandkids are way too young. Just worked out that way. But it brings me to my other item of business. You and I had a conversation back ten years ago or so about how this thing of ours would carry forward. And this change at the top, with Moses gone and Haircut in the group, well it seems to have got everybody more focused on the whole succession thing. I'm told that they are all happy with the way you've been handling things up here in Cooperstown, and they're still comfortable with the original plan if you are. But they wanted me to ask you whether this all still works for you. Does it?"

"Absolutely, sir. This is the best thing that could have happened to me and my family, and none of us will ever forget it."

"That's excellent, and I thought you'd say that. So here's the other question. Your son has passed his twenty-first birthday. Have you had 'the talk' with him? Is he on board?"

"I did, Captain. Didn't tell him what it was all about, not that I really know, but only that it was an obligation that our family had taken on long ago, and that, as a matter of honor, he must continue it when the time comes. And thank goodness by then he had settled down. Honestly, I'm not sure I would have trusted the old Charlie with something like this. But now, I know he'll carry it on and make us both proud. Plus, he is really into learning the landscaping business, something I never thought I'd see, and that makes it even easier. He's working his way up. Did some manual labor for a year or so, and just lately I moved him up to be foreman of one of those crews I told you about earlier. They're over working at the Hall today, putting in some new annuals in that garden out in the back."

"That's really good, Jake. My oldest has been in the know a good bit longer, of course, but he's absolutely committed to carrying this on."

"Maybe we should get the two of them together some time, let them get to know each other?"

"Actually, Jake, I don't think that's a good idea. Nothing personal. But the whole idea of this thing seems to be to maintain anonymity as much as possible. I don't think the guys in the inner sanctum, if that's what it is, would want the two of them to get friendly. It worked for us, because things were just getting started. But I think over time the idea is to keep everybody pretty much in the dark. Except, of course, the top guys have to know about you. We're both getting on in years, of course. Me faster than you, needless to say, but I had a head start. The time will come for them to meet one another, and we know how that will work. Best we leave it at that."

"Understood."

With that, and with an exchange of pleasantries, the captain took his leave, eager to be gone before the two office girls returned from their lunch hour.

"And that," said Adam, "gets me to the second thing I noticed on your dad's list. That last item. The auction. He obviously had some reason to connect that with whatever else he was doing here. That last clipping proves it."

"Yes. But I think you are missing the big picture here," Liz offered, withdrawing the logbook from the first envelope. "Look at the logbook, and look at my dad's notes. Notice anything?"

Adam did as instructed, and it was not long before his eyes widened.

"Wow. Every entry on your dad's list corresponds in time, at least to the year, with an entry in the logbook that has one of these key symbols drawn in. I don't have any idea what the other entries are, and even some of the keys don't match up with your dad's list, but there seems to be some clear correspondence between the keys and these events. You've had longer to think about this. What do you make of that?"

"Honestly, I'm not sure. I know my dad was a big baseball fan. He was a big-time donor to the Hall of Fame, a benefactor member or something like that. He had a closetful of their shirts and jackets—more of that stuff than he had company gear, I think. He'd go over there at lunchtime when he wasn't jammed at work and just hang out. And he was always watching some game on TV, even some that must have been played twenty or thirty years ago. I remember it used to drive Mom crazy, but she learned to put up with it, I guess. I don't know where he got that from, because as I remember Granddad, he never had that interest. He'd watch farm shows until the cows came home—literally—and he was a diehard Giants fan—the football team—but I hardly ever saw him watch a baseball game except maybe the World Series. But Dad, he was always interested. Maybe he picked it up in school. And, of course, we do live in Cooperstown, so he would have gotten a lot of what you might call positive reinforcement. Famous players through town, a big annual deal over at the Hall, and all of that."

"So as I understand what you're telling me, it looks like about a hundred years ago, your family took on some sort of obligation to some people they didn't know, guarding some kind of treasure they never saw. And everybody had funny names and it was all governed by some kind of secret code. And now you're telling me that you think it has something to do with baseball, and more specifically, with a century of baseball scandals. Do I have that right?"

"The basics, yes. The only thing I'd change is to be clear that the evidence seems to suggest, at the least, that my father made some sort of connection to baseball. Whether that was real, or just something he imagined, I can't say."

"Okay, but here's a question. Presumably, your father had known about this obligation since sometime early in his adult life when he heard about it from his father, your granddad. And he'd been fulfilling that obligation himself since, what did you say, 2008 or even earlier? So well over a decade. And for all that time, he'd been this huge baseball fan. But over all of those years, and all those log entries, he never made the connection between the two. Right?"

"Right."

"So what changed? Assuming you're right about his notes being made all at the same time, and therefore quite recently—and something I noticed that you didn't mention is that several of those printouts have date codes in the website footers and they are all dated last year, shortly before he passed—why did this light suddenly start flashing Morse Code in his head telling him these two big things in his life were actually one and the same, or at least closely interrelated? I mean, your family has been involved in this thing since at least 1934, and he'd probably been in on it for years himself. What happened that made the connection for him?"

"Now," Liz replied, "you're down to the first real question in all of this, and it's one I have been thinking about a lot. And here's where I am on that. Taking your assumption that these codes are for different people, if you look at the logbook since my dad took it over, there have been only two people who have asked for the keys, or whatever that symbol signifies. No telling who they were. This guy 'Tres' seems to have been a regular of sorts in recent years, but other than that, it's been a long time since anybody else was logged in. Then there is that very last entry, somebody calling himself 'Lot Lizard.' He'd, and I am assuming these are all men, but it doesn't matter . . . he'd never been there before. First-timer.

"Here's what I think. I think my dad was different from his father and Grampa Jake because he actually followed baseball pretty closely. Watched it on TV, read about it, and for all I know played fantasy games on his computer when he should have been working. The point is, he actually knew the game.

"I think he recognized 'Lot Lizard.' I think that's how he made the connection and why he made it when he did. Then it was just a matter of some online research, and we know for a fact that he did that, and boom—there's the connection. And maybe that's what he wanted to tell me there at the end but never got to."

"So you're thinking this 'Lot Lizard' was a player? Maybe somebody whose face he recognized from all of his time over at the Hall of Fame?"

"I don't know. Could be a player, or maybe a club owner . . . really anybody prominent and connected to the game. To me, at least, that's what makes this make some sense. It doesn't explain what it's all about, or who is involved in it, but I do believe it has to do with baseball. And it seems pretty clear that your collection of papers and Jocko's Journal were some sort of catalyst. That's why I read your book, and that's why I came to your book party. I want to try to unwind this thing and figure out what it's all about. I thought you might like to help out."

It was a pure joy driving through Upstate New York on the new interstate. *Glad I didn't have to do this a few years ago*, he thought. *That would have seemed, no, that would have been, interminable. Thank God for Dwight Eisenhower.*

Alas, the joy did not last long. Once he came to the turnoff for the state highway, he was back on a narrow, rutted two-lane. The signage was terrible, but that didn't really matter to him since he knew that his destination lay at the very end of this road. This was his second time coming up here this year, though the first on this particular business. He wondered for a moment why he had not made the trip more often, but as the miles passed slowly by, he realized that he knew the answer. You had to really want to go to Cooperstown. It wasn't one of those places you just happened to pass through.

He also knew he'd likely be making this trip with some frequency in the future, so he decided to enjoy it as best he could. *At least*, he thought, *I can pay a visit to the Hall of Fame.*

Coming into town from the south, it took him only a couple of obvious turns to reach the corner of Main and Chestnut. He had solid directions from there and was able to find parking close by his destination, the offices of A. Holt Greenstick, Landscapers. He walked the short distance to the building and entered through the double glass doors. Two women looked up from their work as he came in.

"Good afternoon," he said. "I hope you can help me. I'm looking for Charlie Fairchild."

The younger of the two workers stood. "Charlie's in his office," she said, pointing to an open door several feet to the man's left. "Can I tell him who's asking?"

"Actually, he doesn't know me. But his father and mine were long-time friends. I was in town for the Hall of Fame, and I wanted to stop by and say hello."

The woman, who was in actuality the company's bookkeeper, poked her head into her boss's office and passed the message along. Charlie followed her out and offered a hand to his visitor. "I'm Charlie. And I have a pretty good idea who you are. Please do come in." With that, they went into Charlie's office, and he closed the door behind them. "How is your dad? I'm thinking since you are here that maybe he's not very well."

"No, Dad passed away a couple of years ago. He was a hard liver, you know, and I think it finally caught up with him. He was living in a nursing home down in Florida toward the end, and we knew it was coming."

"You know, I think I first met your father many, many years ago. I have a vague memory of a man who had dinner with us out on our farm, and I think that must have been him. I guess he and my dad had some real adventures back in World War I. Of course, Dad probably did a little embellishing on all that. Met him again three or four years ago."

"I never had the pleasure of meeting Jake. But like you, I certainly heard lots of stories. You know, my dad told me more than once that Jake had actually saved his life. Listen, I've never done this before. I guess I am supposed to say this weird thing to you. He melts rainbows paying heed. Mean anything to you?"

"Devilish journeymen toil," came the scripted reply. They proceeded to complete a ritual that would, soon enough, be familiar to both of them.

"Do you need the keys?"

"No. Actually, I just came up to give you the new code names. I guess you log them in. I'm not supposed to ask for the keys unless I am instructed to do that. The new names are Haircut, Horse Lover, and Blade."

Charlie made a note, unsure, but thinking that he should probably not reveal the location of the journal to his visitor.

"I'll make sure they get into the log. And I guess I need to get your code name as well."

"You know, I had never even thought of that. What was my dad's code name, if you can tell me?"

"Successful. He called himself Successful."

"Hmmph. That's clever." He paused for a moment. "Let's call me Successor."

"That works. I'll use that from now on. Anything else we need to do?"

"Nah. I know you're busy. There's an exhibit over at the Hall that I want to visit, and then I need to be on the road before it gets too late. Till next time, then?"

"Next time." They shook hands, and Charlie's visitor left. He closed his office door again, pulled out the log, and made the requisite entry. I wonder who these guys really are, he thought. But before long, he was again immersed in his work.

———

"Seems to me the keys are the key to the whole thing." Adam had a knack for stating the obvious. He and Liz had reconvened the following morning over bagels and eggs at one of those trendy East Side cafés.

"Well," Liz replied after throwing him the look his comment deserved, "we have the keys. What we—I—don't have at this point is the lock. Or more correctly, the door. It seems to me there's a good chance that you're going to find those papers you wrote about, or something to do with them, behind that door, wherever it is, and whatever it leads to. And it seems pretty clear as well that the door itself is somewhere in Cooperstown. I know the town, but you seem to have an eye for this sort of thing. And that's why I showed up yesterday. To see if I could convince you to take an interest in this and come up north to help conduct a search."

"So," Adam said, "you're thinking of doing a treasure hunt."

"Exactly. There's a secret here that my family has been keeping, or helping to keep, since the 1930s. I don't know what it is. I don't know why we were chosen. I don't know why we are still doing it, or were until my dad passed. I don't know what he was going to tell me around the time he died. And I don't know whether finding this door will answer any of those questions. But I need to find out whatever I can. Will you help me?"

Adam sat quietly for a long moment, pondering his response. This could be a real wild goose chase, a waste of time. And he remembered his last visit to Cooperstown, which had ended in an abrupt and unexpected way. It had left a bad taste. But also a taste for . . . not revenge, exactly, but validation. Maybe that was the word. Besides, he was getting to like the company.

"Yes, I'll come up there," he said at last, to Liz's obvious relief. "But I'd like to give Jason a call and see if he can come over there as well. He's pretty handy if we need to do anything like, say, assist the door in opening if we find it. That okay with you?"

"You mean there really is a Jason? And his name really is Jason? I truly thought you had made that up as part of the story."

Adam smiled. "There is indeed a Jason, and that really is his name. Jason Drumm. Lives up near the border with Canada. You okay with that?"

"Hey. The more the merrier, as the saying goes. Besides," she went on with a twinkle in her eye, "maybe he's cute."

"Yeah," said Adam, watching the bait wiggle on the hook but not biting. "There's that. But what I'm really thinking is this. You have the keys to this door, it's true. But, depending on where the door is and what's on the other side, you might break the law by going through it. And you would have a really tough claim of ownership to anything on the other side, even just to look and see what it is. But if those Hancock papers are actually there, which, again, we suspect but don't know for sure, there's at least an argument to be made that Jason is there to retrieve his stolen property. It's a tenuous argument, to be sure, and not having the original of Jocko's journal makes it even more so. But at least it's an argument. Of course, all of that assumes that anyone finds out what we're doing and can make a claim themselves."

"See? I knew there was a reason I needed you to come along."

<hr>

"Hank," Charlie said to his oldest offspring, "You're twenty-one now, and I want to tell you how proud I am of you and the way you've grown into a fine young man. It gives me the confidence to have the conversation that we're about to have."

"Dad, come on! You think I don't know about that stuff? Things are different now. Just last week . . ."

"Stop right there! That's not the conversation I was thinking of, and that's absolutely not something I want to know about! There's something you need to know, a kind of a family secret, and one way or another, it's going to impact the rest of your life." He had his son's attention now.

"Many years ago, not long after your grandparents moved out here to Otsego County and started the farm, your granddad got a visit from an old war buddy of his. He used to call him 'the captain.' I have met the man myself a couple of times, though I don't know his name. He was just always the captain. But I remember sitting at dinner one night when he visited for the first time, and he told stories about how Dad, your grand-dad, had saved his life during the war, and how he'd always been grateful for that. The rest of it, I heard only later, mostly when I turned twenty-one and my dad sat me down for the same talk I'm about to have with you."

Charlie proceeded to fill his son in on the basics of the commitment Jake had made to the captain and his unknown employers, the ways the family had benefitted in the years since, and the details of how the arrangement was to work.

"Now," he continued, "and this is the important part . . . the idea was that this arrangement was going to go on for many years. And these guys had developed a way to keep it going. They would change from time to time themselves, and that's why Granddad needed to keep a roster of who was in and who was out. But he agreed, and he made it binding on the Fairchild family, that we would remain the only keepers of the keys. We would pass that responsibility from oldest son to oldest son down through the generations. And that's what I am starting to do today.

"If you agree to take this on as a lifetime obligation, and you give me your solemn word of honor on that, I will show you where I keep the keys and the logbook, and I'll show you where the door is. It's a pretty good secret. And then, when the time comes, and eventually it will, well, you'll just take over the job and then you pass it along to your own boy when he's ready. And—I cannot emphasize this enough—even though you have the keys and know where the entrance to the storage area is, you can never go inside. You can never know what's in there. Never. Or we could lose everything. I know it's a lot to think about, but I need to know if I can count on you for this."

"Wow . . . ," Hank replied, then after a moment, he added, "Of course you can. I mean, it sounds fascinating, and mysterious, and strange all at once. But yes. I'll keep it going. But how do I do that? Do we know the names of these guys? I guess if there's a list in this logbook, I guess we must."

"Well, not exactly. They have actually gone to a good bit of trouble to remain anonymous. Let me explain to you how this works."

Reaching First

Today, even Max was in a reflective mood. What turn of the wheel had brought him to this time and this place?

Chance is a funny thing. It gives to some, takes from others. For Max, chance had been a benefactor. His small-town Pennsylvania upbringing had set him on his career course, accompanying his father from an early age to the barns where he was first exposed to the silver-tongued fast talkers peddling cattle or used tractors or antique butter churns. He had always been amazed at just how many antique butter churns there were in Pennsylvania.

He had been far more amazed at the auction talk itself. How did they do that auction cry? How could any human tongue do such a thing? How could lips move that way without spoiling what the tongue could accomplish? "One dollar bid, now two, now two" was about as far as he could get on his own at first, and even that was lost as he tried to match the speed of the local auctioneers. So, he made a point of dragging his father forward to sit in the front row, at auction after auction, until the callers began to recognize the young fellow who was trying to mimic their speech and their movements. Soon they would welcome him by name, and some even started saving him a seat up front if he and his father were late arriving. There he would sit, often on his own, taking in the cadence and learning the routines of the room. Before long, he was taken on by one caller as an apprentice and, as he grew older and his skills developed, was even given the chance to sell the occasional item on his own. Eventually, the "kid caller" became an attraction in his own right.

But in the end it was also chance that had allowed him to escape the barns and the feedlots and the estate sales of his youth. It was chance that had brought Richard Marbury to central Pennsylvania one April day—the same Richard Marbury whose name graced one of New York City's premier auction houses. It was chance that had caused the engine of his sleek black Mercedes sedan to overheat while on his way through town, and chance that he had chosen to pull into Jack's Super Service across from the auction barn. It was a dead-level certainty that Jack did not have a hose in stock suitable to repair the split one that had caused the problem, since Jack maintained little parts inventory of any kind, and certainly none for a Mercedes. But fortune intervened once more when Jack, after a quick phone call, allowed as how he could obtain that hose from a buddy in the next town and have the car ready to roll in about three or four hours. And once more when, not knowing who his customer was but merely seeking to help him pass the time, Jack pointed across the road to the auction barn, where the parking lot was beginning to fill, and suggested it as a center of local entertainment if his visitor was of such a mind.

It was not exactly what one might call a busman's holiday, because the contrast between the staid multi-digit events at Marbury House and the raucous bidding wars of a rural barn where five dollars was often an extravagant offer, and for some a day's wage, was stark indeed. But there was a fundamental underlying sameness to the two, and Marbury decided his course, signed for a numbered paddle, settled into a metal folding chair, and took in the scene. Soon he, too, was lost in the singsong of the auctioneer. And that is when the unexpected happened.

The next object on the block was an old guitar of some sort—not a Gibson or a Martin or any other make that Marbury recognized, but just an old banger that showed signs of having been played hard for many years. And as it was placed before the crowd, the auctioneer moved aside, and up stepped this kid. Couldn't have been more than sixteen. Dressed in overalls and a plaid shirt, so he looked just like one of the crowd, but there at his neck was a white bow tie. His hair looked like it had been cut with shearing scissors, and it probably had. It appeared he'd slicked it down with some sort of grease, an effort that was mostly, but not entirely, successful. But he had a big smile and he showed no fear. So, some style, some poise, a little flair, and an aura of self-confidence. Pretty good for a kid. What really got Marbury's attention, though, was the way the bidders in the room suddenly sat to attention and how quickly the undertone of conversation ceased. It was almost as if they had come just for this moment, as if all else had been mere prelude. As soon as the young fellow opened his mouth, Marbury understood.

To be an auctioneer was a noble calling, for it was the responsibility of the auctioneer to find and achieve the true worth of whatever object lay before him or her. An auctioneer needed a gift of speech and an eye for value, but also a sensitivity to the human character, that of the buyer, and that of the seller. Not anyone could do this job, but with proper training, many could, and some could do it well. To be an exceptional auctioneer, though, to rise to the elite tier as Marbury himself had done years ago, one needed more. One needed an effervescent appreciation of the object on the block, an innate sense of where the sentiment in the room resided at any given moment, and a sharp eye for opportunity on those few occasions when it lay itself open before you. More than that, one needed a signature style, a voice or a manner that made the bidders yearn to be buyers, if only to share the moment with you. The basics could be learned, but only one born with these gifts could be great.

And that is what had captured Richard Marbury's attention in that old auction barn that afternoon as he waited for Jack to fetch and install the new hose. It was not just the raw enthusiasm of this young auctioneer or his boyish charm or his effort at a touch of style, though all were reflective of something below the surface. It was the way he could draw the bidders, and even some who had not intended to be bidders, into his small niche at the front of the room, as if in some way they had to occupy it with him. And it was the musicality of his chant, which far exceeded that of the old guitar he was selling. You knew it was an old piece of farmhouse flotsam, but listening to this kid, you wanted to believe Johnny Cash had played it at Folsom or Willie Nelson had worked a hole into it and filled it with autographs. The kid sold that five-dollar wall hanger for seventy-five, and if he didn't have a heart, he might even have gone higher.

Marbury had not come to town to scout talent. He had not known the town was there, had had no intention of stopping, let alone spending three hours on a rickety old chair in a drafty old barn. But by the time Jack had returned and installed the new hose in the Mercedes, Marbury had introduced himself to the young auctioneer, offered to train him in all the finer points of the business, and hired him on as a new apprentice. Max Tomhoff rode shotgun in that Mercedes all the way to New York City, and he never looked back.

———————

"Boys, welcome to A. Holt Greenstick Landscaping, and welcome to Cooperstown. I gather you have been here before," she said with just a hint of irony.

Adam and Jason had driven to town the day before from their separate points of origin and, having passed the gauntlet in the outer office, were seated across the desk from Liz, now the company's CEO.

Jason picked up the thread, and the hint. "Well, we did have a chance to visit over at the Hall of Fame a couple of years ago," he deadpanned. "Nice collection."

"All right, you two. Let's get down to business," Adam interjected.

"Right," replied Liz. "Just to recap for you, Jason, this company was started by my great-granddad, Jake Fairchild, back in the 1930s, and we've been in this same location, same building actually, ever since. I think we'd all agree it was a strange time to be starting up a business, what with the Depression and all, but that's what happened. And it appears that he did that with some encouragement, and probably some help, from some wealthy backers who have remained anonymous down through all these years. I have no idea who they were. But they had to be influential, because right away the company got some really major contracts. They . . . I guess I should say we . . . did the primary landscaping work for the Village itself, which means all the parks and public areas, for the ball field when it was made into a modern ballpark back around that time, for the Hall of Fame after that was built, for the big resort hotel on the lake, and some other places. It's a small town, but that was a big deal, especially for a company nobody ever heard of. And for the most part, we still service those properties to this day. My point is, these people must have had some serious pull.

"But," she said, looking at Jason, "as Adam has probably told you, there appears to have been a quid pro quo of some sort. A few months after I took over for my dad, who died of a stroke last year, I came across a set of keys and some papers that had been tucked into the back of a drawer in this old desk. And as best I can tell from the papers, our family has been keeping watch over some sort of secret all these years. I don't know if that is some kind of treasure, or a cache of papers of some sort, or a famous stolen diamond. It could be anything. But it is pretty clear that whoever those men were, their successors were still accessing something right up until the time my dad passed.

"The week he died, Dad told me he wanted to meet over dinner to talk with me about something, but we never had that dinner and I never learned what it was. However, in the same drawer with the keys and the older papers was another envelope with a list my dad had made, apparently not long before he died. It was a list of baseball scandals with dates that matched a lot of those in the older papers. It wasn't a perfect match, and his list only corresponded with a certain type of information. But it was close. And the last entry on his list was the auction down in New York City where they sold off the papers, or whatever it was, that you and Adam claimed to have found. And there was a copy of the article from *The Times* about that sale. But even then, I didn't make any connection to you until I happened to read Adam's book. I try to read anything that talks about Cooperstown, and someone in town had mentioned it. I had to read it twice to be sure it really matched my dad's notes. And then, of course, there was the Hall of Fame connection, or at least the one you guys apparently suspected. That's when I went down to the City to meet Adam at his book signing. In the meantime, in the several months since Dad passed, no one has reached out in any way to ask about what I found in the drawer, or at least no one I know of."

"So," said Adam, picking up the narrative, "that's kind of why we're here. We have a set of keys, a starting point around the time when lots of big changes were made to the town, and some pretty strong hints that we are probably looking for something, probably at least some papers, relating in some way to scandals in baseball. Whatever it is, some people have gone to very great lengths to assure that it remains secret, although at the same time, as I think about it, they seem to have wanted to preserve it. Maybe out of a sense of history. That would certainly fit with the Jocko papers and their anonymous buyer. You know, Jason, we thought it was the people at the Hall of Fame, and maybe it was. After all, this is Cooperstown. But this seems to have started years before the Hall was built. My guess is that if we solve one mystery, we'll solve the other at the same time."

"Okay," said Jason. "So this is some sort of quest. Something like that. Where do we start?"

<hr />

Hank Fairchild looked up from his desk as a man with a large brief-case entered his office. The man stood around six feet tall, had white hair with traces of what might have been blond, wore thick glasses with heavy black frames reminiscent of Charlie Sheen in the movie *Major League*, one of Hank's favorites, and featured a mustache that almost looked like it belonged on someone else. He had what might be described as a craggy look about his face, and some serious age lines.

"Mr. Fairchild," the man began, "we've not met before. You can call me Lot Lizard."

Hank sat up in his chair. He knew the name. The name had been in the logbook for all the years he had been maintaining it. And now, in a single sentence, the name assumed a human form. It made some things suddenly seem real, others somehow different.

"He melts rainbows paying heed." The stranger began the familiar ritual.

"Devilish journeymen toil," came the response.

"I rented view plus Uncle Hooch."

"Oh battle unhappiest. Sir, if you would be good enough to step back into the outer office for just a moment, I will be ready to help you."

Lot Lizard returned to the reception area, closing the door behind him, and took a seat on one of the three well-worn visitors' chairs. Shortly after, Hank opened the door and gestured to his guest. "I have what we need," he said. "I'll show you to the place, then leave you to your work."

Once at the doorway, Lot Lizard took the keys, opened the lock, entered the darkened space, and closed the door behind him. As usual, Hank found excuses to hang around the area until the visitor reemerged, his briefcase seeming somehow much lighter than before. All quite routine, or at least as routine as these little encounters tended to be. The man made his goodbyes and disappeared as quickly as he had come.

Yes, it was all routine. And yet, this time Hank had a sense that he knew who this guy calling himself Lot Lizard really was. He was sure they had never met, but there was something strangely familiar about him. And for the next several days, somewhere in the darkest recesses of his brain, he worked at the problem as one would a forgotten word or a friend from long ago. And then, suddenly, a breeze of recognition came up and swept away the darkness.

He knew, or at least he suspected, who this latest visitor had been.

It was at that point that his mind really began to churn.

<hr />

Adam took the cue. "When we last talked, Liz asked me to give that very question some thought. Where do we start? How do we narrow this down? One obvious thing I think we can take for granted is that there is a doorway somewhere in Cooperstown with a lock that fits one or another of these rather oversized keys. And just as obviously, we can't try those keys on every door in town. So we need a plan of some sort to guide the search.

"Now, it seems to me that there are some coincidences that can help with that. Namely, the startup of the company and the first dates in the old logbook both date back to the 1930s, and that was also the time when lots of things were happening around town here. I did a little research on that. There was a big renovation of what is now Doubleday Field—a new field, a new grandstand, new bleachers, new parking. It's pretty clear that the folks here in Cooperstown were starting to embrace the idea that this was the home of baseball. Then they started building the Hall of Fame here, too. And that big hotel, the one over by the lake, was right in the middle of it, because the guy who owned that—Clark, I think his name was—well he was the guy who was building the Hall of

Fame. They were upgrading the water and sewer systems, and that was a lot of construction. This place must have been torn to hell. It would have been the perfect time to build a little secret vault somewhere in town, probably tied into one of those projects. And I'm guessing that's just what somebody did.

"Wherever this magic doorway is, it could be inside any of the buildings, or even the outbuildings, that were constructed back then. But I am thinking it probably is not. Because if it is, they wouldn't have decided to set up a landscaping business as a cover—and that's what this is, Liz, no offense. They'd have started a maintenance service of some sort—plumbers, electrical, janitors, whatever. People who would have had a reason to wander around inside spaces that were otherwise private. But they started, or got your family to start, a landscaping business. And then they got you all of these big accounts that you've kept for almost a century. That has got to be significant. And I think that's how we are going to solve this thing. We are going to take a tour of all of the oldest A. Holt Greenstick accounts—and not just the biggest ones, because they could all have been nothing more than bright shiny objects intended to deflect a search—and see if we can't find the door we are looking for."

Liz thought for a moment, then said, "Adam, I think you are really on to something. Working outside, we don't deal with a lot of doors ourselves. But we certainly do see them here and there. I'll put together a list, including a few of the private houses that we have maintained for a long time, and we can start on that in the morning. Why don't you guys take a walk around town, maybe stop in at the Hall or run out to the Fenimore, and let's meet for dinner around six or so. There's a nice Italian place on Main, Calabrese's. Not fancy, but the food's good, and the owner is an old friend. Plus, they have a really good wine list, and I may need a good glass of wine by then."

"You aren't the only one," said Jason, breaking his prolonged silence. "This is a lot to take in."

It was the mustache and the glasses that had thrown him. Not that the man had them, but that they were wrong for him. Unnatural. And prominent enough to draw the eye. Take them away, add in some thin-rimmed eyewear, and he thought he had his man. He googled a name, clicked on a bio, pulled out the attendant photo, enlarged it on his screen, and sent it to the color printer. Then, amused by a memory of having done something similar as a youngster and having been caught and punished, he drew in a mustache similar to the one he remembered his visitor as possessing and blackened the frames of the eyeglasses in the photo with a marker. Damn! This was a guy with a serious baseball connection; that's why Hank recognized him.

Hank's next step was to pull out the old logbook for a closer inspection. He might have a pretty good idea who Lot Lizard was, but there were a lot of other names entered into the book over the years, and he had no idea who any of them really were. The true identity of even his most frequent visitor, who called himself Tres, was a complete mystery to him. Chasing those names would be a dead end for sure. But he did have something else. He had the dates, or at least the years, when one or another of these men had borrowed the keys, not only from him, but from his father and his grandfather. If he could figure out some connection between Lot Lizard and those dates, or more correctly, between baseball and those dates, since Lot Lizard, he could see, had not been involved in this enterprise until perhaps thirty years before, then he might be able to reason out what might be on the other side of that door. Sure, the easy thing would be simply to open the door and look for himself. But Hank was a man of honor, and that he had pledged never to do. No one, however, had ever instructed him not to wonder about it.

What could this be? What could he and his forbears have been guarding for all these years? It could, he supposed, be memorabilia of some sort. Babe Ruth's bat, Ty Cobb's spikes, that sort of thing. But hell, the Hall of Fame is just down the road and it is full of that stuff. So not likely. Same, he figured, for record books, autographs, probably even baseball cards. That stuff was everywhere in town and hardly merited this kind of attention. No, it had to be something deeper, something worth hiding away from the world.

It occurred to Hank around that time that baseball was really good about keeping records of just about everything, and that recordkeeping included what amounted to time stamps. Baseball had a timeline, and, as it happened, so did Hank. He had the logbook. Maybe he could find a correspondence between the two. He turned back to the computer, went to Google, and typed in "timeline major league baseball." It took the search engine less than a second to return six million and seven hundred thousand hits. Or so it claimed.

Hank wasn't that curious. But he was curious enough to make a start. There was a Wikipedia entry, but it amounted only to a graphic showing the dates when various teams had attained major league status. It was, he guessed, interesting to know that the Troy Trojans and the Worcester Worcesters had once been regarded as tops in their game. But it was clearly not what he was looking for. Next up was a list of dates featured by Ken Burns in his documentary film series on the game. They included a variety of events, many centered on things like when Babe Ruth was traded or when Yankee Stadium opened. Nice, but again, not *the* list he suspected he needed. Then something called Timetoast.com offered an interactive timeline of the game, but that one focused a lot of attention on firsts—the first stolen base, Joe DiMaggio's hitting streak, and so forth. No obvious connection there. It was when he came upon the extraordinarily complete listing at a site called Timelines.ws that he began to form the glimmer of an idea. That particular listing went on and on, noting significant births (*e.g.*, Jackie Robinson, Harry Carey), deaths, hits, games—you name it. *All of this*, thought Hank, *along with all of the individual records, team records, it's all public information. The fact that I am reading it here proves it. There would be no reason to keep that information in deep storage, let alone deep secret storage. No*, he thought, *I am looking for something else. And maybe there are some hints to it here, some passing references to things that might have a lot more to them than meets the eye. The Black Sox. Pete Rose's gambling problem. Maybe I need to tweak my search terms just a little.*

That was when he returned to Google with a new query: "timeline major league baseball scandals."

Bingo! Only about two million hits this time, but not far down the list was a link to an item titled "MLB History: 20 Most Shocking Scandals in Baseball History." That timeline, with its accompanying thumbnails, went way back, even into the 1870s, but it also listed a lot of more recent scandals, though truth be told, Hank didn't think some of them amounted to much. But they had dates, and he made assiduous notes of those. Then he went to some of the other sites Google had captured. Before long, he felt like he had a pretty comprehensive list of scandals. He took out a yellow legal pad and arranged them into a rough timeline of his own, then he opened his desk drawer and pulled out the logbook.

The day dawned sunny and bright, and the temperatures promised to cooperate. They had a lovely day on which to commence their quest.

Liz pulled out her list. "Let's start with a couple of houses that are nearby. Actually, just around the block. They back onto the ballpark, and the families that own them have been with us from the beginning. One of the things you will quickly learn about Cooperstown is just how many families have lived here almost forever. Anyway, I have already called both owners and told them I had some visiting firemen in town and would like to show off our work. We've all known each other forever, grown up and been in school together. So, no problem."

That portion of the tour lasted only a short time. There were a couple of outdoor sheds and, of course, some basement doors facing out into the yards, and the "inspection team" very subtly tested the keys in these. But as expected, the keys, which were distinctly oversized, did not so much as threaten to open any of the locks they encountered. Big keys, small locks.

From there, the group circled around to Doubleday Field, the site of the annual Hall of Fame Classic, a sort of all-star old timers' game that had replaced the traditional major league contest some years earlier, and a large number of other contests. This was a more hopeful venue and presented a greater challenge to the search. They tried the outbuildings, the restrooms, the concession areas, the groundskeeping office, the dressing rooms. No joy. They wandered the perimeter and the field itself, looking for hidden entrances, alcoves, locked gates—in short, anything they could find. Still no joy.

"This is a complex facility," said Adam after an hour or so, "and I don't know that we can write it off entirely. I mean, there could be a door inside one of these rooms that we couldn't get into, although that would seem to defeat the purpose of having so many keys. But if it's here, we have obviously missed it."

"Probably time to move on," offered Jason as Liz nodded agreement and again consulted her list.

"Let's try the Hall," she suggested. "I know it would please you guys if we found it over there."

They walked the couple of blocks to the Hall and its offices. Liz made a call on her cell phone to alert someone at the Hall of their presence, lest the security staff become concerned about a small group that seemed to be poking around.

"Honestly, guys, I don't think this door we're looking for is inside the Hall. If it was, as you said, Adam, why would these people need a landscaping company? If they are some kind of baseball bigwigs, baseball royalty, they'd have far better access to the inside of that building than anybody in my family. Plus, if it was really secret, and if some or all of them were recognizable even to my dad, how would they ever access their little hideaway without drawing massive attention to themselves? So I think if it's there, it will be somewhere outside the building."

That made sense to everyone, so they concentrated their search on the perimeter and the adjacent grounds. They began at the median on Fair Street, just east of the Hall complex and not technically part of it. But this was Village land and itself included in a company maintenance contract. In the center of the median was a statue of James Fenimore Cooper, after whose family, among the earliest settlers, the village was named, but there were no doors to be seen. Then it was on to the Hall itself, a somewhat convoluted building on the inside, but a much simpler one without. They tested all the doors they encountered, examined the statues of Johnny Podres and Roy Campanella in the rear of the building and the stone path between the two, looked for any evidence of hidden entrances, and, as they had at the ballpark, came up empty.

"Let's go grab some lunch at the Doubleday, and we can move on to The Inn. That's another old client, though I think it was still a private home when we started there back in the thirties. These days it's your basic fancy B-n-B. Lovely old building, but not much to it. Then if there's time, we can move on to the resort. That's going to take a while, because the building is old and complex and the grounds are extensive. We might find some pretty old doors and outdoor structures over there, though."

———— ⚾ ————

Hank had been in front of the computer for less than two hours, but already he had found a great many news articles, magazine pieces, and in some cases even books that talked about baseball-related scandals that seemed to correspond, at least roughly, with many of the dates in the log the family had been maintaining. Some pre-dated the 1930s, when the recordkeeping began—obvious ones that everyone knew about, like the time the Chicago White Sox, forever afterward known of course as the Black Sox, had taken money from gamblers to throw the 1919 World Series, or another one involving gambling and Pete Rose, a prominent Cincinnati player back in the day, but also some really obscure ones, like the one about an umpire who was thrown out of baseball for life back in the 1870s for taking bribes to influence games, or the night the Cleveland Indians gave away cheap beer to fans and ended up with a riot at their stadium. He was surprised to see just how much weird and awful stuff had happened down through the years.

There were also, he noticed, some years where someone had accessed the keys but for which he could not find any information about wrongdoing or scandals. Given how much he *had* found, that was quite curious, and it got him thinking about the recent visit from the guy calling himself Lot Lizard. The most recent scandal he had come across in his research was the one where the Houston Astros were using cameras to steal signs from opposing catchers, then signaling them to batters by banging on trashcans, even in the World Series. There was even a question about whether one of their players, Jose Altuve, who hit the walk-off home run that eliminated the Yankees in a league championship series, and who then grasped his jersey so that teammates could not rip it off as commonly happens, was wearing a buzzer so he could receive the signs. But that all came out back in 2019, which corresponded with the last time he'd been visited by the fellow he knew as Tres. There was nothing like that going on now, at least nothing he knew of.

So what might this latest visit have been about?

The answer eluded him for quite a while, and truth be told, it was not his highest priority. Things had been pretty busy around the office lately. Plus, he was breaking in some new employees and had been neglecting their training and the need for some temporary enhanced oversight. He needed to turn his attention back to business and put this baseball mystery, if that was what it was, out of mind for a while. And that is precisely where it stayed until he had the time, one Sunday, to catch up on his reading.

Hank was one of those people, and they are legion, who subscribe to *The Times* but then become overwhelmed by the sheer volume of the newspaper as it builds up each day into a mountain of old headlines, old news accounts, old editorials, old crossword puzzles, and old advertising. Catching up on those rare down days when it was possible, typically gray and rainy weekend days, was akin to nothing so much as an archeological dig through layers of long-past events and the fleeting flotsam and jetsam of pop culture. And it was on just such a day that Hank, having turned over the stack of papers to put the oldest on top, came across a brief article reporting on the outcome of an auction of baseball memorabilia, mainly papers of some sort, at Marbury House down in the City. It had something to do with Ty Cobb, a name Hank not only knew well but had seen once or twice in his research, and some anonymous buyer had paid millions of dollars for it. No one was sure who. On a hunch, Hank checked the date of the sale and realized it had been just a few days before he had been visited by Lot Lizard. Hank then read through the remaining two or three feet of newspapers, keeping an eye out for more information, but there was no follow-up information of any kind, either about who had purchased the collection of papers or what was in them.

Hank came to believe that he, and perhaps he alone, had the answer to at least one of those questions.

—◈ ◈—

It was nearly two o'clock when they reached the grounds of the resort, and the frustrations of a thus far failed search were beginning to show.

Still, the intrepid trio soldiered on. Well, in any event, they found the energy to circle the mammoth building from its southeast corner to . . . its southeast corner. There were quite a number of doorways along their path, and they tested each of the ones they found locked, all to no avail. Liz suggested they also try locks on the lower level inside the building, which they proceeded to do with the same outcome. It was possible, they thought, that there was at least one service level still further down, and for a moment that seemed promising. But Jason then pointed out that if one of their keys did not give them access to such a level, it was almost certainly not going to lead them to the hoped-for prize.

To finish the search of the resort, they went back outside and walked the grounds, testing the locks on a couple of well-camouflaged outbuildings and looking for any trap doors or other subtle points of entry they could see. There were none. Then, with a final burst of energy, they walked out to the road and over to the adjacent golf course, where they once again searched in vain.

"I don't know about you guys," said Liz at this point, "but I am bushed. I can barely move. But for a beer and maybe dinner, I can probably make it back to the hotel. What do you say?"

That was an easy one, and the three treasure hunters retraced their steps, then found themselves a small table on a veranda outside the less formal of the hotel's main restaurants, one that offered a beautiful view of Lake Otsego, the centerpiece and likely *raison d'être* for the resort. They ordered some snacks and a pitcher of one of the local brews on offer and settled in to review the day's labors.

"Well," said Adam, "that was certainly a colossal waste of time."

"Oh, I don't know," Jason replied. "We now know of a great many places where there is *not* a lock that can be opened with one of these keys."

"Plus," Liz chimed in, "on the positive side, we have covered pretty much all of the biggest places we might think of to search. I mean, we do have some smaller properties that we have serviced for a very long time, and I suppose it could be at any one of them. And maybe our mistake was in thinking we'd find the door at one of the most public and obvious places. But we're not completely out of options. Remember, it is almost a certainty that the door is here in or near town somewhere. We might have been very close already, and simply not looked in the right direction. Maybe tomorrow we can be a little more systematic."

"About tomorrow," Jason interjected. "This has been fun, and it was great to meet you, Liz, and even to see you again." The latter comment was directed at Adam. "But I need to get back out to the farm. Rooster is doing his best, I'm sure, but I can't leave him out there on his own forever. So I will need to head out sometime before noon tomorrow."

"Understood," said Adam, "though I hate for you to miss the big reveal if it ever comes."

"I'm sure you'll let me know if you find something interesting. You'd damn well better!"

"Of course," promised Liz. "Hey. Shall we order some dinner? It's particularly pleasant out tonight, and the food here is quite good."

After the shrimp cocktail and chilled oysters that they shared, the mint and garlic-crusted rack of lamb (Adam), coq au vin (Jason), and king salmon with lump crab tortelloni (Liz), the thyme roasted heirloom carrots, and the hand-cut fried Kennebec potatoes with smoked sea salt and curry ketchup—all washed down with a private label Napa Cabernet—it is no wonder that coffee alone was all the temptation they could each handle to finish the meal. Chairs pulled back in a line and legs extended to facilitate digestion, or perhaps simply because all three were too tired to bend their knees or remain fully upright, they gazed across the lake in the deepening twilight.

It was Jason who raised the question that had occurred to neither of his companions. "What's that?" he asked, pointing at a tall structure a distance away along the eastern shore.

"Oh," replied tour guide Liz. "That's Kingfisher Tower. That's been there forever. Some of us locals just call it the Castle. It's not a real castle, of course. Edward Clark—the first Edward Clark, the one who partnered with Singer and made all the money—built that back in the 1870s. I don't know if he liked to go there and look at the lake from the top of the tower, or if he was just creating some eye candy for tourists. I don't know if they even had tourists around here back then. But it's become quite a local landmark."

"Well," Jason interjected, "if you wanted to hide something in plain sight, that looks to me like about the best place I've ever seen to do it. Can people get into the place? It looks like there might be some big, old doors over there."

"The general public?" Liz returned. "No, it's closed to the general public. And the only way over there is by boat. There's a little dock of sorts, but it's in full public view, and, like I said, you're not supposed to be there. Now, as it happens, back behind the tower itself, there is a bit of a lawn and a landscaped area. And as it happens, the A. Holt Greenstick company has a contract to maintain those grounds. Had it since the 1930s, I think, or at least for a very long time." By now, Liz was smiling as widely as her two dinner companions.

"Got a boat?" asked Adam.

"As a matter of fact, we have a service boat we use to work over there."

"I think," said Jason, "that first thing in the morning, before I head home, we might take a look at that building and its big, old doors, if you are of a mind to do that."

Liz was quick to respond. "I think we can arrange that. Then, just maybe, we won't have to call and tell you what we found."

It was quickly agreed that they would meet for breakfast around nine at the rather more formal restaurant one level up, which offered an extensive buffet service.

"Okay," said Jason as he stood and stifled a yawn. "In that case, I'm off for the evening. I'm still an old farm boy, and my body clock sets off alarms at about four thirty in the morning and pulls my plug long before this. Besides, after that meal, I can barely hold my head up. I'll see you two lovebirds in the morning." And he disappeared into the nearby entrance to the hotel.

What an odd turn of phrase, thought Adam. *Lovebirds, indeed.* Adam tended to think of himself as unattached, though perhaps more by circumstance than by intent. Sure, he missed having any close family members, especially now that both of his parents were gone. But if he stopped to think about it—and he seldom did—he had always convinced himself that he enjoyed his independence. And yet, he had to admit he was attracted to Liz as he had not been to a woman in quite a while. He could not tell what she was thinking, because like him, she was sitting quietly, taking in the view. But he began to wonder if perhaps Jason had sensed something in him before he had sensed it in himself.

Hank was back at his computer and poking around the internet some more, building out what he thought was probably a list of baseball scandals that had something to do with his occasional secret-agent-type visitors. He was becoming convinced that he and his family had been protecting a storehouse of information that someone in baseball did not want getting out. And he could see how that desire might apply to some of what he'd been finding. Which games did Pete Rose really gamble on? Or was it all a setup of some kind, even a ruse to force a much-disliked player out of the game? What else might Marge Schott have said? Was Altuve wearing a buzzer? There could be secret passages off of any one of these rabbit holes.

But others did not seem to fit the pattern. He was puzzled, for example, about how anything related to the Beer Night riot in Cleveland could be so sensitive it had to be locked away forever. That one had happened when he was a kid, and honestly, he'd never heard of it until he started this little research project. Of course, he thought, it was the Indians who were involved, and back then, they might as well have been a minor league team for all the attention they warranted.

The best summary he found was on Wikipedia. According to that writeup, the Indians had been having cheap beer promotions to draw fans as far back as 1971. It wasn't working. Their average attendance was about seven thousand fans at a game, mostly regulars and few enough in number that the players recognized a lot of them on sight. The team was awful, and they played in this cavernous stadium right on the shore of Lake Erie. Hank had actually been there for a game once back in the early nineties when he'd been in Ohio on business and the Yankees were in town. The place, he remembered, was old, grungy, smelly, windy, and cold—even in July. And it seated about eighty thousand people, or more than ten times the number who generally showed up. Those Cleveland fans must have enjoyed feeling lonely in a crowd, he mused. Officially it was called Municipal Stadium, but everyone knew it simply as The Mistake By The Lake.

In 1974, he read, the Indians decided to have a dime beer promotion one night in June when the Texas Rangers were in town. The usual price was sixty-five cents for a twelve-ounce cup of suds, so this was a great discount. And the Tribe was generous. True, a fan could only buy six beers at a time, but there was no limit on the number of times he (or she) could do that. Oh, to be an Indians fan on such a night. The promotion itself was planned well in advance. It took time, after all, to lay in that much beer.

The Indians' timing was not fortuitous, however. The same two teams had squared off in Texas the week before, and there had been some serious bad blood generated. Punches had been thrown by both sides, and the Indians had been pelted with food and beer by Rangers fans. And when Texas manager Billy Martin, whom Hank knew to have had one of the worst tempers and fastest mouths in the sport, was asked in an interview if he had any concerns about visiting Cleveland so soon afterward, he replied that there was no cause for concern as there would not be enough fans at those games to worry about. Cleveland media picked up the comment and challenged fans to respond. More than twenty-five thousand of them—nearly four times the average attendance—showed up and started swilling beer.

The game apparently had its moments. In the early innings, Hank read, the Rangers ran roughshod over the Tribe, and the fans satisfied themselves with an occasional foray onto the field. Early on, a woman ran onto the field, stationed herself in the Indians' on-deck circle, and bared her breasts, and later, after an Indians home run, a naked man ran out to second base to celebrate. An inning later, a father and son ran into the outfield and mooned fans in the cheap seats. And this was no weekend debauch; this was on a Tuesday. People in Cleveland really knew how to party.

But it wasn't until the bottom of the ninth that the real fun started. The Indians rallied to tie the game and had the winning run on second base. Just then, there was another incident involving a fan in the outfield, at which point Martin and his players charged out of their dugout in his direction, wielding bats. Alas, they had misjudged both the situation and the fans, a large number of whom, in an advanced state of inebriation, also charged the field in response, some of them armed with knives, chains, and remnants of stadium seats that they had by then dismantled for the purpose. Those in the upper deck, seemingly disappointed that from their distant vantage points they were unable to reach the field easily, had no effective recourse but to throw bottles. About two hundred fans surrounded the Rangers players, and that group was swelling in number. Chivalrous to the last, the Indians players ran onto the field, carrying bats of their own, not to attack their opponents this time but to encircle and defend them against the fans. Like a wagon train circling for defense, the home team formed a perimeter. Then both teams retreated to the dugouts, and then to their respective clubhouses, which were quickly locked down. Indians players later escorted the Rangers to their bus.

That was not the end of the rioting, though, as Hank learned to his astonishment. Fans continued to work off their beers by throwing cups, rocks, radio batteries, food, and chairs. One chair hit the chief of the umpiring crew in the head, and a rock struck his hand. Despairing of restoring order, he declared that the Indians had forfeited the game to Texas. About twenty minutes later, the Cleveland police arrived and things calmed down at last. But the disturbance then moved to a nearby public park, where it continued for a while longer. Cleveland's general manager at the time, Phil Seghi, put a coda on the night when he blamed the umpires for losing control of the game. But the team did seem to have learned a lesson of sorts. When the next Ten-Cent Beer Night was held in July—and yes, they apparently did it again—about forty-two thousand fun-seeking fans showed up. The cheap beer, however, was limited to two cups per person. Lee MacPhail, the American League president, was rather droll about the whole thing. "There is no question," he observed, "that beer played a part in the riot."

It was all pretty amusing, at least from Hank's perspective a half-century later, and it took him a good while to stop chuckling. But that's when it hit him. This was embarrassing to baseball, sure. But it was all out there in public from the get-go. The whole thing was in the papers and the sports magazines and on TV. And it was in Cleveland, AKA,

The Big So-What? Why on Earth would something like that merit being buried in a secret archive? Unless, of course, there was more to the story.

—◆——◆—

Jason did not think twice when Adam and Liz arrived together at breakfast the next morning. And if some sixth sense had somehow led him to make that off-hand reference to lovebirds the evening before, it failed altogether to alert him to the fact that something vital had changed in the hours since dinner, that two parallel lives had been redirected onto a common path.

"Another gorgeous day!" Jason noted as Liz and Adam sat down across the table from him. "So Liz, do you folks ever get any other kind of weather over here? Maybe I should move further from Canada."

"Believe me, you guys just hit it lucky. When it's nice in Cooperstown, it is truly nice. And when it's not, it's probably a lot like . . . where did you say you live?"

"DeKalb Falls. It's way out in western New York."

"Enough chitchat," said Adam, intervening in this stream of niceties and weather trivia. "I'm still looking across the lake at that weird tower over there, with the big doors and the old locks. I don't suppose I could interest either of you in hitting the buffet tables and getting on our way."

"Absolutely," Jason replied. "I do have to get on the road by about noon. Plus, just walking in past all that amazing-looking food almost made my legs too weak to get all the way over here to the table."

"It does look good," agreed Adam. Liz just smiled and pushed back her chair.

The buffet itself was quite a remarkable spread. From the omelet station and the waffle baker to the array of sausages and bacon types to the colorful pastries to the juice bar—even to the fresh fruit over to one side—the group could have lost its will to leave the restaurant, lost whatever momentum it had for its quest, and gained a collective few pounds, all in the space of a couple of hours. But the smell of the fresh coffee that awaited them back at their table seemed to snap them out of whatever food-induced trance they were in. Breakfast disappeared fairly quickly, energy and focus were restored, and off they trekked over to the docks

75

at the foot of Pioneer Street, where they climbed aboard the great yacht *Greenstick*, which, in truth, closely resembled the back end of a landscape service's truck. And, of course, that is pretty much what it was.

Liz cranked up the boat's two 300-horsepower inboard engines, and, seated amid a clutter of lawnmowers, string trimmers, leaf blowers, and assorted gardenalia, they headed toward Kingfisher Tower on the far starboard shore.

"Liz, did you remember to bring the keys?" Jason queried in jest.

"Yes, Jason. I remembered the keys. But just in case, if you look under that seat you're on, you'll find a machete. And in the next compartment over, we keep a white hockey goalie's mask. Say, is today the thirteenth?"

Adam could no longer contain himself. "Dude! Wasn't that your favorite movie? Character was named after you or something?"

"Okay, okay. I surrender!" Jason offered with his hands in the air.

While all this banter was taking place, the boat had moved close to the landing beside the tower, which was not actually all that far away from town.

It was, when you came down to it, a rather bizarre, almost whimsical, little building. On one side, facing west toward the lake, was the tower proper, some sixty feet tall and twenty feet square, topped by a steep tile roof with a decorative metal spike of some sort that probably served as a lightning rod. Windows dotted all four walls of the tower. On the opposite, or easterly side, of the structure was a large portal that resembled the entrance to a Medieval cathedral. On the south side were three stone wedges, basically mini-buttresses, that doubtless held the tower upright, while on the north was a small build-out featuring two arched windows. Adjoining the tower on the water side was a small dock, and it was toward this that Liz steered the boat. Adam and Jason tied the craft to the pilings fore and aft, and the three of them clambered over the side and onto the wooden slats. They were sturdier than they looked.

"When we are working out here," Liz said, "we usually tie up a little ways behind the building. That's where all the landscaping is, and there's a spot over there where we can use a ramp to offload whatever equipment we need. Nothing heavy, but then, mostly it's just that lawn that you could see when we were approaching. But we are over here at the tower once in a while as well, spraying for weeds or what have you, so no one will pay us any mind. Let's start here with the door to the tower, and then, if we need to and we're really careful, we can work our way around to the other side."

There was a large lock on the door that looked pretty old—old enough to have been installed as far back as 1876, when the tower was constructed. Liz pulled out the keys and tried them in the lock, one after another.

"Not even close," she observed with just a touch of surprise in her voice. It seemed she had convinced herself that this tower portal would be "the" door. Clearly, it was not.

The trio then picked their way around the tiny peninsula to the other side of the building, with its own ancient timber door. Another lock, another pass with the keys, another failed attempt.

"Arggh!" she exclaimed. The surprise had morphed into frustration. "This is such a perfect place. How can the keys not fit? Although, if you think about it, for these guys to use the tower all these years, well, they'd have had to have permission from the Clarks. And they're not even baseball people, let alone cabalists. I know that Stephen Clark built the Hall of Fame in town, but the townsfolk have always assumed that was more of a business decision than anything else. It sure has worked out well for all of us. And there is always a Clark chairing the Board of Directors at the Hall, but again, we all write that off as a kind of philanthropy or stewardship. That family has probably started and backed more museums than almost anybody in creation. So maybe there was a flaw in our reasoning, and we just jumped to a conclusion without thinking it through."

They looked around for some other, less obvious place to try the keys to this fantasy kingdom but had no luck at all. Disappointed, they piled back into the good ship *Greenstick* and set a return course for Pioneer Street, the jewel that is Cooperstown arrayed before them and growing ever closer.

Passed Ball

Max knew to expect his next visitor, but beyond that, he had no idea what to expect. What in the world would the Chief Investigator for the Senate Select Committee on Sports and Antitrust want with him? At the quiet knock on his open door, Max looked up from his desk.

"Mr. Prevost? Please do come in. I'm Max Tomhoff. Please have a seat."

"Jim Prevost," the man said, offering his hand, "but everybody just calls me CI. The perils of being in a job for too long, I guess. Thank you for seeing me."

His visitor selected a chair at the small table in Max's office and lowered himself onto the cushion. He was, thought Max, a gray man. Gray by age, gray by coloring, gray by his facial expression, and gray by the rich fabric of his dark suit, though white by his obviously expensive shirt (a Zegna, Max guessed) and red by his necktie and pocket square. He resembled nothing so much as the caricature of a high-powered lobbyist—more that than the richly clad dandies and collectors who tended to populate his auction room on the big days. He looked very . . . Washington.

"Can I offer you some coffee?" Max asked in an effort to break the ice that caked off of his visitor's visage.

"No, but thank you. I won't take much of your time. Not today, anyway. Really, this is something of a courtesy call and a heads-up. As you may know if you follow things on Capitol Hill . . ." He paused to allow for any sign of recognition from his host. Seeing none, he continued,

"As you may know, our committee has been charged with looking into any number of issues relating to professional baseball. Price fixing for tickets, contraction of the minor leagues, collusion on player salaries, pressuring local governments to build new stadiums by threatening to move franchises. Really just anything about the business of the game that might call its special status into question. Do you know about that, the special status, I mean?"

"Not really. I'm afraid I'm not much of a baseball fan. Or any sports for that matter."

"Well, very briefly, back more than a hundred years ago, around 1914 or so, there was another so-called major league called the Federal League. That group of teams decided they could build their league the fastest by opening their wallets and stealing away players from the older leagues, the American and the National. It wasn't the first time somebody had tried that, and they did get about fifty or so players to jump over there for lots of money. Well, the Americans and the Nationals weren't going to take that sitting down. They fought back pretty hard, and in the end, this new league just didn't draw very many paying customers. So, in 1915, the newcomers sued the older leagues in federal court for what they argued was an antitrust violation. Remember, this was back in the days of Teddy Roosevelt, who prided himself on being a trustbuster.

"The judge who heard the case was a guy named Kenesaw Mountain Landis, and he just sat on it. Didn't make a decision, didn't do a thing. A few years later, after a big gambling scandal in Chicago, Landis was actually named the first Commissioner of Baseball—maybe coincidence, maybe not. But that was still in the future, and in 1915, he apparently figured that if he just waited them out, the parties would find a way to settle their dispute, and that's just what happened right at the end of the year. The major leagues made some concessions, and the Federal League faded away to nothing. All, that is, except for the team in Baltimore, the Terrapins, I think they were called. That Baltimore team filed its own antitrust case against the American and National Leagues, claiming they had an illegal monopoly. The forced failure of the Federal League was Exhibit A. Now, Baltimore won that case at the trial level, but in 1922, the Supreme Court ruled that the major leagues were not engaged in interstate commerce and were therefore exempt from the Sherman Antitrust Act, the law under which they'd been sued. Oliver Wendell Holmes wrote that decision, and to a cold read, it doesn't begin to match the facts. It's pretty obvious that major league baseball teams travel, recruit, broadcast, and do just about everything else they do across state lines. So, there's been a lot of disagreement with that decision over the years, although it has stood up in a couple of subsequent tests in the courts. Seems like all the justices must be baseball fans. As a result, if anything is to be done to change it, it will have to be Congress that does it.

"Anyway, my boss, who chairs the Select Committee, has a special interest of his own in baseball and a suspicion that the time may be approaching when that antitrust exemption will disappear."

"Well, I have to say," Max said, thinking he ought to participate in the discussion at least a little, "that is all very interesting in its way. But I don't see what it has to do with me, or with Marbury House. As I indicated, I don't even follow the game."

"Precisely right. But as we have been digging into all of these legalistic kinds of questions," replied his guest, "we have come across a potentially related phenomenon. There is, as you surely know well, a large and highly lucrative market in baseball memorabilia, both historic and contemporary. And we have reason to believe that this market is laced with counterfeit objects, fraudulent claims, and perhaps even money laundering. The committee has not addressed this area yet, but this is something in which my senator has taken an intense personal interest."

Max stiffened and sat up in his chair.

The visitor raised his hand, palm open and outward. "No. Before you ask, we have no reason to think you or this auction house have engaged in any wrongdoing. Or, I should say more correctly, any *intentional* wrongdoing. Some months ago, you auctioned off a collection of baseball memorabilia for an astronomical amount of money. What was it, eight million or so?"

"Something like that." Max did not remember all of his auctions. There were just too many. But he did recall that one.

"I am here to let you know that we, meaning the Senator and I, will be taking a close, and, at least at the outset, a highly confidential, look at both ends of that transaction, but especially at the sale. As I recall, that lot went to an anonymous bidder. We are going to want to know who that was."

"Now hold on," Max began to sputter.

Again the open, outward palm. "I know. Anonymous is anonymous. Well, when the United States Senate comes calling, with subpoena power if necessary, these things sometimes change. And really, I do mean this to be a friendly visit. The Senator asked me to run up here and give you a heads up before any of that happens, so you can have the time to talk with whomever you must talk with—your boss, the buyer, your in-house attorneys, or anyone else—and do whatever you must do to be ready when we come knocking on your door for real. And we will be doing that, sooner rather than later."

With that, Max's visitor rose from his chair, proffered his hand again, and slipped out of the office.

Shit, thought Max, though he was always careful to avoid using such language aloud. And his mind became a whirl of to-do's.

<hr />

"Okay," said Jason when they had set foot back on dry land. "I think I am going to head back home. It's a long drive, and I'd like to get back in time for the late afternoon chores. If you guys find anything exciting, do be sure to let me know."

And with that, he set off back to the hotel to collect his belongings, pay his bill, and reclaim his pickup from the parking lot.

"And how about you, Adam? What are your plans?" Liz gave him a look that was at once quizzical and full of promise.

"Plans? Who plans anything these days?" he answered with a smile. "Actually, I was thinking I would take a wander through the Hall of Fame building just to see where the doors are and which ones have locks."

"Big locks that take big keys?"

"Yep, those are the ones. Care to come along?"

And off they went. Liz had maintained the lifelong membership in the Hall that had become a Fairchild family tradition, and with the flash of a card, they passed easily through the admissions area. Then it was on to the third and uppermost floor, checking first for any doors around the perimeter and then for any interior closets or other locked points of entry they could find. Similar searches followed on the second floor and the first, then up the ramp to the smaller displays and the research center. They saw lots of doors, even some marked for authorized entry only, but none with locks anywhere near big enough for their keys. Many were electronic locks and took no keys at all. There was no way to know what lay behind those doors, or up in the restricted offices of the archive, or for that matter in the adjacent building that housed the executive offices of the Hall—an area Adam knew better than he might have wanted to—but given the dynamics of the arrangement with the Fairchilds and the apparent use of a landscaping company as cover, all of these options seemed unlikely. So, before long, the pair of amateur detectives found themselves back out on Main Street. They found a convenient bench and sat down.

Liz opened the conversation. "I have been racking my brain trying to think of other obvious places that my dad, my granddad, and Great-Grampa Jake would have had access to that might have a door like we are looking for, and I can't think of any we haven't already tried. I think that leaves only the smaller or less obvious places that have been with us from the beginning. There are a few. There's the Village Hall, for example."

"Where's that?"

"Look up and across the street to the right."

"Oh."

"And there's the offices of the Clark Foundation. You can't really see them from here, but they are just down there to the right, in the next block. Right across from the Village Hall. And there's Cooper Park. That's the big park across from the James Fenimore Cooper statue that we looked at yesterday. There's the Episcopal Church over on First Street. I'm not sure how long that's been there, but I think there was always a church of some sort on that spot. There's a bit of landscaping over at the water plant, which goes back to the 1930s. But I really doubt they'd have used that. It's not very centrally located. And there's Lakefront Park. We actually walked alongside that one when we went down to the boat. But that's pretty low ground over there. Wouldn't be a good choice for this.

Beyond that, there are just a couple of residential clients and we're out of options."

"I'm in for continuing the hunt," said Adam. "Sounds like I might need to stay around for four or five days to check out all of those places."

Liz started to correct his estimate but caught herself when she realized what he was really suggesting. "Yes," she said. "I think that sounds about right. But that resort is going to cost you a fortune for that long a stay, even if you are a rich and famous author or you live on granola bars, corn dogs, and Big Macs for the whole time. Why don't you come out and stay at the farm? It's a big old house and just me rattling around in there now since Mom moved over to a seniors home in Oneonta. There's even electricity and indoor plumbing."

"Well," he smiled, "as long as there's electricity and indoor plumbing, I think that might be nice."

"It's settled then. I need to go back to the office and finish up some paperwork that's been hanging since you guys got here. Why don't you wander around town a bit, maybe even check out some of the more public areas we were just talking about. I feel like I need to hold onto the keys, at least until we figure this thing out. But if you see any doors with big locks, make a note and we can check them out. Give me a couple of hours, then we can grab the cars and I'll show you the way out there."

Liz headed back to her familiar turf, while Adam set off to prowl around more of the Village and its environs.

<hr />

Hank was troubled in a way he had not been before.

To his core, he felt the obligation he had assumed upon reaching his twenty-first birthday. His father had made clear the family's indebtedness to a group of unnamed men who had set it on a course to prosperity in the midst of the Depression, and the promise that had been made. It was always with him, and it had never occasioned the least bit of discomfort. He had, as the protocol required, passed the same sense of commitment to his own son when Eddie had come of age, and was gratified that he had accepted it willingly. In fact, it had occasioned a visible sense of pride. Of course, none of them knew just what it was they were helping to protect.

When Eddie had been killed overseas, Hank had been devastated. He was, he felt, never quite the same afterward. He loved Liz, and he was proud of her achievements and especially of the way she had stepped up as she grew older and took on more responsibility for the business. She was a quick study, and a diligent worker, and he was sure everything would be in capable hands when the time came. But as he had fallen into the depths of despair and then climbed the slope back to a sense of normality, he had never once focused on one of the consequences of Eddie's death. He had passed the secret of the hidden vault on to his son, but except for Hank, it had died with him on that distant battleground.

And now, as Hank knew but had not shared with anyone else, his own time was winding down. Years of ignoring the urgings of his doctors were catching up with him, and catching up fast. That was itself yet another layer of worry. Lot Lizard's visit had been something of a wake-up call, and his research in the days since had been focal. He thought he knew, at least in general terms, what he was guarding and for whom he might be guarding it. But there were rules, one or two of which he had now inadvertently violated, and he had no way of reaching out for guidance. The "rules" seemed to require that he pass along the responsibility of controlling access to his oldest *son*, and he had done just that. But those rules were laid down many years ago, at a time when women were not expected to follow sport or even to work outside the home. The men who made up those rules probably thought that every man would have a son and that the only women one encountered at a ballpark were those of questionable morals. It was a different time, a different era, a different ethos. Now, today, he had no oldest son. No son at all. And Liz, the one offspring he did have, had given herself over to the business and was getting to an age where she, too, might have no one to pass the secret to. Yet he had no way to contact those above him in the chain of responsibility to seek their guidance as to what he must do. He did not even know who "Tres," his most common occasional intermediary, really was, let alone how to reach him. It was all on Hank to make a decision.

And make a decision he did. He determined that the closest he could come to fulfilling his obligation was to share the matter with Liz and to charge her with continuing the family's role of keeping the keys, the log, and the secret of where the outer door to the hidden vault could be accessed. He needed a few days to plan out just how he would do this, but he knew that the time for action had come.

"Liz? Hey, it's Dad. I got a couple of things I want to talk with you about. Private, family kind of stuff. It's been a while since we sat down, just the two of us, and broke bread. How about this coming weekend we drive over to Oneonta, just to get away, and have a nice dinner. I'm buying."

"That sounds lovely. Can we go to the usual place over there?"

"Absolutely."

"Perfect. Pick me up about 5:30?"

"You bet. Love you, Sweetie."

"Love you, Dad."

It was the last conversation they were to have.

———

In the event, it was not Max who responded to the Senate inquiry, but the outside attorney for Marbury House, Phil Houston, or Philly-Hugh, as he was known to friends and colleagues. Of course Marbury House would do all it could to cooperate, he told the subcommittee's Chief Investigator once he had had a chance to confirm the man's identity, though there was some information the firm would be unable to share absent a subpoena for same. He then instructed Max to travel to Washington, so as to keep the matter as far from Marbury House as possible, and to share as much of the requested information as he could under guidelines that Philly-Hugh then set out in writing.

So it was that Max found himself stepping off an Amtrak Acela train at Union Station on his first-ever trip to the nation's capital; walking past the station's retail corridor with its mixture of high-end merchants and basic station services, through the capacious Main Hall and the aptly named Colonnade; and finding himself in bright sunshine at the center of a circular drive. Avenues led off in every direction as taxi, Uber, and Lyft drivers competed for space outside the terminal. It could all be quite confusing, but Philly-Hugh, who traveled to Washington frequently, told him to just look up and straight ahead and he'd be fine. Following that instruction, he raised his gaze and saw straight ahead and beyond the maze of traffic the dome of the US Capitol.

Max's first challenge was to find his way to the Dirksen Senate Office Building. The local shorthand for the House and Senate Office Buildings, all named for former members, was HOB and SOB, respectively. And Max had to chuckle at the thought that whoever named this one after the late and notoriously irascible Senator Everett Dirksen of Illinois had had the last laugh. Dirksen SOB indeed.

Outside the station, Max asked a Red Cap attendant for directions and was told that the Dirksen Building was located at First and Constitution. "That's Northeast," said the man, trying to be helpful. "That'd be toward your left if you're headed that way," he said, pointing south. "And Constitution's about two or three blocks down that way, straight ahead." Max thanked him and headed off into the confusion of streets, street signs, vehicles, the tents of homeless people, and the general cacophony of one of the city's busier quarters at midday. With all the roads, sidewalks, seemingly competing or misdirected traffic lights, vehicles coming at speed from unexpected directions, and other distractions, all he had to go on was the vision of the dome in the distance and a determination to work his way closer.

Once Max had made his way south across Massachusetts Avenue, the main through-street in the area, he was able to collect himself. He discovered to his immense pleasure that he was actually on First Street, NE, and headed in the right direction. *Thank you, Google Maps.* As he progressed, though, there were few immediate landmarks. To his left was a great expanse of parking lots, all surrounding a small building that appeared to be a restaurant, and beside it, a utilitarian-looking government building of some sort. Across the street to his right was nothing but park land. The cross streets, he found, were named for the letters of the alphabet, or perhaps they were simply named for the quality of their performance. The first one, D Street, for example, might have earned its grade from the vast vista of parked cars. The next one was better, with parking on the near side but a bunker-like Senate office building across on the south side. Better, but not great. C Street.

B Street, he discovered, was actually named Constitution Avenue, and as promised, consigned in eternity to the northeast corner was the

Everett Dirksen Senate Office Building. In fact, the building filled the entire block, at least along First Street. With all of the security in place nowadays, it took Max a little while to find an entrance that was open to the public, but he was soon enough able to pass through the metal detector and past the police dog into a very impressive public office space. The corridors were bustling with important people, some truly so and others only wishfully so. Looking for a way to the fifth floor, where the subcommittee had its offices, and not especially interested in climbing the stairs, he was denied access to the first elevators he found. Senators only, the operator told him. Max could not recall the last time he had actually seen a human elevator operator, but there she was. Walking a bit further down the corridor, he then found a bank of lifts open to the public—he looked for a sign that read "Taxpayers Only," but did not find one—and rode to his desired floor. He exited into a wide corridor lined at distances with fancy signage marking the offices of the senators, and nondescript but functional signs indicating committee and other offices. Finding the one he sought, he entered, introduced himself, and was directed to a leather sofa to wait.

"Gentlemen," said the man known to Hank as Lot Lizard, "thank you for coming in to meet with me. It's a little early in the afternoon, I know, but I'm sure you will agree that we must honor our little rituals." With that, he produced three thick hand-blown glasses and an untapped bottle of very well-aged Macallan single-malt whiskey. Removing the cork, he did the honors.

"I give you the GameKeepers."

"The GameKeepers," his two guests repeated, and all three drained their glasses. Some rituals could be a pain in the ass, things like code names and secret phrases. But all three men agreed that this particular one did not fall into that category. Lot Lizard left the uncorked bottle on the mahogany conference table and opened the discussion.

"I don't need to tell you we have a problem. Well, more correctly, baseball has a problem, and it has the potential to become our problem. You know as well as I do that this Senate Select Committee investigation is picking up some momentum. That damn senator the Majority Leader stupidly named to chair it is actually taking the job seriously. He wants to challenge the antitrust exemption, and he is out combing the country for evidence of unfair competition and, from what I hear, any other sort of skullduggery he can dig up or, I fear, manufacture. And as we in this room know better than anybody, if he digs deep enough, there is dirt to be found.

"In this circumstance, it seems to me that our course of action is clear. For one thing, I think we should distance ourselves from the Cooperstown operation for a while. No visits up there under any circumstances. With your permission, I will pass that instruction along to Tres. There is actually some good news on that front, at least for us. We learned recently that Henry Fairchild, the fellow who has been minding the store up there most recently, has passed away. Stroke. That's sad for the family, of course, and later on it will create some challenges for us when we are ready to resume that operation. But for now, it means that no one up there has direct personal knowledge of who any of us are. I've been up there, Tres has been up there a few times, maybe one or the other of you. But even if Fairchild managed to arrange a successor, it won't be anyone who can pick us out from a photo.

"The other thing we need to do is to see if there is any way we can discredit or shut down this investigation, or at least make sure it gets channeled into some direction that gives the Senator the show he seems to want, but keeps us and the game safe and well. I think it's one of those situations where our best defense is the proverbial bright shiny object. Let's throw some meaningless chum in the political waters—some trivial scandal or some little bit of collusion that can be set up and shown to be isolated—and see if we can't get the sharks swimming in a harmless direction. You may have some thoughts about what that might be. I do not, as yet. But that's what I thought we might want to discuss today."

Their agenda clear, the three men got down to some serious discussion. They determined almost from the outset that they would have to find a scapegoat, someone prominent enough in the game to provide the needed misdirection and yet sufficiently inconsequential to isolate the damage. Perhaps for the first time, this particular group of three wished they had the one thing that was now denied them—access to the Cooperstown archive.

———

The Chief Investigator sat behind a battered old desk in a surprisingly utilitarian office. Gone were the expensive hand-made clothes and the fancy pocket square, replaced by an off-the-rack brown suit and an open collar. Max thought the wardrobe change purposeful and consistent, designed in both instances to establish the man's power. *I can dress better than you on your turf*, it seemed to say, *and need not dress to impress you on my own.*

"Mr. Tomhoff, thank you for coming down to DC. I do appreciate the gesture."

"It's my pleasure," replied Max. "Our Mr. Houston thought it would be a good idea, and, since I have never been in Washington before, I was rather pleased at the prospect. Assuming, of course, that ours is a friendly conversation."

"I know of no reason it should not be, as long as, that is, you are bringing me the information I requested."

"Yes, I have brought it along. Or at least most of it."

At this, the man raised an eyebrow. "Go on."

"First, you asked how we acquired the materials that we included in that auction lot. They all came from a single source, two sisters in far Upstate New York, Jenna and Elaine Drumm, who claimed to have found them buried under rubble in an old barn on their property. Before accepting the lot, we did as much due diligence as possible. We confirmed their address, we confirmed that the property had been owned by the family during the time period when the papers were apparently compiled and that it actually had a barn or some other old outbuilding, and we confirmed through court records that they had inherited that property and everything on it from their father when he had passed away. With a barn find, that's about the limit of what one can do."

"And did you contact these sisters to advise them of our investigation?"

"Per your instruction, we tried to do that. But they were no longer living at the address in question, the business they jointly operated had changed hands, and no one knew where they were. Our impression was that they had simply taken the proceeds and decided to move away from their old, rural life, or perhaps just to travel. But that is pure surmise on our part. Perhaps you will have more resources to bring to the search."

"Well, we'll see. It is certainly odd that your sellers have apparently dropped out of sight. But no one seems to be missing the documents, and they are not on any lists of stolen collections, so we may take their acquisition by Marbury House at face value. Assuming, of course, that the documents are genuine."

"On that score," Max continued, "we undertook our customary research. We had the various signatures and other content authenticated by the best sports memorabilia firm in the country, Bonomo, and they came back with a solid confirmation. We had the inks and paper tested for age and composition, and again everything checked out. We invited a representative from the Baseball Hall of Fame to review the documents for content and significance. They were sufficiently impressed that they sought to arrange a private purchase before the public auction, but the sellers were not interested in that. And the truth is, they probably got a better return that way. We had other experts review the materials as well, but the report was the same in every instance. So we proceeded with the sale."

"And you have paperwork on all of that?" CI asked.

"Everything you asked for." And at that, Max opened the briefcase he had been hauling around since leaving his office early that morning and handed over a thick sheaf of papers. "You will find it all there."

"Very good," mumbled CI as he shuffled through the papers. Then more affirmatively, "Excellent. Excellent. Very thorough. Thank you. But now we come to the central question. Who purchased the papers?"

"Well, that's the problem area. We do not know. If a prospective buyer comes to us and asks to bid anonymously, we try to accommodate that. People do it for all kinds of reasons—security concerns, marital disputes, political considerations, tax matters. None of that do we regard as the business of Marbury House. We are concerned with the bona fides of the purchaser and his, or her, or, I must add, its, because we have many corporate and institutional bidders, ability to pay the price of a successful bid. So we run credit checks and the like until we are satisfied on that point. But we do not, as a firm and long-standing matter of House policy, reveal the names of our anonymous bidders."

"And there's the problem," the man behind the desk interjected.

"Well, let me continue. We do not reveal the names of our anonymous bidders except as required to do so as a matter of law, which is to say, under court order or a subpoena."

"So what you are telling me is that, should the Special Committee issue a subpoena demanding the delivery of that information, Marbury House would comply with that subpoena?"

"I am informed by Mr. Houston, our outside counsel, that that would indeed be the case."

"Understood."

"I might add, just informally, though, that once you do that, you may find the result less than fully satisfying."

"Ah. You don't actually know who your buyer was."

"I am not prepared to say that. I am only telling you, as advised by our attorney, that your quest may be somewhat more complex than you anticipate."

***

"Liz. Hey, it's me." Adam's voice was a little nasal-sounding and broke up from time to time. Cellular reception in some parts of Cooperstown was not always reliable, and out in the surrounding countryside, it was downright chancy. As it happened, Liz was in a remote corner of the farm when the call came in.

"Hi! I wondered if you would be calling today. I'm out in one of the sheds, and I can barely make out what you're saying."

"Well, find a hilltop or something, because I think I may have figured out part of our little puzzle."

"Give me a minute." Liz walked outside and started watching the bars on her phone. She found a spot. "Okay, what have you got?"

"You remember those really weird lines of text on that little scrap of paper?"

"Yeah."

"Well, I think it's an anagram, a word puzzle. The meaning is not in the lines themselves. They are pure nonsense. But if you start seeing what other words you can make with the words in each line, it gets much more interesting. They are lines from a poem. And get this. It's a poem about baseball. So that fits."

"Wow. Are you sure? I mean, how did you figure that out?"

"I was playing around with the word puzzles in the newspaper over the weekend, and it just sort of hit me. Those lines might be like one of the anagrams in the paper. So I sat down with a pad and a pencil and tried to pull out the other words that might be in each line. There are some tricks to that, you know. Like counting the number of times various letters appear. It's a known fact that certain letters, like E or O or S, appear more often than others in English language words."

"My God," Liz remarked. "You really are a nerd. A word nerd! I never knew there was such a thing before I met you."

"Yeah, well. What can I say? You don't always make a lot of money as a writer, as I can personally attest, but if you keep at it long enough, you do learn a lot about words. Anyway, I went to the shortest line on the page, figuring that would be the easiest place to start. That turned out not to be a good decision, because there wasn't enough to work with. So then I backed off and took a look at the whole thing. I spent hours with it, until I finally had what I thought was a valid five- or six-word phrase. I plugged that into Google, and the rest of it fell right into place. They are all lines from this poem, but they don't all come together. They're from different parts of the poem. And guess what."

"Guess what? After all this build-up, all you can say is, 'Guess what?' I may love you, Adam, but you are treading on thin ice here."

"Okay, okay. Sorry. The lines seem to point to a specific location. I think they are telling us where the secret room or vault or whatever is located. We were actually there, and somehow we missed it. We overlooked it."

Adam read Liz his translation of the four lines of poetry, which she recognized immediately. And he told her the spot he thought the poem was pointing to. Everything he said suddenly made sense, and it made sense as well of many other aspects of this little mystery.

"You coming up to play Geraldo Rivera?"

Adam laughed. The reference, he knew, was to a heavily hyped television program back in 1986 in which Rivera, a television personality of the era, set out to open a vault in the old Lexington Hotel in Chicago, once a hangout of the famed mobster Al Capone, on the theory that Capone's many secrets would be found there. Since those secrets might include anything from hidden money to dead bodies, Rivera had on hand a medical examiner and some IRS agents. Something like thirty million people tuned in for the spectacle. Who knew what might be in there! But as it turned out, there was no *there* there. The vault was all but empty.

"How do you even know about that? I was a kid back then, and like everybody else, I was watching that stupid show. But you're not old enough to remember that."

"No, I didn't see it. But it was kind of a running joke in our family. Any time a package showed up, or any time one of us kids would go to open up a birthday or Christmas present, Dad would say it might be Al Capone's vault. And then he'd go off on a riff about Geraldo Rivera. So, you want to come up for the last stage of the search? You owe me a visit anyway."

"Give me a couple of days. But if you have a chance, you might take a look and see if you can figure out what we missed."

⸻

The Senator was in one of his brusque moods. "So where are we on that Marbury House thing?" he queried.

"About where you'd expect, Senator. The guy from the auction house came down a few weeks ago, and between him and the lawyer, they gave us just about everything except the identity of the buyer. But they were pretty good about that, too. Basically, as you'll recall since you signed off on it, they invited us to subpoena the information so they could claim they were forced to disclose it. The usual. As you might expect, though, they didn't actually know who bought that stuff. All they had was the name of a Bahamian company, something called GKeypers, Inc. Naturally, GKeypers was a shell corporation owned by another Bahamian company called Keypers OTG, and Keypers OTG, you will not be surprised to learn, was owned by the same company that's been behind all of the other major purchases of this kind of material that we have been able to document, Srepyek-G, Inc.—also based in the Bahamas. That led us to an offshore account at Banco Bahia in . . ."

"Nassau."

"Exactly. They're not very imaginative, and they do seem to favor the Bahamas."

"So this is yet another acquisition by our friends, whoever they may be. Enough of this crap. Every time we follow one of these trails, we keep running into these same people. They seem to have a taste for files and research on baseball scandals that have never been made public. At least, that's what it looks like. But who the hell are they and what are they up to? It could be a collector with really strange taste, but then, why all the secrecy? It could be a blackmail ring, pulling embarrassing or incriminating photos or documents, or even confessions, out of the files they buy and cashing in from people who want to keep that material hidden. It could be some Mexican or Colombian cartel laundering its cash, and then working like some sort of sports memorabilia chop shop, selling off bits and pieces of their take that no one would recognize with or without the context. It could be any damn thing!

"Enough. The banks down there are pretty hard to crack, even now in this so-called enlightened age of international banking. But we have some indirect leverage down in the Bahamas through the storm assistance fund, over which I have a certain measure of control, and I also know a guy at the Central Bank down there, or he used to be. I want you to go down there and nose around. If you push the suspected money launderer angle, they might be willing to help you out. Tell them I'm going to be chairing a new and deeper subcommittee investigation of offshore banking and drug money. That'll get their attention. Give them what we know about these transactions—dates, amounts, transferees. Make it look like a legit and serious inquiry. Find out who signed the paperwork for the account, how the funds arrived. You know the drill. You'll probably need a forensic accountant, if only to talk to these guys in their own language. Take Mitchell with you. We can spare him up here for a few days.

"Depending on who you end up dealing with down there, they might turn around and warn their client that we're looking at their records, but that might very well work in our favor. Force them to make a mistake. In any event, we wouldn't be able to prevent it without going through law enforcement channels, and I don't want to do that. Not yet. Then, if you find out it's something else altogether, you can just express our delight that they would never be engaged in something so nefarious and walk away all friendly-like. Just make sure when you do walk away, you have the real name of that account owner in your pocket."

———

The Chief Investigator had learned the hard way that it was wise to check with a friend at the State Department before traveling to a place that was unfamiliar to him. Once, when he was younger and far less savvy, the Senator, then a congressman, had dispatched him to Santiago, Chile, on some fool's errand, and off he'd gone, not taking the time to process a key fact: The country was controlled by a dictator, Augusto Pinochet, who was inclined to police his opponents with the assistance of death squads, and who had even commissioned an assassination on US soil, in Washington itself. When CI got off the plane in Chile, he had picked up a tail, a very visible tail, whose presence assured that no one he needed to speak with on behalf of the congressman would speak with him. Then, one night, his tail disappeared. Just vanished. That was the night he got mugged, and was barely able to make his way to the embassy and any sense of safety. After he healed for a couple of days, the ambassador had arranged an escort for him, and he made it to the airport and onto his outbound flight, shaken but basically intact. Lesson learned.

The Bahamas sounded safe enough. Boaters from Florida seemed to head over there all the time. But just to be on the safe side, he checked in with State. Good thing he did, because the department had issued a Level 2 Travel Advisory for the islands. It read in part:

Exercise increased caution in the Bahamas due to crime. Some areas have increased risk.

Country Summary: Violent crime, such as burglaries, armed robberies, and sexual assault, occurs even during the day and in tourist areas.

Although the family islands are not crime-free, the vast majority of crime occurs on New Providence and Grand Bahama islands. US government personnel are not permitted to visit the area known by many visitors as the Sand Trap area in Nassau due to crime. Activities involving commercial recreational watercraft, including water tours, are not consistently regulated. Watercrafts are often not maintained, and many companies do not have safety certifications to operate in The Bahamas. Jet-ski operators have been known to commit sexual assaults against tourists. As a result, US government personnel are not permitted to use jet-ski rentals on New Providence and Paradise Islands.

Exercise caution in the area known as "Over the Hill" (south of Shirley Street) and the Fish Fry at Arawak Cay in Nassau, especially at night.

He sent Mitchell an email with a PDF of the warning. Then he sent an advance notice of the trip to the congressional liaison at the embassy to ask about the possibility of obtaining the use of a sidearm during his time in-country. This was not going to be the sun and sea vacation he had first thought it would. There was one perk, though. The Senator had tapped some private funds and told him he and the accountant could take a couple of rooms at the Hilton resort, right on the beach. That provided some security and presumably some good American meals, and it also freed him from the restrictive rates and rules that applied to travel by government employees. Sometimes it was nice to be working for Congress, which had a way of generally exempting itself from the laws and rules it applied to everyone else.

<hr>

It was an unusually hot day in Nassau, and the tarmac at Lynden Pindling International Airport in Nassau was hot and sticky under the tropical sun. The turboprop island hopper from Miami had to rev its engines after landing simply to keep rolling to the terminal. The building itself was not large but was modern compared to others in the Caribbean, its design suggestive of a cross between Eero Saarinen's 1960s scheme for Washington's Dulles Airport and a shopping mall. The mall was clearly the dominant partner in this marriage.

Stepping off the plane into the C Concourse, the duo turned right toward the entrance to the Bahamian immigration and customs services.

Barely had they entered the space when they were approached by a tall black man in a tropical suit. "Mr. Prevost, I believe? Please," he said, his island accent discernible in a single word, "come with me."

"Are you from the embassy?" CI asked.

"No, no, man," he laughed. "No. I am with the Financial Services Board of the Bahamas. Actually, I am the Chairman of that Board. We are . . . I think you would call it an umbrella group for all of the financial services industries in the Bahamas. A combination, really, of industry leaders, government officials, legal and accounting specialists, and the like. Your senator called and asked me to extend the courtesy of having someone greet you upon arrival. I saw no reason to dispatch an underling. Now, please do come with me."

The chairman then led his visitors through a gate at one side of the immigration area, nodding to a uniformed official who approached, gave their government passports a cursory glance, stamped them both indicating entry to the country, smiled, and saluted. The group then progressed down to the baggage claim area, where their bags were already set aside near a conveyor belt. They collected those, and then followed the chairman through the customs area, where the same ritual of deference was performed, and out into the torrid heat that was impervious to seasonal change. A white limousine appeared before them as if by magic.

"I know you are to stay at the Hilton complex. My own office is not far away in the same direction, and I would be pleased to offer you transportation. Please let my driver take care of your bags."

Not more than ten minutes later, the vehicle pulled up outside the main entrance to the hotel.

"Thank you, sir, for this very great courtesy," said the Chief Investigator, making to exit the car. "I will make a point of telling the senator of your act of kindness."

"That will be appreciated, and please do give him my regards. But I am happy simply to make you feel welcome in my country. Here is my business card. I know very little of your assigned task, but if I am able to assist in any small way, please feel that you can reach out. I will instruct my staff to facilitate that."

"You are too kind. Thank you."

One unexpected benefit of his increasing closeness with Liz was the new appreciation Adam had developed for time on the open road. Exiting the City and driving Interstate 87 north to Albany was a traffic nightmare much of the way and most of the time. But west on the interstates from the state capital to Colliersville was always quick and easy, unless there was weather, and the two-lane from there to Cooperstown was sometimes slow but unavoidable in any circumstance. The more he made the trip, though—and as the months passed, it became a regular part of his routine—he began to venture further west, even, sometimes, into the wilds of northern New Jersey, then to turn north through Milford or Liberty or Roscoe or Margaretville, the latter of which always got him humming Jimmy Buffet songs. The old, two-lane backroads of his home state were slow, especially during those times of year when farmers needed to move combines, or whatever those big things were, from one field or farm to the next. The log trucks, crawling up and down hill and around yellow-lined curves, were a pain in the behind, but otherwise he found himself enjoying slowing down and the chance it gave him to think and dream and plan a future he had never anticipated. That future was about to take yet another turn.

"Okay!" he said, opening the door to Liz's office without the formality of being announced. "Did you find it?"

"Whoa, cowboy. Slow down! Come over here and plant a big one." The pair shared a long embrace before Liz picked up the thread of conversation.

"You know, it was very clever of you to work all that out. And what a great idea about what it all meant. I could see right away exactly how you got from those lines of poetry to the spot you identified. It was so obvious, and it really meant hiding the thing in plain sight. The only problem is, I don't think the Chamber of Secrets is located there. I looked all around that place, inside, outside, up, down, and sideways, and I didn't find any entrance to any kind of passage anywhere. We can go look again, and maybe you'll catch something I missed. But at this point, I simply don't believe it's there. Nice try, though."

"It has to be there. That's the only possible meaning of that anagram."

"Unless, Hon, it is just that. Just a nonsense anagram they used to identify each other. Maybe they weren't as clever as you give them credit for, as clever as you are."

"I don't buy it. No offense, but you must have missed something. It has to be there."

"Hey, be my guest."

"I will. I'll get into whatever I can get into over there and have a good look around. First thing in the morning. For now, it's been a long day's drive, and we have some catching up to do. It's been two long weeks. Let's go grill some steaks at the farmhouse. I brought along a really nice bottle of an Oakville Cab, and we can get a pleasant buzz on to start the evening."

"I can't."

"Can't what? Can't have dinner? What, do you have a date?"

"No, I can have dinner. But I can't have the wine."

"I thought you liked reds. Sorry. We can grab a bottle of white on the way."

"It's not that. I just can't be drinking right now."

Adam looked at her quizzically.

"That," she said, "is the other thing I need to tell you."

<hr />

"Senator, that guy from the Financial Services Board was really something. And by the way, he sends his regards. Mind if I ask how you know him?"

"Poker."

"Beg pardon?"

"I ran into him years ago when I was in the House. Back then, there were a lot of problems with money laundering through banks in the Bahamas. Some of it was even tied into that law firm in the Panama Papers, the one that was working for all those drug cartels and dictators and dirty execs and political slush funds. Anyway, some of us went down there unofficial-like to see if we could find a way to help their government see the light, or at least understand that Uncle Sam was getting serious about that shit, and they would not want to end up on the wrong side of whatever sanctions or other policy we ended up implementing.

"I think he was with the Central Bank at that point in time. Don't recall exactly. But since we were not down there on official business, we had to do things somewhat informally. And one night, one of the Bahamian guys suggested that we might have a productive conversation with some of his well-placed buddies over a friendly game of poker.

"Now, I've gotta tell ya, there are some serious poker players down there. And all of them being bankers and captain of industry types, even on a small scale, they love to run up the stakes." He laughed. "I had to hit up a couple of donors when I got back to DC.

"I can usually read the table. But these guys, they had some poker faces like you wouldn't believe. All except one. There was one guy at the table who couldn't bluff for shit. He was so bad, you couldn't have done better against him if he was wearing mirrors for eyeglasses. His face was full of tells, his voice sounded different, he even held the cards differently when he had a good hand. I knew right then and there that this was a man who could not tell a lie, or at least I'd know it when he did. There are times when you need an honest man with honorable intentions to accomplish an objective, so I made him my friend.

"Of course, there are also times when you need a dishonest man to accomplish what you seek. And in a place like that, there is, or I should say, there was, almost nothing of value you could achieve without such men. So I made them my friends as well.

"When you come down to it, politics is about knowing just what you want to accomplish, then choosing the right kind of friends to help you get it. In this instance, what we needed was someone who would hold the honor of his country and its banking system in high esteem, and would want to avoid any sort of high-profile embarrassment. Sounds like a whisper hinting at money laundering was just the ticket, and I take it you found him helpful?"

"Yessir, we did. I think it was because he was outside the government, working in outside channels. But every door we needed to knock on, well, he was able to crack it open. The government, the bank, just everybody. Mitchell got in to see people at the Compliance Commission and something called the Financial Intelligence Unit. And by the way, Mitchell here was great—obviously knew what he was doing, and he didn't waste any of the opportunities we had. I got a meet with the Inspector of Financial and Corporate Services, kind of like the chief investigator for the Securities Commission down there. I told him we had pretty similar jobs, and we hit it off real well. And he also set up a meeting with the Permanent Secretary in the Department of Financial Services and Trade, kind of like the chief of staff, I think. I probably told him more than he told me.

"But of course, the point was never to tap those guys, any of them, for anything we might find actionable. So we saved the best for last. Day before yesterday, your friend set us up with a meeting with the president of Bahia Bank. He didn't tell him what it was about, because he actually didn't know. We were pretty careful what we said to everybody else, in case it came back around to your friend. So in we waltz, and we sit down at this fancy conference table—sanded down and polished up from the wreckage of some old pirate ship. Perfect. Just your perfect howdy-do for some typical Yankee fact-finding junket. But then I started dropping the names of everybody we had just been around to see. The regulators, the Ministry, the government investigators, the compliance watchdogs. And you could actually see the blood draining from this guy's face. And then I told him what we wanted, and just how anxious we were to get it, and just how powerful our boss was, and just how concerned everybody who was anybody in the Bahamas was about being aboveboard, which was true if he checked it with anybody we talked with, because that was where we steered every one of those conversations.

"Well, of course he hemmed and hawed for a minute about bank privacy and Bahamian law. And we let him go on with that, and we didn't make a single counter-argument. Actually, we just sat there in stone-faced silence. And, of course, made a show of taking a few notes. You'd have been proud. And like we figured it would, the silence started to get to him, and who knows what kind of thoughts were circling around in his head. And finally, really without another word, he got on the intercom to his secretary, asked her to have some flunky come in, had us tell the flunky exactly what we wanted, and then went to the men's room for an extended stay while we hung around and waited. About a half hour later, the guy's secretary brings us a brown envelope with a file folder inside. We had to agree not to carry it out of the building, but we got the chance for a nice, long, uninterrupted look. Mitchell did most of that, and I think he was a little surprised. Mitch, why don't you pick it up from there."

"Sure. Well, Senator, in the world of offshore accounts and hidden dollars, this turned out to be amateur hour. Either these guys were merely going through the motions in a half-hearted effort to cover their tracks, or they were really bad at it. I mean, even staying with the Bahamas after that major banking overhaul they did back around 2000 makes me wonder just how serious they were. And that whole structure of dummy corporations we found a couple of weeks ago? That was virtually the whole deal. The top company in the pyramid was the account holder of record at Bahia, and it was the entity that made all of the deposits and authorized all of the payments and withdrawals. And by the way, there were lots of deposits and payments, but no outright withdrawals.

"Now, we should go back and check against some other transactions we've found that paid for some of this baseball material over the years to be sure. Truthfully, I am still a little fatigued from the trip. But if I remember correctly those other transactions, there were payments out of this account that seemed to match up with at least some of them. I can let you know for sure in a day or two. They went to various auction houses, memorabilia dealers, a couple of people who I think owned ball clubs at some point. But there were also payments to a couple of private detective firms, an agent or two maybe—though I don't know many of those names—and a bunch of lawyers. It looks like they are using this Bahamian account and all of these shell companies to buy up some sort of baseball records, none of which, for some reason, ever seem to come on the market afterward.

"Now, it could be some billionaire collector who has a really odd set of interests and a big man cave. But those people, they are usually a lot more sophisticated in this sort of dealing, and if they were trying to dodge taxes here or anywhere else, they'd have buried it under tons of lawyering and banking, then they'd NDA it out the wazoo. And there is none of that here. Plus, we're not really talking about a lot of money. That account never has more than a few million in it, and often it's way less than that. Compared to the stuff we usually look at, it's chump change. So there has to be something else going on."

"Let me chime in here, Mitch," interrupted CI. "There was one other thing. We had a look at the signature card for the account. Really, it was a stack of cards, and they go back decades. So this has been going on for a very long time. And there were some interesting names on the cards, baseball names for the most part. There always seem to be three people with access to the account, but they rotate in some fashion, so it's hard to be sure just how big this group is. On balance, I would say pretty small—half dozen or fewer—but that could just be the tip of some bigger iceberg, the leadership of some bigger organization or something like that. We have a list of them for you. But the most interesting of all was one of the current signatories on the account." He proceeded to give his boss a name.

The Senator smiled. It was not a good look on him. "Okay, so it sounds as if maybe they are hiding, but not running. We need to figure out what to make of that. Nice work, gentlemen. Mitch, you get me that other information when you can. Then I think I'll take it from here. Thank you. That'll be all." It was the Senator's way of dismissing staff members. "CI, would you hang on just a moment?"

"Sure, boss."

Once Mitchell had left, the Senator turned to his trusted aide.

"Let's see if we can get into this from the other end as well. When we talked to the auction guy, one of the things he told us about how they handled that last bunch of material was by running it past some expert at the Hall of Fame for an assessment. So somebody over there must have a pretty good idea of what was in that collection, even better than the auction house, and maybe even why somebody might want to hide it. See if you can find us someone at the Hall to talk to, will you?"

CI nodded and left the office through a side door.

———

Everything about this was new to Adam. He had made it through the better part of his life without feeling a strong attachment to a woman.

The proverbial confirmed bachelor, used to living on his own terms. Yet he felt that attachment to Liz. Keenly. And then, just when it seemed he had accommodated himself to that new reality and its potential implications, he found himself in still more *Terra Incognita* on his map of life. Fatherhood! How was this possible? Well, he knew, of course, how it was possible. But still.

The shock of the news, which Liz delivered in a surprisingly matter-of-fact manner, was rapidly displaced by concern. Liz was at the high end of what was generally regarded as childbearing age, and he vaguely knew that could be dangerous, for mother and child alike. But she reassured him—or tried—with a report that she had been to the doctor a couple of times, and that everything so far looked just fine. She simply needed to be more than usually careful in her habits.

"You haven't said yet whether this is a good thing. Is it?" Liz was trying to get a sense of the path ahead and of the as yet uncertain nature of the footing.

"Are you kidding me? It's great! I mean, give me a minute here. You just hit me with the shock of a lifetime, and I have to catch my breath. But I can't think of anyone I'd rather play Mom and Dad with than you. Give me a big one, Momma!"

Liz complied.

"Not that it matters, but do you, er, do *we* know the sex of the baby?"

"No, I'm not that far along. Still a few weeks to wait. But I wouldn't want to find that out on my own, even if I wanted to know. And I'm not completely sure I even want to know in advance. So let's make that decision together?"

"Absolutely. Now, how about some vitamin pills and orange juice to celebrate?"

She smiled. "I'll skip the vitamins for now. And you may add vodka to your orange juice as long as you do it when I'm not looking."

———

Roger Coppersmith had been to the Capitol Building many times, though always as a tourist. As a politically neutral nonprofit, the Hall of Fame did not involve itself in efforts to influence public policy, with the notable exception of any proposed changes to the tax code that might be to the museum's benefit or detriment. And the last time something like that had been up for consideration, it was back in the days of Roger's predecessor as Chief Operating Officer. So Roger's trips to Washington generally centered around the local museums, which he enjoyed on their own merits but also enjoyed visiting for ideas about exhibits and the like. The curators and facility managers at Air and Space, Natural History, American History, American Art and the other Smithsonian museums could be imaginative from time to time, and their collections were unequaled. But it was some of the smaller, private museums, like the Phillips Collection or the Children's Museum, where you found the real innovators. And this time, there was an added advantage: the whole affair was a legitimate business expense.

When CI had contacted the Hall as the Senator had instructed, he was a bit circumspect about the purpose of his request, alluding only to the role of the museum in evaluating and acquiring baseball artifacts. No one in Cooperstown was quite sure why the Select Committee should take such an interest in the Hall, but in discussions with their general counsel, Gene Seyforth, the general feeling was that the museum leadership should cooperate fully and openly, at least until the figurative third-base coach started flashing some sort of hold sign. In the circumstances, the feeling was that it would be best to respond from the top of the organization rather than by dispatching someone further down the food chain. That would surely be taken as a sign of good faith, and follow-up visits by more specialized staff could always be scheduled afterward.

Roger willingly took on the assignment. He left home around five on that Tuesday morning and drove to Albany, then across the Hudson to the Amtrak station in Rensselaer. There he caught the first train of the day to Penn Station in New York, where he changed to an Acela Regional Express for the ride to Washington. He arrived in DC in the early afternoon, with time to spare before his scheduled three o'clock with the Senator, which had been arranged not in a committee office, and not even in one of those big and fancy Senate offices where the solons like to greet and impress their constituents, but in the Senator's private office, which, because of his seniority, was in a corner of the Capitol itself.

"Mr. Coppersmith! Please come in. I apologize for dragging you over to my little hideaway, but there is some business on the floor today that may require my urgent attention, so I am trying to stay nearby."

"Not at all, Senator. I've been to the Capitol before, but honestly, I never knew these offices were here."

"Yes, it's our little secret. You won't tell, I hope!" The smile this time was genuine.

"No, sir. Your secret is safe with me."

"Well, that's good, Roger—may I call you Roger?—because in a way, that's what I want to talk with you about. Secrets, and the keeping of secrets. Secrets about baseball, in particular."

Coppersmith sat up in his chair.

"I'm sure you know that the Select Committee, which I chair, is taking yet another look at the antitrust exemption that has long been enjoyed by Major League Baseball. It was always a legal fiction, of course, that professional baseball did not meet the test of being interstate commerce and hence was not subject to the antitrust laws. And over the years, Congress and others have had occasion to revisit that determination. But it has never been reversed. Yet here we are, in an age of billion-dollar contracts for network broadcasting rights, of streaming video that reaches every corner of the world, of national advertising campaigns across numerous baseball stadiums, of bidding among teams in disparate states for the services of free agents and coordination of effort in the drafting of amateur and international players, and so much more. Honestly, Roger, if that is not interstate commerce, I don't know what is. Big league baseball today is not an industry of strictly local organizations providing strictly local entertainments, and I doubt that it ever was.

"And yet, it may not follow that the exemption should be overturned. For one thing, the precedent itself is now well established, and that is worth something. And it is surely true that a withdrawal of the exemption might have dire and unforeseen consequences for the business side of baseball. To be sure, those of us who love the game—and I count myself among them—do not want to do fundamental harm to the National Pastime. Baseball is one of those things that hold this country together through good times and bad, that tie us to our shared history and culture.

So if we were to make any changes on the antitrust front, I, for one, would want to make sure we did so in a cautious and nuanced manner."

The Senator paused to gather his thoughts, and Roger took the opportunity to try to establish some rapport between the two. "Senator, I am certainly aware of the issues around antitrust, and I know a bit of the history, both when Justice Holmes made that initial ruling and then in some of the later challenges. And I find myself in the middle, torn between my friends in professional baseball, who swear that they are dependent on the exemption for their commercial success and who are amazingly supportive of the Hall of Fame, and my appreciation for all of the changes to our way of life that you have just set out. So I have a foot in each camp, and I guess I am hoping that no one pulls too hard."

The Senator chuckled at the image. "Then, Roger, I think we are in very nearly the same place. But I confess, that is not exactly the reason I asked my aide, Mr. Prevost, to reach out to you. I need something a little different. In the course of taking a very broad look at the business of baseball, and by that, I do not mean only that of the professional leagues and their teams, but all of the business that circulates around and through the sport, we have come across an anomaly of sorts that we are struggling to understand.

"As you know perhaps better than most, there is an immense trade in baseball memorabilia—in baseball cards, photos, books, autographs, souvenirs, even stadium seats and all sorts of ephemera. And we have come across a series of cases in which some person or persons or even institutions, we do not know who, paid what seem like exorbitant sums to acquire seemingly obscure collections of documents about baseball, and then, basically, to squirrel them away. These do not appear to be commercial transactions in the normal sense, because the materials are bought, but they are never, ever sold. They come into public view through an auction or some other form of sale, they are purchased, and then they disappear, seemingly forever. Certainly, this is not always or even nearly always the case. Yet it is common enough to have drawn our attention. Frankly, we are concerned that someone is using baseball memorabilia as a mechanism for laundering money or engaging in some other form of villainous behavior.

"The problem is that we do not know exactly what is in these various collections of disappearing documents. So, if you will permit me a Holmesian moment, we do not understand just what game is afoot. It could be entirely innocent—just a secretive collector with a specific passion. Or it could be something altogether different—some kind of blackmail, fraud . . . We simply don't know."

"I understand what you are saying, Senator. But I do not see how you think we can help you. Are you thinking about some kind of sting operation or something?"

"No, no! Not at all. This is a Senate Select Committee, not the FBI. No, nothing so aggressive. But some time back, one of these transactions occurred through an auction at Marbury House in New York City. There was a collection of historical papers of some sort, and they went for something like seven or eight million dollars. The buyer was anonymous, and after the sale, the papers disappeared from view. Unless you have them, no one knows exactly what's in them or where they are."

Coppersmith raised his hands in the air in a gesture of innocence. "No," he smiled, "we do not have them. But I do know of the auction lot you are talking about, and I might be able to enlighten you about them just a bit.

"As you can imagine, the Hall is something of a go-to place when someone has serious questions about historical materials relating to the game. So quite naturally, when that collection of materials came to Marbury House, their Acquisitions Department gave us a call and asked if we might send someone down to evaluate the goods. And, of course, we complied. We dispatched an archivist and a historian who studied the papers in that collection in great detail. They were surprised by some of the content of the papers, but at the same time, they were convinced of their authenticity. In fact, they were so enthusiastic about that set of old records that we actually tried to arrange a private purchase through the auction house. Unfortunately, they were unable to convince the seller to part with the collection for any price we could afford. So the auction proceeded, with the result just as you have stated."

"Do you know who has the papers?"

"No sir, I do not."

"Do you know what was in them? We read the auction listing, but it did not actually reveal very much."

"Now, there I can help you to some extent. There were some old military documents from World War I, some correspondence to and from some prominent baseball people, and a fairly large trove of notes from a baseball writer of the 1930s who was going around researching material for a series on the first class in the Hall of Fame—*our* first group of inductees. The gist of it was to suggest, but not to prove, if I recall correctly, that one of the early stars of the game, Ty Cobb, might have been complicit in the exposure of another early star, Christy Mathewson, to the poison gas that eventually led to his premature death from TB sometime in the 1920s. The reporter was going around interviewing surviving veterans of a particular training unit, but he never actually wrote the story. Passed away on a train, I think, in the midst of his travels. And that's pretty much what was there."

"And that sold for eight million dollars?"

"Apparently so. Now there were some quite unique letters in that grouping, with some valuable autographs. And the military documents themselves were pretty interesting, as I understand it, because if valid, they would suggest some things about the conduct of the game back around the time of that war. The implication is that records might have been altered, both military records and baseball records, and that there was a very high-level cover-up of certain events."

"But that was more than a hundred years ago."

"Precisely."

"So even supposing that the auction price represented a realistic indicator of the value of these things, and I am not convinced of that, why would someone make such a purchase, then bury the goods? I don't get it."

"Hmmm. Well, a couple of possibilities come to mind. One is that somebody might be writing a book or a movie or something like that, which they want to base on this apparent evidence. I don't think you can rule that out, but the price does seem to be at least an order of magnitude higher than would typically fit that scenario. Plus, if someone were undertaking such a project, our archive at the Hall is one of the first places they would usually stop. But to my knowledge, we have not seen anyone like that come through the door lately. I could check on that to confirm it, of course.

"Another possibility is that you just have a rich, quirky collector, maybe not even an American. There are lots of rumors, for example, of Saudis and others from the Gulf region using their oil money to acquire all manner of rarities for their personal pleasure. Maybe some prince or some business executive got interested in baseball as a college student, and decided to pounce on these papers. And there is also a lot of Chinese money flowing through the markets these days, although that seems to go more in the direction of Asian arts and antiquities. Offhand, I don't think you can rule that out.

"A third explanation, I guess, is that someone is, in fact, buying this material, and you say there are other examples, for the express purpose of burying it. At the Hall of Fame, our mission is to preserve and display the items in our inventory. But maybe someone else, for whatever reason, has exactly the opposite mission—to acquire materials that are potentially harmful to the game and to take them out of public view, perhaps permanently. I hate to think of it, but such a person might even take these things away and then destroy them to be absolutely certain they are never discovered. I shudder to think of that kind of vandal loose in our sport, but I have to acknowledge it is possible."

"Well," interjected the Senator, "let's pick up on that thought for a moment. Now, you said that this latest trove of papers from the auction was all stuff that was, what, more than a hundred years old?"

"Much of it. In fact, most of it except for the reporter's notes, and those were not much newer. 1930s, I think."

"Right. So here's my question. Why would material that is a hundred years old and pertains only to players who have themselves been dead nearly that long, why would anybody be willing to pay eight million dollars, or whatever it was, simply to take that information out of circulation?"

Coppersmith sat quietly for a moment, pondering this very reasonable question. Then an answer occurred to him. "1994," he said.

"Beg pardon?" asked the Senator.

"1994. As you probably know, one of the longest-running issues in baseball has been in the area of labor-management relations. You probably remember how back around 1969, Curt Flood, who was one of the stars of the game, challenged Bowie Kuhn, who was the Commissioner of Baseball at the time, to make him a free agent, able to negotiate with any team for his services. He essentially sacrificed his career to make the point that the old reserve clause, that common contract language that bound players to their teams indefinitely, was unjust. Flood lost out, but the whole notion of free agency that is such a big part of the game and its finances now goes back to that challenge. It became a center point of labor relations until—and this is interesting in the context of this particular conversation—Congress intervened in 1997, just before Flood died, and passed HR 21—that was the number on Flood's Cardinals uniform—that provided, get this, antitrust law protections for baseball players that matched those of players in other sports that did not have the institutional antitrust exemption you are looking at. That was the real start of free agency.

"Well, in the middle of all of this contentious labor strife, in 1994, the players finally decided they had had enough, and they went on strike. It was the fourth time they had done that over about twenty years, but this time they were serious. The strike started in the middle of August, and that was it. No more baseball season, no postseason, no World Series. *Finito*. The players actually stayed out until early April of 1995, so past Opening Day. As I recall, there was also a big fight over replacement players.

"This was not a popular move with baseball fans, as you can guess. The media tended to portray it as a fight between billionaire owners and millionaire players, and in an era of rising ticket prices, neither side got much sympathy. Giant TV deals got canceled and restructured. There was just all kinds of fallout. And when baseball started up again in 1995 and the 'real' players returned, attendance fell off by around twenty percent, and much more in some markets. There were all sorts of incidents. At a Mets game, three guys wearing T-shirts that read "Greed" ran onto the field and started throwing dollar bills at the players. Some fan in Cincinnati hired one of those advertising planes to fly over the stadium, trailing a banner that basically told the owners and players to go to hell. In Pittsburgh and Detroit, fans threw all kinds of stuff onto the field on

Opening Day. And at Yankee Stadium, the fans started yelling at Don Fehr, the players union president, and somebody held up a banner that read 'Shame on You.' I think Fehr threw the guy a finger. In other words, the whole thing was a PR disaster for the sport. The teams and the players had to work very hard to get their fans back. That's when all kinds of new promotions were developed, when even star players would stand for a long time signing autographs, and when the players, with League encouragement, started flipping game balls into the stands after each inning as souvenirs, something they had seldom done before.

"Now to your question. Remember what happened in 2020, when that virus hit and shut everything down? And then the owners and the players couldn't figure out how to agree on starting back up? And then came some more contentious labor talks—as bad as in the old days—the next year? Even a lockout. And by then, unlike 1994, there was a lot more sports programming on television. People were even starting to watch soccer. The game was on the brink of disaster once again. Might not take but one little push and, lo and behold, the commissioner decides at the last minute to move the All-Star Game out of, where was it, Atlanta because of politics. That really alienated some people who had stuck with the game through everything.

"Then comes your auction. And what's for sale is a potential rewriting of baseball history in which the first real role model of the game, Christy Mathewson, is in effect a victim of the guy remembered as maybe the biggest bad guy of the game, Ty Cobb. Basically, a morality play in which evil triumphs. I am not saying that was the case. I don't know. But I am suggesting to you that if someone really was out to protect the game in some way, perhaps even from itself, in that context and at that moment in time, acquiring that particular collection might have made a lot of sense. If it hadn't been Mathewson in particular, and maybe the same for Cobb, whatever happened might have been just another incident. But it was Mathewson, and it was Cobb, and even today, at such a sensitive moment, that might make it something more."

"You know, Roger, that actually does make a lot of sense. And I am wondering if there might be similarities in the other cases in our files. But that is one for us to sort out. Utterly fascinating."

"Senator, let me just mention one more thing. Probably not relevant to you and your investigation. But as you know, I am the Chief Operating Officer of the Hall, the nuts-and-bolts guy. This sort of thing usually crosses my desk only when it needs a signature. But in this case, after the sale, we were approached by some farmer from Upstate New York who claimed that the papers were stolen from him, and that they actually belonged to us, to the Hall. He had some sort of weird, cryptic journal that he claimed proved his case. It was obviously bogus from the start, though we never figured out what his real game was. We managed to get him to hand over the journal so he couldn't use it in a play against anyone else, and then we tossed him out on his ear. I mention this because when he came to meet with us, he brought along a writer friend named Adam Wallace. And Wallace has subsequently published a book that treats this fraudster as a legitimate guy out to help the Hall get justice, and paints the Hall itself in a pretty negative light. I figured you should hear that from me, rather than later from someone else."

"Very interesting. I'll have Mr. Prevost get a copy of that book. Wallace, you say? Maybe there is something in there—not the claims about the Hall, but something else—that we can use, though after your description, it's hard to imagine what. Roger, it has been a pleasure and an education. Thank you so much for coming down to DC to meet with me."

"My pleasure, Senator. And if you ever find yourself in Cooperstown, I'd love to give you a personal tour of our facility. There are some really interesting artifacts that are tucked away simply because we lack the space to display them, but they are on the VIP tour and I'd love to show them to you."

———

"Adam!" Liz sounded breathless on the phone. He barely recognized her voice. "Adam, you have to get up here right away!"

"Sweetheart, what's wrong? Are you okay? Is the baby okay? Talk to me!"

"I'm fine. We're fine. It's not that."

"Well what is it? What's going on?"

"Adam, I found it! I found the door! And you won't believe where it is."

⸻

The man known to some as Lot Lizard had just received some very troubling news, and it was about to get worse.

"Are you sure? Are you sure that's what he said?"

"Absolutely," replied Roger Coppersmith. "That's what the man said. He intends to reopen the entire question of the antitrust exemption. He went on and on about all the changes that have taken place since that was established. Free agency, network TV and streaming of games, intercity travel. He almost used the word collusion when he mentioned the amateur draft and recruiting international players. It seemed like everything the owners and the leagues, and maybe even the players, had done to impose some kind of regularity and control on the game was on his list."

"And you think he was serious?"

"Well, I'm just an old country museum steward. I am not one of the powers of big league baseball. Far from it. But if I were one of those fellows, well, my first call when I left that office would have been to my lawyers to start building a defense."

"Roger, we both know you are not some country bumpkin. Nice try, old friend. And if your ears were twitching, some others would best be twitching along with them. I wonder if those guys know anything about this yet."

"I have no idea. And I can't be the bearer of that news."

"No. But I can. And I will leave your name out of it. Not to worry."

"I thought you might want to do something. Reason I called. And now that that's out of the way," he continued, "I'll tell you the really strange part of our conversation. Somebody down there in DC—I am guessing the Senator himself, but it could just be one of his staff looking to stir things up—somebody down there has gotten all excited about some crime syndicate or secret organization or some such that's going around buying up all kinds of documents and other papers that might be embarrassing to baseball, and then burning them or stashing them away where they'll never come to light. They were just spit-balling on that, I think. They don't really know what's going on. He said it was likely to be just some rich eccentric collector, but he also threw out some other ideas—money laundering, extortion, or just somebody trying to protect the franchise from itself. But they are pretty clearly onto some pattern of unusual and often very expensive purchases of certain kinds of memorabilia, apparently over a long period of years, and it all disappears into some deep dark hole. I know for sure we never see it at the Hall."

"Wow. That's fascinating. What kind of stuff was he talking about? Was there some example they're chasing down?"

"Actually, there was one. You remember that auction at Marbury House a couple of years ago? When was that . . . 2021? I guess they had been looking into that one. In fact, that seems to be how they came to contact the Hall. Back before the sale, the auction people had asked us to authenticate the papers in that collection, and I think they must have mentioned that to the Senator. He seemed to know a lot about it, everything, it appeared, except who bought it. Apparently the auction house was not very helpful on that."

"That's really strange," offered Lot Lizard, careful not to betray a catch in his throat. "Was the collection worth what was it, seven, eight mil? What the heck was it?"

"Well that's the thing. It was a lot of documents that were mostly over a hundred years old. There was this embarrassing incident at a military training camp back during World War I. Really, if it was true—and who can say—it was more than embarrassing. There might have been some real bad stuff involving Cobb and Mathewson, and a big cover-up by the government and the military and even the game. I remember Ban Johnson's name was mentioned, and where that man went, well, anything could have happened. He was a real conniver.

"There were some letters with serious autograph value and some interesting old documents, and beyond that, it was just a bunch of reporter's notebooks that were barely legible. So, to answer your question, yes, there was some evident value there, mainly for the autographs. Maybe three or four mil in today's market. The rest was all just ancient history, interesting but not worth the price it brought. We had actually tried to acquire it privately ourselves for the Hall once we had a look, and we made a reasonable offer, but the seller wasn't buying. Guess that proved smart as it turned out."

"But why would anybody pay that?" asked Lot Lizard. "I mean, a money launderer—and I am just speculating here, because that's not a world I know—but somebody like that might be willing to eat the loss to convert a pile of cash, but they'd have to turn around and sell it to make that work for them. And one of us would have heard if there was somebody with resources who was collecting and selling at this level. What the hell is going on?"

"Well, that was a question the Senator put to me, and I'll tell you what I told him. 1994. Remember how bad things got after the August shutdown that year? Remember how the press played that as billionaires fighting with millionaires, and nobody could identify with either side? MLB lost about a fifth of its fan base, and the ones who stayed with the game were pissed as hell and pretty unruly. It took years and a lot of money to get past that anger and create some new and better memories. And here we are a generation later, and the owners are making money hand over fist and the players, at least the good-quality veterans, are doing great, too. Even the young kids are getting half a mil a year. The union is making noises, kind of like they did back when Don Fehr was there, but a lot of folks seem to assume that's just posturing. Things are too good for everybody to mess them up. Then, BOOM. That Chinese virus comes along and everything shuts down. Baseball and basketball and all the sports, but everything else as well. People were basically locked in their houses for more than a year. I mean, how many times can even the biggest fan watch Game 7 of the 1971 World Series and not go stir-freaking-crazy? Except maybe in Pittsburgh, I guess. And just about the time they started getting back to their real lives, NASCAR comes back, and the PGA comes back, and hockey and basketball are planning their comebacks. And who is fighting the next war between billionaires and millionaires? Baseball. What was it Boswell said in the *Post*? 'A baseball crime in broad daylight.'

"Now what I said to the Senator was that somebody who saw the coming damage and really loved the game might do almost anything to stop anyone from throwing gasoline on the fire. And if the basic character of the game is being seriously challenged, and if someone were to come along and make public that particular collection of papers, with its conspiracy theory overtones and allegations of a cover-up that went back in the day to the very essence of the game, you don't think the press would eat that up? Wouldn't matter if it was true or not, and they'd find some hook to make it sound current. And if the government was shown to have been a co-conspirator, or even the instigator of something like that, given the little I know about the lack of confidence people have in government today, it would be on front pages for months. Baseball might never hear the end of it, might never recover. And as I told him, preventing that might be worth serious money to somebody.

"I didn't say this to the Senator, because I didn't think of it at the time. But you could say something similar about somebody who had a real axe to grind against the game—maybe an ex-player who thought he'd been mistreated or, well, who knows, but somebody with the money—could have bought up that set of papers and realized what was there, and might just be sitting someplace waiting for the right moment to dump them and get even.

"Anyway, that's not our problem, and it may not be a problem for the guys who run the game. I don't know. I just thought it was kind of interesting and that you might think so as well."

"Man, I really need to ponder that one. That is weird. But of course, we do live in a weird world. Hey, Rog, thank you so much for the heads up on the antitrust thing. I'll make sure that word gets to somebody who can use the information. And as I said, I'll do it in a way that protects you as best I can. Just so I know, when you talked to the Senator, you didn't sign a nondisclosure agreement of some kind or swear an oath not to discuss the conversation, did you?"

"No, nothing like that. He didn't ask, and I didn't get the sense he was too worried about it. I mean, the proceedings of the Select Committee will probably be mostly public, and if they're not, we all know, and he certainly does, that someone will leak them. Besides, they'll have to bring some MLB types in to testify. Even players. Those politicians down there love to have famous athletes as witnesses. They get to ask for autographs."

As Lot Lizard ended the call, he felt his blood running cold. *Perhaps,* he mused, *the code name I chose all those years ago was more appropriate than I guessed.* There was no nearby rock on which to sun himself back to warmth, so a finger or so of that Macallan single malt would have to do. Perhaps more than one. Then, he had better get to work.

———

What a day for the traffic to back up heading north out of the City. He'd forgotten it was Friday, and all the Catskill and Vermont warriors were making an early escape. It was dark by the time he reached the farmhouse.

Liz was showing now and displaying the slightest mama-bear waddle in her gait. She met him at the car with a hug and a kiss, followed by a cat-ate-the-canary smile.

"This must be good," said Adam.

"Oh, you have no idea," she replied. "Come on inside and let's have some dinner. I made a pot of spaghetti sauce, and I've kept it hot. Just need to throw on some pasta. There's a nice bottle of Sangiovese with your name on it."

Cooking was serious business in the Liz Fairchild household, as Adam had learned to his great delight. It was a good match. Eating was serious business in the Wallace household. So the two of them puttered around in the kitchen, mixing a salad, boiling a pot of water, tossing in a full box of angel hair pasta (Liz was obviously eating for two at this point), and converting a fresh ciabatta loaf into some well-seasoned garlic and herb bread. By the time they sat down, Adam had almost lost his train of thought. But he recovered it quickly.

"Okay. I'm here. We're eating. And the curiosity is killing me. If you love me, this is the time to spill the beans."

"All right. You remember how dowdy our offices were down in the village? Honestly, I don't think they had been painted since the Great Depression, or even systematically cleaned beyond sweeping up and dumping waste baskets since, I don't know, the turn of the century. Like I told you before, that's what happens when you have a bunch of men in charge of things." She looked up with that wry twinkle in her eye that

Adam had come to know when she was baiting him. "They just look past things like dark or dingy or disgustingly dirty year after year.

"Now, you've seen it here at the house. Mama Liz is starting to nest. We need to be thinking about safety for a little rugrat—gates on the stairwells, plastic plugs in the outlets—all that sort of thing. And at least one of us is." Again, Adam did not take the bait. He wanted desperately to get to the meat of the story, but he didn't want to interrupt.

"Anyway, since I spend so much time at the office, I started seeing that old place in a different light. And I decided it was past time to do some fixing up. We don't get a lot of clients coming into the office, but we get a few. And I began to realize how embarrassing it was to bring them into that space and how unpleasant it must have been for the staff to work out in the main area year after year surrounded by filth and clutter. So I started out there. I got some new furniture—desks, chairs, cabinets, even phones—and I have a whole new computer system and new software on order. We closed up for a couple of days, and while the space was empty, I had a commercial cleaning crew come in and do their thing, and I had it repainted. Even put a new sign up on the wall.

"Then Mama decided to treat herself. I kept my dad's old desk. Just couldn't bring myself to part with it. But I got a couple of new side chairs, and I got one of those fancy ergonomic desk chairs, and let me tell you, they ought to make one of those that pregnant ladies can strap on their backs so they can just sit on it any time. Really comfortable for somebody in my condition. Then I had the cleaners come in again, and then the painters.

"Now you remember all those bookshelves in there, crammed with catalogs and old records, and property plats and the like. I had the guys empty all that stuff into boxes and move it out into the business end of the building. I thought about replacing all the shelves at that point, but I decided that was self-indulgent and I had splurged enough. So I asked the painters to put a nice new coat of Greenstick Green on them. Did you know we actually have our own color? Anyway, the shelves were all jammed together around the walls, and they had to turn them all about ninety degrees and move them out into the room so they could get to everything to paint it.

"Well, when they got to one of the shelves, they just couldn't budge it. It was built right in. But they figured they could get to all of it except the back, which wouldn't matter, when they moved the next one aside. And when they tried that, something weird happened. The shelf just kind of rotated around without anyone lifting it up. Turned out it was resting on a steel bar of some sort that was cantilevered out from the built-in shelf. And there were three heavy-duty, I guess you'd call them articulated hinges that had been recessed into the sides of those two units. The other thing was—and as many times as I had looked at that unit or moved stuff on and off those shelves I had never noticed—the unit did not quite reach the floor. It sat on four rubber casters or wheels. So when you released a very subtle catch on the next set of shelves and pulled on the right side of that last shelving unit, it just swept open and to the left. If somebody hadn't hit that latch by mistake while they were trying to move stuff around, we might never have noticed all this.

"And here's the good part. Behind that set of shelves, the one on casters, was an old steel door with a great big lock set into it."

"Jesus!" exclaimed Adam. "It was right under our noses all the time! So did you open it?"

"No. I pretended I knew all about it, told the painters it was just an old closet nobody used anymore, and had them paint over it with the same color they were putting on the walls. Then, once I was alone, I rotated out that set of shelves and tried the keys, and I found one that worked. That's when I stopped and called you. Mama may be brave and tough, but if that door opens into some dank, dark hallway with the rancid smell of dead rats, Mama wants her man around. Tomorrow's Saturday, and the office is closed for the weekend. So, we can have the place to ourselves and go exploring."

Chin Music

"Grab a chair, CI. As you can see, I took the liberty of ordering us some lunch."

Lunch with the Senator was, as CI knew better than anyone, always the same. It always started with a bowl of Senate Bean Soup—a thick admixture of navy beans whitened by a hot water rinse, ham hocks, mashed potatoes, chopped onion, garlic, celery, a bunch of parsley, and butter, with a bit of salt and pepper tossed in for good measure. Beans, garlic, butter, and a sedentary profession with occasional bursts of rhetoric: What, CI thought from time to time, could possibly go wrong?

Before his election to the upper chamber, when the Senator had been a mere congressman, he had always looked across the Capitol and yearned for a daily lunch in the Senators Only dining room, where the soup was a popular tradition. So it had been something of a rite of passage when, on his first day in the Upper Chamber, his senior colleague from his home state had introduced him to the fare in its natural habitat. By 2012, when the Senate leadership decided to close the Senators Only dining room as an economic measure, he was hooked like a street junkie. The Senator had to have his soup, and not out there with the public. So every day, at the appointed time on his calendar, a junior staff member—referred to around the office as the Soup Nazi, a modest homage to the nineties television sitcom *Seinfeld*—made sure to have a piping-hot bowl of bean soup for the Senator, and one for each guest he might be entertaining, set out on the conference table in his office. And, since the Senator was also partial to club sandwiches stacked high with turkey and bacon, mayo on the side, that, too, was always on the table, one for each diner. As in many more substantive matters, the Senator was fully confident that his personal tastes were universally shared. Or he simply didn't care.

Finishing his soup, the Senator reached over and claimed CI's mayo container, slathering its contents on the second half of his sandwich much as he had his own on the first. CI had learned to enjoy his club sandwiches dry.

"Time is starting to press, CI, and we need to move this thing toward some sort of conclusion. So, what have we got so far?"

"Okay, let's start with the straight antitrust material. . . ."

"Screw that," the Senator interrupted. "If we want it, antitrust is a slam dunk. The evidence has been clear for a hundred years, and it just keeps building and building. Proving antitrust was never an issue. The issue has always been political will. You need to have a majority of the House and Senate actively wanting to rein in these baseball billionaires, and you need a president who was never a team owner himself and might sign the damn legislation. It's easy to get close, and after the debacle of the last couple of years, we might be near that time. But at this point, I'm not sure I give a shit. And I am certainly not willing to do any serious horse trading to make that happen. So let's move to the other thing. That's where I can maybe use some leverage."

"Well, there are some intriguing hints on that, but so far, nothing definitive. I went back up to Cooperstown and suggested to our friend, Mr. Coppersmith, that, while he had been very helpful to us, the time had come to connect me with whoever it was up there who had actually laid hands on the auction stuff at Marbury House. I wanted to talk to that guy. Turned out that the guy was actually a woman, one of their in-house historians for what the baseball types call the Deadball Era, back before about 1920. I spent an afternoon with her and walked away with something less than a complete inventory, but more than a cursory understanding, of what was in that collection.

"From what she told me, there were some Army documents showing that a bunch of players who were eventually named to the Hall of Fame—which wasn't started until about twenty years later—so some pretty prominent players, served in a National Guard unit down in

Georgia where they were training on poison gas. It was baseball trying to help out the war effort, and not incidentally get the government off its back, by creating a kind of publicity stunt. Problem was, there was never any publicity, the unit itself was apparently disbanded early, and nobody knows why. In fact, this historian told me that one of the local papers down there, the *Augusta Herald*, actually did a great big feature section on that camp the very same week the players were there, naming all the officers and describing the units, and even carried the lineups for a ballgame between that camp and some naval base from nearby. But apparently, there was nothing about the famous ballplayers being at the camp, and none of those boys showed up on the team roster. So, those papers seem to be the only evidence this ever happened, which accounts for their value to somebody for some purpose, whether that is yet, or never, to be revealed. Something must have happened down there, but there's no telling what . . . unless it was in those papers."

"Coppersmith said something about Cobb and . . . Mathewson, I think, when he was down here," the Senator interjected. "Something bad. I didn't really pick up on it at the time."

After pausing to make sure his boss had finished his thought, CI resumed. "Yeah, it was Mathewson. There were also some letters that seemed to relate to all this, but never actually said anything about it. And the bulk of the collection was a bunch of notebooks from some reporter who might have been chasing the story but never lived to write it. Guy was pretty old, and he dropped dead on a train, apparently. Now, if there was actually a high-level cover-up of some sort, you might be tempted to question how he died. Protecting national security and all that. No telling who might have heard what he was up to. But nobody had any reason at the time to even think of that, and some rural quack just wrote it off as a heart attack.

"That's where we get to the Wallace book. Everybody seems to have taken that as just speculative fiction—all that stuff about Christy Mathewson and Ty Cobb. But the more I think about it, and especially after talking to this historian at the Hall, I'm starting to think that Wallace might actually have seen the whole file of stuff, and he might even know more that he decided not to write about for some reason.

We put it off before, but it might be time to go have a chat with Mr. Wallace."

"Perhaps, perhaps," mused the Senator. "But the guy's a writer, and those people can be like hot stoves. You need some protection if you're going to touch them. What else?"

"Most of the rest is just rumors. I keep hearing a couple of names . . . Luna is one, and Steever. They keep floating around, and the context always seems vaguely nefarious. But there is never anything more than that. There have probably been guys with those names or something like them around the game in the last couple of decades, but I haven't been able to tie either name to any known scandal. They're just wisps of suggestive cloud drifting across the face of the moon."

"Cut the poetic crap, CI. I know you were once a lit major. Just be glad I gave you a lifeline out of that life!" It was a common bit of friendly banter both men recognized for what it was. CI had proved his loyalty and abilities often enough that neither felt a sting, or the need for one. Besides, it was true.

"What else?"

"Different topic, but the one other thing I keep hearing goes back to all the fighting around Curt Flood. Flood, remember, is the guy who had the balls to challenge the reserve clause and stick with it, and the top baseball guys, well they didn't take kindly to that. Played pretty dirty, I think. There were years of fights with the union, lawsuits, player strikes, race-baiting, personal attacks, collusion, side deals, promises allegedly made and broken and vigorously denied, and lots of big personalities all around. A lot of stuff that passed for normal back then but could surely paint baseball in a pretty bad light by today's standards. In the end, Flood lost his case but won his point, but by then he had basically lost his career, too. Never the same, and the pressure on him must have been massive and constant. Well, with all of that going on for so long and with fights on so many fronts, you just know there were lawyers involved. And law firms never throw anything away. So, somebody, somewhere probably has some records of all the backroom dealings, maybe some documents, some investigative reports . . . could be anything. And it could generate some real leverage. I could—"

"Now that I think of it," the Senator inserted, "I know who that somebody might be, or rather, might have been. Nice fellow, long gone. But the law firm. . . ."

He spent a moment lost in thought, and CI knew better than to interrupt.

"Okay, here's what I want you to do," the Senator said at last. "Let's go down two tracks. First, get me a list of all the partners at this law firm." He wrote down the name on a slip of paper and passed it across the table. "There are a lot of names on the door, and the way these damn things keep changing and merging, there could be more or different ones now than there were back when my buddy was there. This would have been the name about ten years ago. Martindale's or some other source will have a record, and once you find the right firm, making the list should be an hour's work, if it's anything more than just Xeroxing. Get me bios on those people, too, and spouses. I'm sure to have a connection to somebody there, and given how old those records are, we might even be able to get a look without having to issue a subpoena. The less of a paper trail we create at this time, the better.

"Then, I think the time has come to see if we can learn anything from Mr. Wallace. But he can't have any idea whatsoever of our real interest here. Maybe find some way to reach out to him directly, but be absolutely certain to arms-length us. If that doesn't work, just go to our usual Plan B. But be very careful. The last thing in the world that I want is for him to think he has the scent of a new story. Finish up, CI. I've got work to do."

———

It was a bright, sunny day outside, with temperatures in the mid-seventies. But inside, the office was dark. Lacking windows other than the big north-facing one in front, it was dependent on artificial lighting, especially in Liz's inner sanctum.

"Was that a new logo I saw out front? Big willow tree?"

"Actually," Liz replied, "that's not a willow. It's a Palo Verde. Desert tree, mainly. Sure as heck doesn't grow around here."

"Then why use it?"

"Never studied Spanish, right? Palo Verde translates as Green Stick. So it's actually the perfect image to go with our name. Part of my new freshen-up for the business. But it's a weird tree in its way. The reason for the name is that the trunk and branches are all green, not brown like almost everything else. The green is chlorophyll, the same stuff that's in green leaves, and the trunk and branches, the green sticks, actually produce something like two-thirds of all the photosynthesis for the tree."

"Fascinating," Adam replied, rolling his eyes just a bit.

"Hey. You asked. What'd you think? It was just a pretty picture?"

"Okay, okay. Let's get down to business. Show me the magic shelf."

Liz moved her desk chair to one side, fumbled with a release mechanism on the second shelving unit from the right, then pulled on the right side of the endmost unit. Out it swung, just as advertised. And there, behind it, redolent in a new coat of Greenstick Green semigloss, was a steel door with a big old lock.

"Damn," blurted Adam. "There it is! Let's do this!"

Liz pulled out the lower right-hand drawer of her ancient desk past what seemed at first like a full stop, reached in, and extracted the box with the ring holding the three large keys. She opened the box, isolated one of the three keys, and handed it to Adam along with its companions. He, in turn, pushed the key into the lock, surprised for a moment that it slid in easily, though by then he knew that it would. A turn of the wrist to the right, a loud "click," and the door swung away, opening to the left on an invisible hinge. It creaked a little as it went.

"That hinge could use a little oil," he deadpanned. 'What kind of maintenance do you people do around here?"

The open doorway admitted light from the office, but that light died quickly once inside, suggesting to Adam a deep, dark space of some sort.

"Honey, grab a flashlight, will you? I don't think the one on my phone is going to do much good in here. This looks like it leads to a cave or something."

"A flashlight? We're a landscaping company, as in plants and outdoors. We work in sunlight!"

"Enough!" They both smiled.

"Let me grab one from the shop next door. Hang on."

"And see if they have some kind of compass, too. Let's see if we can figure out where this goes. Probably not much of a GPS signal in here for my app."

After about five minutes, Liz returned with a powerful LED flashlight in hand, together with an old-fashioned magnetic compass she had found in a drawer and a pair of Greenstick hardhats. "Thought we might need these, too," she said, keeping one of the hard hats for herself and passing the remaining bounty to Adam.

By this time, Adam had discovered a steep flight of concrete stairs about ten paces into the darkness. Newly equipped, he judged it safe to continue. He and Liz descended the steps, twenty in all, and found themselves in a hallway of sorts, a long and narrow concrete-lined tunnel that led into the distance. Adam shone his light forward and thought he detected a series of reflections in the ceiling.

"There's got to be a light switch around here somewhere."

He scanned the nearby floor, walls, and ceiling with the light. "There!" he exclaimed. At the seam where the left-hand wall met the ceiling, he had detected an old metal conduit, the kind that builders used to use to carry electrical wiring through mechanical spaces and workrooms. He turned around and traced the conduit, thinking that he would find a light switch at the end. He was partly right.

The conduit continued upward to the top of the stairs they had just descended, and sure enough, up at the top, a short length of the tubing led downward to a metal box with an old-fashioned switch on its front, the kind where you turned a dial to the on or off position. He had missed it in his original canvass for a simple reason: Rather than sitting in the open doorway in easy sight and reach when entering from the steel door, the light switch was on the opposite side so that its presence was hidden whenever the door was opened. But he was surprised to notice that the main conduit itself continued all the way to the outside of the wall of Liz's office, then disappeared within.

"Looks to me like you and your family have been paying for the electricity for this place, whatever it turns out to be. Hold on a minute."

Adam hurried quickly back up the steps, slid the door so that it was about three-quarters closed, and flipped the switch. The revelation was immediate.

"Look at that!" he exclaimed as he made his way back down the stairs. The lights were of an ancient design, but they worked to light the steps, to light the area where he and Liz had been standing, and to light a tunnel that seemed to stretch almost to infinity or New York City, whichever came first. He turned off the flashlight and jammed it into his pants pocket.

"Ouch!" Adam had forgotten just how much heat could be generated by a high-intensity LED light in a metal housing if it was left on for five or ten minutes. "Damn!"

Liz laughed. "Maybe it's a good thing I'm already pregnant, Mr. Wallace."

"Point taken," he smiled back. "But that sucker's gonna smart for a while."

"Look at that. Those look like the old Edison-style bulbs, and it's hard to see much detail from a distance. But look how far they go. Did you bring bread crumbs?"

"No. Only a couple of Paydays and a bottle of Saratoga spring water I stashed in my little pack here."

"We doing this?"

"We're doing this."

"Then let's get going."

One thing you could say about this journey: It would be difficult to get lost. They were in a narrow corridor, lined on all four sides with concrete: block on the walls, poured on the floor, and slabs on the ceiling. The corridor was about four feet wide and maybe eight feet high, and was cooler throughout than the ambient air outside, not surprising since they were ten or fifteen feet underground, assuming, as seemed to be the case, that they were moving away from the stairs on a level surface. Interestingly, as they noted to one another, despite having presumably been closed up for the better part of ninety years, the air inside was not stale or even unduly humid. There was a barely detectable movement of air in an indiscernible direction. They had yet to see a vent, but in this light, that did not mean there were none.

"Somewhere up ahead or nearby," observed Adam, "there's a ventilation system at work. Chances are you are paying for that as well. Hold on for a second."

Adam took the compass out of the pocket where he had stashed it, mercifully not the same pocket where he had jammed the flashlight. "Let's see what we get. Your office building faces, what, north?"

"Almost. It's some variety of north-northwest."

"Okay, so if this corridor comes ninety degrees true off the back wall of the building, then we should be going something just east of due south, right? Let's see." He held the compass level under the nearest light bulb and gave it a brief moment to settle. "There it is, about ten degrees off due south. And still going. We should have brought a tape. About how far would you say we've come? Hundred feet?"

"Maybe a little more. I'd say go back for the tape measure, but curiosity has the best of me right now. We can always come back and measure, or even just walk it off to estimate. But let's keep going. This is just too weird."

They walked about twice as far again as before, and calculated that they were perhaps a football field distant from the Greenstick offices, but they could actually no longer see the entry stairway in the distant gloom, and thus could not be at all sure. Then, up ahead, the corridor appeared to end against an unmarked concrete wall. Suddenly, they were not quite so sure they were on to anything more than an elaborate feint of some sort, as much a figurative end of the road as a literal one. It was not until they came within about two light bulbs' distance that they saw this for what it was, a turn to the left into which the corridor continued. Just around the corner, on the left-hand wall, was another dial-like light switch. When rotated, it revealed another string of Edison bulbs, though one that seemed much shorter. The fourth bulb down the row appeared to have burned out.

"I think we must be getting close to whatever this is," Adam offered. "But where the heck are we? What's behind your office? What are we under?"

"Well, there's a little service area—utility connections, dumpsters, and that sort of thing. And some parking for our trucks. Then there's a pretty narrow road and a little bit of a greenway, really just a visual barrier that hides the back of our building. Then there's this big paved parking lot. Big enough for a few hundred cars."

"Parking for what? Cooperstown isn't exactly noted for its ample parking opportunities."

"That's easy. It's the parking for . . . Oh, my God! Adam, do you remember a couple of months ago when you called me with that cockamamie poem idea and we went off on that wild goose chase?"

"Of course I remember."

"And what was the translation of that line from the poem that set you off?"

"It was part of that sign and countersign thing that I thought was some kind of anagram. I thought the whole thing came from that famous old baseball poem, 'Casey at the Bat.' At the time, it seemed to fit everything together, but now it just seems foolish."

"Maybe not so much. Do you remember the last two lines of the coded exchange?"

"They are drilled into my psyche. I sleep with them at night . . . when I'm not with you. 'I Rented View Plus Uncle Hooch, Oh Battle Unhappiest.'"

"And when you worked out the anagram?"

"Well, when I thought I did. Yeah . . . 'He Pounds With Cruel Violence, His Bat Upon The Plate.'"

"And you leaped to the conclusion that the door to the treasure was right near home plate, and you sent me off on a search of the ballpark, and there was nothing, right?"

"Right. And I still feel foolish about that. I obviously had it all wrong."

"Well, maybe not so much. The parking lot is for Doubleday Field. And home plate at Doubleday Field is at the near end of the ballpark. Adam, we are probably about to head directly under the grandstand at Doubleday Field in the direction of home plate. You had the location dead right, but it wasn't the location of the doorway. It was the location of whatever was—is—on the other side. We'll have to confirm all of this with measurements and some careful navigational calculations, but I think we are about to find out just what old Casey was hammering on."

Aside from the power trip that came with questioning a recalcitrant and pompous witness now and again, the two biggest perks of his job that gave CI pleasure were the fat Cuban cigars his boss managed to acquire despite the decades-long boycott of commerce with the island and shared willingly with those he trusted, and the right to put his feet up on the other side of the large senatorial desk whenever the Senator himself chose to hoist his own. As for the cigars, the Senator was quick to recount a story told to him by President John Kennedy's former press secretary, Pierre Salinger himself, and later retold in the premier issue of the magazine *Cigar Aficionado*, of the days just before the president imposed that trade embargo against Cuba that was still in place sixty-some years later. It seems that Kennedy loved Cuban cigars and, while he was willing to impose an embargo on all trade with Castro's island, he could not bear the thought of facing life without his Petit Upmanns. So one evening he tasked Salinger with acquiring one thousand of the prized Cubans, telling his trusted aide that the purchase must be accomplished by the following morning. Salinger worked the problem through the night. And, when he reported for work the next morning and was called into the Oval Office, Kennedy inquired as to his success. Salinger reported that he had actually been able to acquire twelve hundred of the cigars. Kennedy smiled, opened a drawer, pulled out a long sheet of paper, and signed the embargo banning all Cuban products from the United States.

If that old spoiled brat Kennedy could corner the market for Cubans and then shut it down, the Senator figured, then by God, he could ignore the damn embargo, too.

As for the feet on the desk, the only rule was that CI must keep his shoes on at all times, and must never mention this perk to anyone. The Senator didn't really give a damn about the desk, and it was an easy way to show his appreciation to his long-time henchman.

So there they sat, feet up, cigar smoke billowing. It was a typical Thursday afternoon recap session before the Senator headed out for the weekend for a town hall back home, a round of calls to his big donors, a weekend of golf, or just quiet time at his cabin in the hills. CI never knew exactly where he went on his four-day jaunts out of Washington, and it mattered very little to him. The Senator was never more than five feet from his private cell phone, and it never rang more than twice before he answered.

"So what have we got?"

"Senator, as you know, I started with the law firm just like you suggested, and it didn't take long to get that list of partners. Once you picked out the partner to approach and gave me a couple of inducements to use, he was really tremendously helpful. Or tried to be. He told me that there was no way he could check out files, even that old, let alone share them with an outsider. But what he could do was find the files, and then set me up in a private reading room where I would be free to look them over for as long as I wanted.

"The first step was to find out what they had and where the records were kept, being as old as they were. So he called in this ace paralegal named Runa something, and he set her on the search while we chatted. About an hour later she reported back. The computer said they had seventeen boxes of material on matters in which someone named Curt or Curtis Flood was identified as a plaintiff, a defendant, a subject of investigation, or a witness, and that they were stored in an archive in the building next door to the office block where we were sitting. He told this Runa to grab a clerk or two and a cart, go next door, retrieve the boxes—all of them—bring them back, and set up a secure room to review them, then let him know.

"Another hour or so passed, and then Runa reappeared. 'Strange thing,' she said. 'There were only sixteen boxes in storage. They were just where the computer said they should be. But we looked and looked, and there was no sign of the seventeenth box.' So the lawyer says to show him the list, and then he makes a strange sound, kind of hard to describe. And he says to this paralegal, 'Let me guess, but looking at these filing numbers,' and he's staring at the list, 'I'd bet that the missing box is number GLIT94X3.1432.321.' And she looks at him like he's some sort of magician, just pulled a quarter from her ear. And he thanks her and tells her to run along. Then he turns to me and he says he thinks somebody has a problem.

"Turns out the GLIT meant it was a general litigation file and 94 was the year, or more correctly, the last year of activity before it was filed, so whatever it was could have been running for a long time. The 1432 was the matter number, and 321 was the box number for that matter when they closed it. So whatever that case was, it was big enough to fill hundreds of boxes. But the X3, he said, that's the key. That's the code for something super sensitive or, for some reason, super confidential. Somebody, he said, has cherry-picked the file on Curt Flood, and the good stuff is missing. So I asked the obvious question: Do we know who? And by the way, Senator, you owe this guy. He was really working this for us.

"So he goes down the hall to some big administrative office, and I can hear him sweet-talking some staffer in there. And he's gone for a good while. But when he comes back, what he's got is golden. The box was checked out something like twenty years ago by one of the former partners, former as in deceased. Could have been a real dead end, but this lawyer, he's smart. So he had this staffer go into some back-office kind of files, stuff nobody ever gets to see, which is why he was doing all the sweet-talking. And he comes back to his own office with a list, actually a copy of a list. The header has been removed, along with any other identifying marks. Our guy did that when he made the copy. And he gave me the list. Here it is." He handed over the list.

"These were all of the clients of the dead partner, guy named Pomerance, and the years he worked for them. If you look down the list about a half-dozen names or so, you'll see why you owe this lawyer something nice."

A moment passed.

"Son of a bitch! Son of a BITCH! We got you now, you old cocksucker."

"I thought you'd find that name interesting."

<hr />

Adam and Liz held their collective breath as they tried first one then the other of the remaining keys in the steel door at the end of the branched corridor. There was a rewarding click of the deadbolt, and this door, too, swung open to the left with a slight groan. Adam felt to the right for a wall plate and dial, found it, turned it, and the room filled with light. Same bulbs, he judged, but proportionally more of them.

It was pretty clear immediately they had found what they were seeking.

They found themselves in a chamber Liz guessed to be on the order of fifteen feet square. To the right, along the near wall and not far from the doorway, was a small wooden table, sturdy but not fancy and perhaps four feet by three, tucked under which was a wooden chair. Starting in the corner beyond and wrapping around to cover the wall opposite the doorway were ranks of industrial-style steel shelving—the kind with corner posts laced with holes for attaching the shelves themselves using nuts and bolts. There appeared to be nine of these units altogether, each about three feet wide (the basis for Liz's estimate of the room's dimensions), five down the first wall, and four more overlapping the corner turn and running along the second. The shelves were slightly more than half filled with an assortment of boxes made variously of wood, different types of cardboard, and even some plastic. The boxes all appeared to be labeled, but to describe their arrangement as orderly would be something of an overstatement.

Adam paused and sniffed the air. Again, nothing. No telltale odor of mold or mildew. There seemed to be a low hum in the background, either barely discernible or entirely imaginary.

"Here we are again," he said. "A hundred years' worth of paper, stored underground, yet no indication of decay, or at least no smell. And I swear I can hear some sort of ventilation at work. Somebody went to incredible lengths to create this space and to preserve whatever is in it . . . Uh oh."

Liz looked up with a questioning expression, then followed Adam's gaze to the left, to the fourth wall of the chamber. And there it was. A third door.

"Let's see," she said, moving her eyes back and forth. "Boxes of papers or whatever, or mystery door number 3. Papers . . . mystery door. What shall we do?"

They both laughed, and without any real hesitation, Liz fished out the third key, which fit the lock of the third door nicely, and turned it. As she did, both of them noticed an odd thing about this final door. Unlike the other two, it opened back into the room they were already in. And as it did, it revealed something altogether unexpected. For behind that door was another, very different portal—a 1930s-style vault door, heavy-gauge steel with a large combination lock. Stenciled across the top, along with some sort of floral decoration, was the name and location of the manufacturer:

ROSENGRENS
GÖTEBORG.

Lower still was a date of manufacture: 1928. Adam and Liz looked at each other in dismay.

"You don't remember any other pieces of paper in that drawer of yours, do you? Say, something with a combination on it?"

"Alas, no. Nothing like that. And as you can imagine, once I found that box and the envelopes, I took a pretty thorough look around in there."

"Great. And after we are so close. Well, I suggest that we think about this for a while and focus for now on what we do have access to, all of those boxes behind us. At the very least, we should be able to answer some questions, and in the process, maybe something will occur to us."

"Agreed. But do you mind if I sit down? And maybe have one of the Paydays? We are getting a little tired over here."

Adam suddenly remembered. "Please!" he replied as he moved over to pull out the chair. "You settle in and rest, and I'll make a start on the boxes to see what's there."

"Just bring them over to the table one at a time, and we can poke through them. Obviously we're not going to make it through them all, at least not today."

"And we are *not* carrying them back up to your office. That's for sure."

"You know, Adam," Liz said. "We are going to need a plan for this. There's just so much here. Plus, I think Mama's going to need to pee soon. How about this: All of these boxes seem to have labels. Let's take a quick inventory of those and see if we can get a sense of what's here."

Doing that took about ten minutes, and when they were done, two conclusions seemed evident.

"It looks," observed Liz, "as if the labels correspond pretty closely to the list my dad made from his research, a bunch of the scandals in baseball since around the 1930s."

"Plus a few others, actually," Adam responded. "Those wooden boxes, which have to be the oldest of the lot, say they are from the Black Sox scandal. That was around 1919 and 1920, so before this vault was even built. Somebody must have been collecting that stuff for years. I can't wait to get into those and see what's there, because people at the time thought that everything had eventually come out. Obviously not, or there'd be no need to have saved all that for another ten or fifteen years and then moved it in here. In fact, as I think about it, maybe something in there is what led to building this giant safety deposit box in the first place."

"Not to mention getting Grampa Jake set up in business!"

"Plus there's this other box that just says 'Dutch Leonard 20-26.' No idea what that is, but again, it's in one of the old wooden boxes. So your dad might have missed a few. But there's something else odd. Something that's not here." Adam waited a tick for Liz to catch on.

"Damn," she said. "Jason's box is not here. There's no sign of all that World War I stuff you guys came across. It was on Dad's list. In fact, I think it got him to doing that research and writing that list in the first place. But it's not here."

"Exactly. But you know what? Your dad made a connection because he was in a unique situation, plus he just happened to be reading articles in *The Times*. But really, even though the auction was public, the contents of the suitcase never were, except in a really cursory way. Some insiders who evaluated that material for the auction place may have been privy to some or all of the contents, but the public? Never was. Only Jason and I were the exceptions. So, unlike the rest of what's here, it never actually became a scandal, and the only way it would have done is if it got out because somebody released the information. And if there is one thing that's very clear by now—the people behind this place here, whoever they were, were not about releasing information like that, no matter how old or significant it might be."

"Adam," offered Liz. "Think about it. Basically everything in these boxes relates to scandals that everybody knows about. And the one scandal we know about, but others don't, is not here. There might be some interesting secrets inside these boxes. But I have a sneaky feeling that the real secrets are just over there." She pointed to the vault door. "We need to figure out that combination."

———— ⊸⊘ ⊘⊶ ————

When Adam and Liz made their way back down the length of the L-shaped corridor, locking doors and turning off lights behind them, and emerged into the somewhat less claustrophobic ambience of Liz's office, Adam's cell phone began to chirp in a way he knew indicated a missed call. He looked but did not recognize the number. Still, for a writer, anonymous calls were not uncommon. He pressed redial.

"This is Adam Wallace. You called my cell."

A male voice on the other end of the call paused for a moment, then replied. "Yes, yes. Mr. Wallace. Thank you for returning a mystery call. My name is Chuck Zanzibar. I am an editor at Cilwsi.com." He pronounced it SILL-wissee. "Have you heard of us?"

"Honestly, I can't say that I have. Is that even a word?"

"No surprise. And no, it's not a real word. It's an acronym for Call It Like We See It, which is our basic philosophy. We are an online sports magazine, actually just a startup at the moment. We're trying to do for long-form sports writing what some others are doing for sports news. But with more zip than *The Athletic*."

"And by zip, you mean . . . what exactly? More sex? More fake stories?"

"No, no. Nothing like that. We just think a lot of what's out there is too stodgy for a young audience, and we're all about a young audience. I'm calling you because our website is going live in two weeks, and we still don't have a zinger of a story as a main feature. But I just read your book about Cobb and Mathewson and how all of that stuff got covered up by Baseball and the government. I love the cover-up part, and that could be just the ticket for us. I mean, the book is already out there. But I was hoping there might be more to the story. I was hoping you might have a lot more information about the whole thing—what secrets are yet to be revealed, who is keeping the cover-up going, that sort of thing. If you have something like that, if you know something really wicked cool, and if you could get us, say, three thousand words, give or take, by this time next week, I could pay you . . . five thousand dollars. Get it to me in three days, I could go, say, seven thousand dollars. The word count is not crucial, since we're online, or will be, but clarity and bright language will be important for our readers. Can you do that?"

Adam paused for a moment's reflection. Maybe it was the fact that only five minutes earlier he had emerged from a cave of secrets suspected but yet to be revealed. Maybe it was the eagerness of this caller or the pressure for haste. Maybe it was the fact that it would be all but impossible to conduct any sort of due diligence on a startup company that did not even have a live webpage at this point. Or maybe it was the fact that, unlike any other similar solicitation he had received, this editor did not seem to care much about what, specifically, he might write about. But something in this call did not ring true. Plus, of course, Adam had a related, but quite a different, project already underway.

"Thank you for that offer, Mr. . . . Zanzibar was it? That's very generous. But I just don't have anything like that. If I did, you can bet I'd have put it in my book. So, I'm afraid I am not the solution to your problem."

"Are you sure? I could go . . . ten thousand dollars for the right material. I am sure I could talk our angel investor into that."

"Again, that's very generous, and believe me, I am flattered. But I just don't have any information of the sort you are after. But I appreciate your calling. And I now have your number if I come up with any ideas in the future that I think might interest you. Oh, and best of luck with your new website. You are getting into a very challenging business."

"I wish the answer was different, I really do. But I understand. Thank you again for returning my call."

And with that, CI turned off the burner phone, got up from the bench along the new River Walk, and tossed the device into the Anacostia River, where, even money, the toxic sludge on the bottom might melt it before sundown.

―――⋙ ⋘―――

Adam stayed with Liz for another day or two, and they did make one more trip down the secret stairway. But Liz was feeling tired after that, and Adam worried that the entire thing might be too taxing for her. So he made excuses to do other things, not least of which was a potential redecorating project. There was, after all, a baby on the way, and hard decisions had to be made about whether to give their new son or daughter the use of Eddie's old room, Liz's late brother, and if so, how to transition it from a young man's private space, complete with precisely the posters and other art and artifacts one might expect to find in such a temple, to something more suitable for a newborn and youngster-to-be. Adam left the big decision to Liz, who made it with a display of grace and a suggestion that her new family find a suitable place of remembrance elsewhere in the house for Eddie. As she pointed out, it's not like this would be the first time the house got made over for a new generation of Fairchilds. Well, she corrected, Fairchild-Wallaces. After that, it was simply a matter of paint.

Once that was done, Adam returned to the City to get some work finished, with a promise to return as soon as Liz felt up to another round of exploration. They promised each other it would not be more than a few days.

<hr />

It was three weeks later, or thereabouts, but the soup and the club sandwich tasted the same.

"So what happened with our friend, Mr. Wallace?" This from the Senator.

"Not much, I'm afraid. I actually talked to the guy. Made like I was the editor for a new online sports mag, and I offered him ten thousand for a brief write-up of any interesting dirt he'd left out of his book for whatever reason. Wasn't a taker. And that was nothing short of free money. So whatever he knew or knows, I don't have the sense it goes past what he wrote. And that makes sense, I guess. If you want to sell books, you want to load in as much hot stuff as you know or can realistically make up.

"So then, like you said, I went to Plan B. I put a tail on him, guy I've worked with before. It actually took two of them, because Wallace lives in this high-rise in New York City. So they had to watch the building entrance but then also the garage where he keeps his car. I had them cover about twelve hours a day. Guy's not into nightlife, and he doesn't go out much at all except for food, so the tail on foot had it pretty easy. But he did head for his car one morning, and my two guys were able to mount up together and catch up with him. He headed north out of town all the way to Albany, then west and up toward Cooperstown. They phoned in every couple of hours, so I'm thinking we got him now. And sure enough he takes the turn up to the Village. But then it got less interesting. Turns out he has a girlfriend in Cooperstown—she has a farm and runs some landscaping company. Looks like the two of them have been busy, if you know what I mean. They drove over to Oneonta the next day to some medical building, and then they were shopping for baby clothes or baby something, but other than that, they spent most of their time at her office in town, and the rest at the farmhouse. It was all totally Norman Rockwell."

"So Wallace is a dead end for us?"

"Far as I can tell, sir."

"Okay, good. Then here's what I want you to do. I want to set a hearing date for about six weeks from now. Make it for the Investigations Subcommittee of the Select Committee. That'll surprise anybody who's paying attention, since technically there is no Investigations Subcommittee. But I'm the damned Chair, and if I have to, I'll create one. Only one member, of course. And getting the attention of certain people is the whole point of the exercise. Get us a room with a short dais but lots of room for cameras. See what's available around then and let me know before you lock anything in. Then schedule it for two consecutive days.

"Once that's done, draw us up a list of parties to be subpoenaed. Day one, I want the two guys from the auction house, that Max guy and the acquisitions guy, and I want Coppersmith and your historian friend from the Hall of Fame. Day two, I want the Commissioner of Baseball. That ought to get their attention. And the head of the players' union. And pick me out a couple of your favorite asshole club owners from the bigger media markets. And just for fun, send one to that Bahamian bank president. He'd never show up, but he'd pick up the phone and make a call to you-know-who. We'll stretch all this out so it has a chance to play.

"Also, let's ditch the whole discussion of antitrust for the moment. That's softball; nobody on our end has any real skin in that game, just other people's money. Plus, that would open the door to my, ah, distinguished colleagues horning in on the hearing. I don't want that. Make it something mysterious and very suggestive. Make 'em think we have more than we do. Maybe . . . 'An Official Inquiry Into Deception and Financial Mismanagement in Professional Baseball.' That should make for some cleaning bills.

"You using that mayonnaise?"

———

Adam and Liz had been down the tunnel, as they came to think of it, only a couple times since that first visit, but it was enough to become intrigued and to convince them of the need to be highly organized as they proceeded. They knew to bring snacks and water, as well as writing pads and a supply of pens. For the most part, Liz became their scribe while Adam muscled around the boxes and dug out their contents.

It was, on balance, a most interesting exercise. For the most part, the boxes contained papers, court transcripts, legal and other files, a good deal of correspondence, a few books, and a great many news clippings and magazine articles, mainly dating to the years before 1995, when the internet was little more than a shared resource among a few favored universities. Later years tended to produce reams of printouts of, essentially, the same sorts of materials. Interspersed with all the paperwork were a few oddities—a box of mismatched baseballs, a baseball glove with some sort of dried, tar-like substance on it, an actual bat with the business end sawn in two, a fairly large rock that seemed to be covered in dried blood. One find was truly gruesome. It was a small box, the kind they sell matches in, and when Adam slid it open, inside he found three severed and long-since shriveled fingers.

It took a long time to go through the paperwork, and in fact, they found themselves skipping more and more. But they slowed down for things like signed written confessions of wrongdoing, some of them known to history and some not, at least as far as Adam could say off the top of his head. The special reports from various attorneys and investigators were dense but informative reading, though even Liz, who knew her way around numbers and business, had a hard time parsing some of the efforts at forensic accounting. It became pretty clear that, at least in the old days, some of the owners were every bit as evil as the players and the media claimed, and that the leagues and the commissioners down through time had had their hands full trying to wrangle the whole thing through one season after another.

By the end of his latest visit, Adam had reached the conclusion that, throughout its history, or at least its latest hundred or so years, baseball was under a more or less constant threat of corruption. Cheating players, cheap owners, opportunistic drug dealers—and there were a lot of boxes about that!—it almost didn't matter. If there was a way to squeeze out another buck from the game, it seemed like somebody would try it. And yet.

"You know," he said as they were wrapping up for the time being, "it still bothers me. As much scandal and corruption as we have been reading about here—and I have to say, it's pretty clear why somebody would want to keep this away from the public eye; it's much worse than what's already got out from time to time and already tarnished the reputation of the game—as much of that as we've been looking at, it bothers the hell out of me that we haven't come across the stuff from Jason's suitcase. I was never really sure just how much of that whole thing I thought was real. But now . . . now I'm starting to think maybe all of it was. Especially if we find it stashed in the vault. And you have to wonder what else is in there that might be so bad that they had to lock it up even tighter. We need to find a way to open that combo lock."

"Yes," interjected Liz, "I've been thinking about that a lot. On the one hand, it's altogether possible that there is no way we'll ever figure out that combination for the simple reason that only the members of this particular little cabal all had it memorized, and they shared it with all the newcomers over the years. That's possible. But it's also risky for them, if only because it becomes a secret easily shared. Any one of those guys over a hundred years could have gone off in a snit and given away the combination in a fit of pique. Unlikely, I know, because they obviously have had some strong bond of trust in this group, but still, not as secure as you might think at first.

"But the other way to do it would be more consistent with their whole approach to security. Get a third party who has no idea what's involved, say some poor family named Fairchild, and give them something, something they can't even know they have, that reveals the combination to any official, sanctioned visitor who might show up many decades after the whole thing was set up. To me, that seems the most likely. And it also means that if we look the right way in the right place, just like the doorway, we'll find it. So let's not give up. Let's put our brains to work."

"I love you when you're smart," said Adam. "Of course, I love you the rest of the time as well."

"Excuse me! Are you suggesting I am not *always* smart?"

Even without military training, Adam knew instinctively when the time came to withdraw his colors from the field. But just in case he had missed her signaling, Liz gave him a good pinch on the arm.

"Senator! Please come in. To what do I owe this honor?" The man known to Liz, and now to Adam, as Lot Lizard was coming around the desk in his capacious personal office as his secretary admitted the unexpected guest. "Can I offer you something? Coffee? A little Johnny Walker Blue?" The first was a mere courtesy, but the second, at upwards of $400 a bottle, was pure suck-up.

"I wouldn't mind a touch of Scotch," replied the visitor. "That's most generous of you."

"Not at all, not at all," offered the host as he poured a finger or two into each man's glass. The crystal, bearing the logo of Major League Baseball, had been a gift. "I don't recall that you've been out this way very often before. I hope it was a pleasant trip. What brings you to town?"

Two predators warily circling one another, only one knowing with certainty that today the other was prey.

"Well, as you may know, I've been looking into some baseball matters, and it won't surprise you to know we have a hearing coming up. The antitrust issues and the rest. And I like you, and I value your counsel. So I was hoping I could just bounce a couple of things off you."

"Absolutely, Senator. It would be my pleasure." He was astute enough to know that by day's end, that characterization might ring hollow. "What's going on?"

"Let's deal with the antitrust issue first. Frankly, it's a slam dunk. Way back when, the Supreme Court said baseball was just a collection of local operators and wasn't really engaged in interstate commerce. So it could not possibly violate the antitrust laws. Bullshit. Professional baseball would have to be played in caves on desert islands and without lights to hide the myriad ways that the major leagues—hell, even the minor leagues from rookie ball on up—are not only part and parcel of interstate commerce, but they are arguably its most iconic form. Everything these teams do—and I am saying the teams, not just the leagues—to make a point, everything they do is interstate in nature, from the day the first equipment truck leaves home for spring training to the day all the winning players fly in for the parade to celebrate the World Series.

"And as for acting in concert to restrain trade, well, it seems to me that MLB fits any definition of a cartel. It negotiates common terms with all kinds of business partners and with the national broadcast networks that carry certain of its games, including the World Series. Those contracts say outright that the national broadcasters can simply override any broadcast contracts the individual teams might have for their local markets. There goes Justice Holmes's reasoning right there. Plus, the cartel enforces standards for the most mundane things, right down to fonts and logo designs, it imposes territorial boundaries among its members, it negotiates and specifies common contractual terms, it requires centralized participation in a common website and mobile app, it operates a centrally controlled recruitment system through its drafts and through all the affiliated minor leagues, which, by the way, it arbitrarily reconfigured not so long ago to eliminate, what, forty-some teams and markets, not to mention several league organizations, and lots of other ways. It even redistributes wealth within the game through the so-called luxury tax. A first-year law student could make that case with her eyes closed.

"It's inescapable, it's unarguable, and I do wish the people who control your game would simply come to terms with it and move on. It makes them look foolish and privileged, both of which, as you perhaps know better than most, are precisely true. It's only money, and your guys are rolling in it. And not only is it an honest policy matter, but it's a winning political one as well. Just ask the fan who has to buy a six-dollar hot dog and a five-dollar bottle of water because they won't let him bring a sandwich into the park. And after the last couple of years, there's not a lot of sympathy out there. So, to get to my point, politically it's a no-brainer. A series of Select Committee hearings on this subject would be of immense public and media interest. Just so you know, we have a long list of people we might subpoena to talk about that.

"Hell. If the FBI ever got into this in a big way, the owners might even be looking at a RICO prosecution. Rigging the free agent market. Cutting back the minor leagues even though they don't own most of those teams. I could probably wake up any day of the week and find three or four brand new predicate acts to justify that, and proving a conspiracy among those guys is as easy as reading the daily papers. They don't even bother to pretend. You know, RICO means treble damages. That'd be billions. Hell, we could build a new aircraft carrier for that . . . call it the *Babe Ruth*, launch fighters like they was baseballs."

Lot Lizard was absorbing this monologue with a growing sense of unease.

"And yet," the Senator continued, "I do not want to go there. At least not now. As vulnerable as your people are right now, I am not one to strike an opponent while he's down. It's an important enough issue that it ought to be a fair fight when it happens."

"Senator, I know some people who will be very relieved to hear that you said that. May I pass it along?" Lot Lizard was grabbing for whatever solace might be within reach.

"Of course," his visitor responded. *You idiot*, he thought. *Why the hell do you think I came all the way out here to tell you that.* "I think that would be okay. Just be sure they understand that I might change my mind about that at some later time."

"Done."

"But that gets us to what I wanted to pick your brain about. In the course of pursuing the antitrust inquiry, my staff came across some other activity that we just don't understand. Initially we weren't quite sure what we had, but we know a great deal more now, and I could use some help from an expert in figuring out just what's going on and what it means. I was hoping you might be that expert."

At this point, the Senator was about to draw once again on one of the deep recesses of his personal experience that was little known to the public. He was, as he'd told CI, a hell of a poker player, and not just in friendly games with Bahamian government officials, where he might purposely lose a few dollars, easily replaced, in exchange for building a relationship or hearing slip a confidence. Some of his colleagues on the Hill knew it; they faced it every third Tuesday evening during the session. But even they were unaware that, before he had run that first campaign for the House, the Senator had toyed, briefly but seriously, with turning pro, though in those days, the professional poker circuit was about as attractive as the rodeo circuit—hidden corners in smoky bars, risking all for an elusive reward, with the entire battle waged in virtually total obscurity. He decided instead to enter politics, with its hidden corners in smoky bars, risking all for an elusive reward, and, but for a chosen few, with entire battles waged in virtually total obscurity. He made the choice secure in the knowledge that his one core skill would come in handy either way: the man knew how to bluff.

And now, here he was, knowing that he possessed far less than a pat hand. He knew some things for sure, not least the fact that the man across from him had his name on a signature card at a certain Bahamian bank. As for the others, he could only guess. Bluff, read the faces around the table, make your move.

"It turns out that there's a small group of men, probably quite wealthy but certainly highly influential, who seem to have set themselves up as the unofficial protectors of the game of baseball. It looks like they buy up any sort of damaging information that comes along about players or teams or the business itself, and they just bury it. It never sees the light of day. They've been doing this, apparently, for decades, so there must be some type of membership recruitment or replacement scheme in place. We figure there are maybe three or four or five of these men at any given time. If there were more, somebody would have heard about it by now. So they are extremely secretive. You've been associated with the game for a long time. Have you ever come across anything like that?"

"No . . . ," said the man across the table. "No, I can't say as that rings any bells."

"Interesting." The Senator reclaimed his time. "Now if these guys want to play hide the sausage with the media or anybody else, that's fine with me. If they're not breaking any laws or interfering with things, who gives a shit how they spend their money? But it's starting to look as if they may have gone a lot further than that. You remember that auction at Marbury House a couple of years ago where they sold off that Cobb-Mathewson collection? That's kind of how we got off on this track, and we have been able to all but figure out who the anonymous purchaser was. We had to track down offshore companies and banks and the like, all of which make it look kind of like a money laundering operation, maybe out of Mexico or Colombia. We'll turn up a name somewhere, and then we can really get into it. And to smoke all of that out into the open, as I said, we're going to hold a hearing or two. In fact, just today we set the date for the first one for about three weeks from now. We figure if we turn over the right rock, even by chance, we'll be able to see what's living underneath it."

"That's really quite a tale, if you don't mind my saying so. Honestly, I don't know how something like that could be going on in the game for so many years without my hearing about it." Lot Lizard was struggling to mask his rising sense of dread.

"Well, I agree with that. I especially agree with it because, truth be told, we are a little further along in this investigation than I have said. We have actually traced through that offshore corporate structure, and we have found the bank in question. It's a really obscure one down in Nassau called Bahia Bank of the Bahamas. And you know what? We also found the signature cards for that account, kind of the smoking gun, you might say. Would it surprise you to know that—"

His host held up his hand. "No need, no need. It's true. A couple of friends and I, and I would really like to keep their names out of this, well, we pooled our money and we did buy up that auction lot. But not for any improper purpose, for goodness sake. We bought it to preserve it for posterity. Even now, we are interviewing . . ." he paused, then stepped gingerly around the trap that he had almost set for himself, "getting ready to interview baseball historians to go carefully through all those documents and determine their significance." Having been so tightly focused on avoiding the trap of his own devising, he failed to avoid the one the Senator had just set for him. Snap.

"Well, that's reassuring, and I am delighted to hear it," opined his guest. "But then, talk to me about this other thing. You used to know a lawyer by the name of Pomerance, didn't you?"

147

"You mean Jimmy Pomerance? Yes, yes I did know him. Really sharp attorney, as I recall. Might have used him for litigation a time or two. But that was years and years ago. In fact, I think Jimmy died a few years ago. Why do you ask?"

"Actually, I can tell you exactly when it was you retained him, or at least when it ended. 1994 or so, wasn't it?"

"Could have been. But that's over a quarter century ago. I can't be sure."

"What was the litigation?"

"Well, even if I could recall after so long, that would be confidential."

"Does the name Curt Flood ring a bell?"

It was everything Lot Lizard could do to control his bowels at that moment. It was as if his entire insides had gone loose, and yet he didn't dare excuse himself. That would be tantamount to surrender in this particular game.

"I knew Curt."

"Oh, you did more than know him. Let's be honest here."

"We didn't exactly see eye to eye on certain issues. But you know that."

"I do." Having read the table, the Senator was confident enough in his cards to launch his bluff. "But you did more than disagree with Mr. Flood. You and your colleagues made his life a living hell, and I'm not just talking about baseball contracts. You pushed and pushed, didn't you? And Pomerance was there with you all the way. It's in his files. Does the file number GLIT94X3.1432.321 mean anything to you?" The Senator had no expectation that a law firm file number would have registered on his prey or, for that matter, that he would ever have seen or heard it. But he also knew the value of tossing out highly specific information, which could easily be taken as a suggestion that he knew a great deal more. It was no accident that he had accumulated great power in Washington circles.

"I don't recognize that at all. But why would I?"

"Why indeed? But let's leave that for the moment. We've been hearing some other things as well." The next move was, he realized, close to betting he could draw to an inside straight, but, again, he felt he had read the table well.

"Does the name Luna mean anything to you?"

He could swear he saw the blood drain from his host's face. The man looked suddenly ten years older.

"No," came the stuttered reply. "I don't think so. Not that I recall, anyway."

"Well, here's another. How about Steever?"

He detected a shaking in the man's right hand. It was time to stop pressing his luck.

"Senator, why are you really here?"

"I thought you'd never ask."

⸻

"You know," Adam said, "I almost had the feeling someone was following me on the drive up here today. I must be getting paranoid."

"Oh, great," replied Liz. "Mental illness in the family."

They shared a laugh, then got down to business, that business being cracking the lock on the vault door.

"I have wasted a lot of time trying to figure this out," said Adam. "In the process, I learned a lot about safes and how these old combination locks work. There's a real system to it—where you are supposed to start, what direction you turn first, how many times you pass 'Go' this way or that, how many wheels there are in the lock, which seems to determine how many times you switch direction. Four times, three times, whatever. And the thing is, every manufacturer seems to apply the rules differently. To make matters worse, we are dealing with a lock from Weimar Germany, even before Hitler, and I couldn't find anything at all about how this company did it. All we know is that it's a big, old honking lock.

"And that's the easy part. Even if you knew how many times to turn it left or right, and which direction comes first in the sequence, you still have to know the combination. Not a minor detail. We need a place to start!"

Liz picked up the thread. "While you were gone this week, I spent a little time down here trying to solve the same problem. I looked everywhere I could think of where somebody might have written or attached or etched or painted or notched it or anything else on a wall or shelf or door. Anything I could think of. And then I went back up to my office, and I basically did the same thing for every little corner of the old desk on the theory that all of the other information was stored there and this might be as well. I pulled out all of the drawers and looked behind them and underneath them. Shone the flashlight into the slots. I couldn't bend down, because I'd never get up. But I went and bought one of those selfie-stick thing-a-bobs and used my phone to take pictures under the desk itself. Nada. Though I did see the label from the place Grampa Jake bought the desk back in the thirties."

Adam had a thought. "Was there a serial number on that label? Let me see the photo."

Liz called up the picture on her phone. Fortunately, she had stored it on the phone itself, and not in the cloud, so she was able to access it down in the vault. But that was as far as their luck ran. No serial number, invoice number, or other hint.

Adam toyed with the keys, as if they might hold the answer. He did a riff on an old Johnny Carson routine in which Carnac the Magnificent would hold an envelope to his elaborate headdress, state an answer, then open the envelope to reveal the question. Only trouble was, Adam wasn't looking for the question. He knew the question. What he and Liz needed was the answer.

"You know," said Adam. "We might have had the right idea the last time I was up here. One of us, and I don't remember who, said something about tying the combination in some natural way to the Fairchild family itself. That's just how those guys might have been thinking back in the day. And on the drive up here, it occurred to me that one way they might have done that would have been to use the highway numbers between, say, New York City and Cooperstown. And then I thought, well, those numbers are all different now, what with the interstates and all. So, what were the road numbers back in the 1930s?

"I actually pulled over at a rest stop and used my phone to find the old numbers. But I ran into two problems right away. First, there are lots of different ways to make that drive, and they all involve different combinations of numbers. And second, it was the 1930s. And Roosevelt was building all of the New Deal parkways, and if you just used the part of the route south of Albany, already you are talking about the Mosholu Parkway and the Saw Mill River Parkway and the Cross County Parkway and the Bronx River Parkway and the Hutchinson River Parkway and the Sprain Brook Parkway, and all of that is if you just stay on the east side of the Hudson. Then you could cross the river up at Poughkeepsie on the FDR Bridge. That opened in 1930, so maybe. If you went the other way and crossed to the west in the City through the Holland Tunnel—and that was brand new back then, too, so maybe they would have gone that way—well then you had the Garden State Parkway. It's a wonder there was a piece of land in the entire Metro New York area that wasn't covered by a parkway. And they all had names, not numbers. So I just gave up."

At that point, the pair retreated in frustration back down the corridor and into the office. Liz had brought sandwiches, and Adam coaxed a couple of canned sodas from the machine in the shop. They sat in thoughtful silence for several minutes.

"Maybe we're making this too difficult," said Liz, breaking the quiet just before it turned eerie. "The one thing we do know about these people is that they were long-term thinkers. The ones who started it can't possibly be alive today, and yet, as recently as a year or so ago, people from this group were still coming here. So they had devised some kind of system to replace themselves in their little group, and also to educate the newcomers or their emissaries on how to access this archive. They had their code names and their challenge-response passwords, and they had my family keeping a record of sorts of who was authorized to get in and who actually came and went. They had the keys, and someone to keep them, someone cut off from the whole organization and unable to identify any of its members—at least until my dad might have done that by accident. And they had the vault door. There was a sophisticated, and yet simple, system for everything else. Why not for the combination? I think the answer has to be hiding in plain sight, and we are just overlooking it because it is so obvious."

"So," said Adam with faux caution, "here we are with you trying to be smart again. Ouch!" Speaking of smart, that pinch surely would, and probably for a couple of days.

"Actually," he said, "that's brilliant. But it still leaves us in the dark. Let's think about what we have. We have the roster of names and visits since the thirties, but that changes all the time, and I don't see anything in the earliest entries that seems to suggest a numeric pattern. Plus, your ancestors kept that record, and we don't know whether they ever shared it with their visitors. So that's a likely dead end.

"We also have the keys. Of course, they don't open a combination lock. And there's nothing on this key ring as I look at it, no engraving of any kind. Plus, we don't even know if this was the original key ring, or if there even was one. Might be something one of the Fairchilds added for convenience."

"Adam, are there any numbers on those keys? When you buy a lock today, the keys that come with it usually have some kind of code numbers on them."

Adam gave the three keys a close inspection. "Damn, Liz! You're right. There are numbers on each one. Let's see . . . CK621R, CK636WJ, CK24KM. There's also a manufacturer's stamp on each one . . . Daly-McCoy Manufacturing."

"Never heard of it."

"Me, either. And there's nothing here that's an obvious clue. But let's crank up your computer and just see if we can find anything about this."

A minute or two later, they were looking at a write-up of the history and products of the Daly-McCoy Manufacturing Company, which, as it turned out, had converted its machinery to make mess kits during World War II but then never reopened after the war. For a short time, however, they had stamped out specialized keys for one of the big lock companies of the day. Someone had posted copies of old company sales brochures, one of which featured keys that looked just like the ones Liz and Adam were holding. And apparently there are people in this world who are lock nerds, because someone else had gone to the trouble of listing all of the style sequences employed by the company. The elements of those sequences were helpful to a point. CK, it seemed, referred to the overall size of a given key, while codes such as R or WJ revealed the type of notching that each style employed. The numbers in between identified particular cutting patterns, of which there were at least 921.

"It might be there," said Adam, "but I don't see it. What else have we got?"

"The only other thing we have that doesn't change through time is the exchange of password phrases. But that already served two purposes, gaining access to the entry door and, probably incidentally, identifying the actual physical location of the archive room."

"I agree. But let's think about this. Why do they have four lines of passwords? Doesn't that seem a bit, what, excessive? I mean, who were they really thinking would try to get in there that a second trick phrase would stop? I can see why they might want to have the second exchange, because, like you said, it confirms the location of the treasure trove. But those first two lines, they're not only weird, but they just seem . . . superfluous. What are they again?"

Liz double-checked. "He Melts Rainbows Paying Heed, Devilish Journeymen Toil. Or in the original, per your translation, The Band Is Playing Somewhere, There Is No Joy In Mudville. If there are numbers in there, I don't see them."

Adam was lost in thought. "Babe, there *are* numbers in there. Even if they wanted to use a double password exchange just for its own sake, they could have taken any four lines or partial lines of that poem, but they almost surely would have taken those lines in succession. And if they had done that and still wanted to end on Casey beating his bat on the plate, which is to say, identifying the location of the room, they would have used the part that came just before . . . Let me see if I remember it . . . 'The sneer is gone from Casey's lip, his teeth are clenched in hate.' And they didn't do that. These very careful, meticulous men chose not to do that. And they chose, instead, to use parts of two other lines. Quick, see if you can call up a copy of the poem on the computer."

A moment later, they were looking at Thayer's best-known work.

"Let's find these lines," Adam muttered. "Here they are . . . all of them, they're all down near the very end of the poem, but they're not in this order. Hmm. I have an idea. Let's count down the number of lines from the top . . . Okay, the band is playing in line fifty . . . Mudville is joyless in line fifty-two . . . Pounding with cruel violence is in line forty-six . . . Ah, but so is the line about the plate. Same line. And I don't know of any combination lock that uses the same number twice in a sequence. But maybe . . . maybe it's the fact that it's really only one line of the poem that matters."

"So," she said, "50-52-46? You think that's the combination?"

"Only one way to find out." They headed for the vault once again.

———— ⚬≡⚬ ⚬≡⚬ ————

No matter the urgency, he believed, life's little rituals must be observed. So the host poured out three glasses of fine whiskey, passed two of them to his guests.

"I give you the GameKeepers." All three joined the toast, then emptied their glasses, the majority unaware of the scale of the challenge they were about to confront.

"Gentlemen," he said as all three men settled into their customary seats, "we have a problem, a large and complex problem."

"This better be important," grumbled the man once known to Hank Fairchild as First Fan, though the two had never met. "This was not a convenient time to travel all the way up here on short notice. What could be so important that we couldn't handle it on the phone."

"I had a visit a couple of days ago from our favorite United States Senator. He wanted to—"

"What?" interjected First Fan. "He came here?"

"Yes, exactly."

"Damn. That's not good. Not good at all. Politicians are all about power, boys. And power is like real estate, it's all location, location, location. You come to me, and it's like acknowledging that I have bigger brass than you. I go to you, I might as well just start suckin'. And that wily old son-of-a-bitch senator, he does not suck anybody or anything. So there's only one reason he would have troubled himself to come all the way out here to see you, my friend. He thinks he has such a huge amount of power over you that he can just be as magnanimous as hell. It don't matter none, because he has nothing at risk. What did that old SOB want?"

"In your own inimitable way, sir, you have precisely captured the situation. The Senator wanted me to know that, even though he could put baseball's nuts through the antitrust ringer, or even RICO if you can believe it, any time he wanted, he was disinclined to do so for the moment."

"And he wanted them to know about it, right? Know they owed him a big favor? Wanted you to pass that secret knowledge along?" First Fan was really into the discussion now. The merger of his two true interests had garnered his complete engagement.

"Precisely. And of course, he didn't volunteer that. Like a fool, I asked if he'd mind if I mentioned it, maybe to the commissioner."

"And did you?" asked Straight Arrow, the third man in the room.

"Not yet. Because it gets worse. And I wanted to have this conversation with the two of you before I do anything.

"There's no easy way to say this next part. He knows about us. Knows, or suspects. He knows about the dummy corporations and the bank account in the Bahamas, knows that we bought that collection in New York a couple of years ago. Even knows," and at this he nodded to the other man with longer tenure among the group, "and I have no idea how, about the lawyer we used to work with way back when we were dealing with Curt Flood and trying to hang a curtain over all of that ugliness. And he dropped a couple of names—Luna and Steever. I don't need to tell you what that would mean. I don't know exactly how much he knows and how much he's guessing. But it all hits pretty damn close to home . . . too close for my comfort.

"The kicker is, he's scheduled a hearing for a couple of weeks from now, and he plans to air all of this. He told me a few of the witnesses he plans to call, and I can assure you, this will be a very public bashing of the game and probably of us as well."

First Fan was losing his patience. "There's more, isn't there? There's something you're not telling us. And I can guess what it is. The Senator wants something. It's the reason he came out here, and the reason he told you about all of this stuff he has. What does he want?"

"He wants to be Commissioner of Baseball."

"Beg pardon?" asked Straight Arrow.

"He wants to be Commissioner of Baseball. Says he's tired of the Senate, tired of Washington. Always loved the game, thinks the last couple of years have had a really negative impact, thinks a lot of people, if given an option, would agree that the current commissioner has outlived his usefulness, not to mention demonstrated a level of incompetence. That's what he says. The Senator wants to be our white knight. He also wants a good salary, the usual perks, and, get this, a one-percent share of each MLB franchise. I figured it out. Altogether a couple of years ago, the thirty teams had an estimated worth of just under fifty billion dollars, that's with a 'B.' In ballpark numbers, he wants a half billion dollars up front, spread across the ownership groups. And that doesn't even begin to address a full point of the ten billion in annual revenues."

"Oh my God," said First Fan. "That's absurd. Why would anybody pay that or anything like it? If they did want a new commissioner, they could buy a good one for what, ten million a year, maybe twelve?"

"Yes. But don't forget about the hearing next month. If he goes ahead with that, not to mention if he changes his mind and decides to pursue the antitrust exemption or, God forbid, starts pushing for a RICO indictment, the damage could be immense. Franchises could lose ten, twenty percent of their value almost overnight. Not just the publicity or the lost fan support, but the damn plaintiffs' bar. Those guys would find some excuse to get their ugly noses under the tent. From his perspective, and I am inclined to agree, he's offering a bargain."

"He's offering extortion, is what he's doing!" shouted First Fan. "Hire me for a shit pile of money and put me in charge of everything and everyone, or I'll wreck you so bad you'll never recover. That's nothing short of blackmail!"

"Wait. I haven't told you the rest. He wants a seat at the table."

"What table," queried Straight Arrow, who seemed the least emotional of the three.

"This table. He wants to be included in this group. He's seen the signature files down at the Bahamian Bank. He knows who we are. And he knows, or strongly believes, that we have been burying harmful information about baseball, information that, if it ever got out, could blow the lid totally off the game and destroy it almost beyond saving. He is threatening to use his hearing to tell all if we don't invite him to join us and give him full access to the material in the archive.

"Now we might, and I emphasize might, still have one thing going for us. I don't think he knows anything about where the archive is located or how it's accessed. Maybe we can find a way to use that to our advantage."

First Fan had had enough. "No!" he said emphatically. "No way I'm going to sit at a table with that man. No sirree! But you're right. We need to move fast to protect ourselves. Maybe we move the archive and leave a few tidbits behind. Maybe we keep everything up there in place, and create a phony archive somewhere else, salt it with some intriguing documents. Either way, we need to create a feint, and we don't have but a few days to do it. One of us needs to get up there and talk to the guy with the keys."

"Well," Lot Lizard said resignedly, "that's the other little problem we have. And this one's on me. A few months ago, Tres checked in. He's the liaison with those folks these days, and he keeps track of things. And Tres mentioned that old man Fairchild, the guy with the keys, had died of a stroke. Just dropped dead all of a sudden."

"Okay, but we have a contingency for that, right? Presumably he passed everything along to his oldest son, just like the agreement says, right?"

"Yes, yes, he did. Years ago, when the boy turned twenty-one. But his son joined the military, and he was KIA."

"Tell me there was another boy."

"No. Only one son. Now, he did have a daughter, Elizabeth. And we don't know whether he brought her into our . . . enterprise or not. It's possible. But there is another possibility, one derived from our own history. You have to remember that a hundred years ago, when our little group was founded and when the original deal was made with the original Fairchild fellow, our predecessors were men of their era, and not the most socially progressive at that. From what I understand, the original obligation imposed on the Fairchilds was that the responsibility for controlling the keys was to be passed along to the oldest son when he reached adulthood. The oldest son. It was apparently very specific. And no one else, no other family member, was to know anything about it. Now times change, and it is possible that this latest Fairchild, realizing he no longer had a son to carry on the responsibility, brought his daughter into the matter. But it is at least as likely that he would have seen doing that as a violation of an agreement from which his family had long benefitted. A real moral dilemma. And she may know all about the arrangement and be waiting for us to contact her. Or she may have no idea whatsoever, and the keys, the log, and the archive itself may be completely unknown to her."

"Do we know where this daughter—Elizabeth is it?—is? Is her name even still Fairchild?"

"Now, that's where we may still be in luck. She's still living up in Cooperstown, and apparently, she has taken over running the landscaping company. Not married, though, which could mean we still have a longer-term continuity issue to address, even if she is in on everything."

"It probably goes without saying," offered First Fan, "that you need to get yourself up to Cooperstown and see what we can do to rescue this situation. In the meantime, let me start working the other side of the problem. You were right to hold off contacting the commissioner before we met. Let's wait on that until I have a chance to sound out some old friends."

—⁍⁌—

"Are you ready for this?"

Adam and Liz were standing in front of the door to the vault. At least they assumed it was a vault.

"Go for it, big boy."

"There's still some guesswork here. From what I read, on about ninety percent of these things you start by rotating the dial to the right first. I guess a wrong turn could set off an alarm, but then, where the heck would it ring? So probably . . . no.

"Okay. The dial is calibrated up to a hundred places. All we need is fifty-two. So far, so good. Let's see . . . Here's the notch on the edge of the dial that's usually the starting point. It's not at straight-up 0/100, but I think that's not uncommon. So, assuming we're right that there are three wheels and three numbers in the combination, then I think I want to go clockwise three times past start . . . Until I reach . . ."

"Fifty," offered Liz.

"Fifty. Done. Didn't feel anything, but don't know that I should have . . . Then counterclockwise twice past start and end at . . ."

"Fifty-two."

"Right, fifty-two. And once more around the clock and then stop at . . . I'm waiting!"

"Forty-six."

"Forty-six." Adam removed his hand from the dial and placed it gently on the top of the steel latch handle. He pressed down firmly and was rewarded as the handle rotated about forty-five degrees. In fact, knowing the Germans, he would have bet it was precisely forty-five degrees. There was a sound deep inside the door. He pulled firmly, and the massive steel door swung quietly open. "We're in!"

The door opened onto an interior chamber that was perhaps five feet across and five feet deep. There was no interior lighting, so Liz flicked on the flashlight. It looked as if the entire area was lined in steel plate, welded at the joints, and welded to the frame of the door. The front three feet or so was an open space, while shelves lined the rear wall of the chamber. Here, too, there were boxes, though far fewer than in the outer room. Liz, who by this time was occupying noticeably more space wherever she stood, hung back and worked the light while Adam gave the boxes inside a cursory examination. He pulled one out into the room and set it on the table. The label read "Hancock WWI."

"Here! This one has to be the papers Jason and I found in his barn." He lifted off the lid of the storage box and was surprised by what he found. Yes, the pay roster and daybook and letters were there, and what looked to be all of JT Willett's notebooks as well. It was all there. But there was more. A diary of some sort from someone named H.R. Barnum. It took just a moment for Adam to realize that he knew that name. It was Abner, the company clerk, the fellow who had held onto the papers that had ended up with Jocko Drumm. And there were copies of some Army investigative reports, from the look of them, some kind of order or official-looking instruction from the Committee on Public Information, the nation's propaganda agency in World War I, and a big file from Major League Baseball itself. And that was just for starters. Puzzled, Adam started flipping pages, moving from document to document.

"Jeez! We didn't know what we had! Look at this." And he showed Liz the items he and Jason had rescued from the barn, the ones that had eventually brought the two of them together. And then they moved to some of the other papers. Words like "propaganda ring" and "spy network" kept popping up. He'd have to read much more closely to be sure. But he thought he was seeing evidence that Christy Mathewson had, in fact, been targeted in a training "accident," but not by Ty Cobb. It looked like he had stumbled onto a German ring of some sort operating in the camp. And if everybody, including the baseball people, chose not to make Mathewson a hero at the very moment of his exposure to the gas, perhaps there was some tie to the game itself. After all, baseball players traveled freely around the country and to all the major cities. It would have been the perfect cover for some espionage. Adam's story-teller gene was starting to resonate.

"I'm definitely coming back to this one. But what are the rest of these? Here's one marked 'Luna, X.O.' and another marked 'Steever.' Hah! Here's a box marked 'DH.'"

"DH?"

"Yeah. Stands for Designated Hitter. Years ago—after the big baseball strike, I think—the American League decided that the game needed more pizazz which they thought meant more offense, especially home runs. So they juiced the ball, and for a while they let the players juice themselves. And they decreed that pitchers, who are notoriously poor hitters, would no longer need to bat. Each team could designate a position player to take the place of the pitcher at the plate. Then, of course, the teams started recruiting guys, mainly musclebound sluggers who could smash the ball out of the park but couldn't field their way out of a paper bag, and making them permanently into designated hitters. Some of them, they were actually afraid to put in the field. Extended the careers of a lot of aging mashers, but in the process it took a whole lot of the nuance out of the game. Now, the National League is doing the same.

"I have to say, I always thought the DH was a crime. Ruined the game. But I am surprised to see a DH box here, of all places. What's that about?"

Adam began to pull materials out of the box and peruse them as he had the Hancock WWI items. He couldn't believe what he was reading.

"It appears," he said to Liz, "that DH here means something a little different. Somebody had a sense of humor. You remember that skater, what was her name, Kerrigan. Nancy Kerrigan. Ninety-four Olympics, I think. She made the team, and it pissed off this other skater, Tonya Harding. Also really good, I think. Well, there was some kind of jealousy thing going, and if I remember right, Harding's ex-husband or boyfriend or some relation actually hired a guy to bust Kerrigan's knee with a steel baton so she couldn't compete against Harding in some big competition. In other words, this guy hired a . . . Designated Hitter.

"As I recall, that didn't go real well for Harding and her crew. But it appears that it gave somebody ideas. You probably wouldn't remember it, but one of the events on your dad's list had something to do with a big baseball strike back in 1994. Season ended early, talks dragged on through the winter. It was a really big deal. In fact, all this stuff with partial seasons and strike threats and all in the last few years was like a rerun in some ways. Anyway, the next year, 1995, they still hadn't settled the thing by Opening Day, so the teams were using replacement players in spring training and a few early games. These were mainly minor leaguers and whoever else they could scrape up, guys who knew they had no real future in the game and so didn't care if the union blacklisted them. From what I'm reading here, it looks like after the strike was settled, and those guys went back to wherever they had come from, well, some of them got kneecapped in pretty much the same way. Somebody hired some muscle to take care of it. New meaning for a 'designated hitter,' apparently. Then, it looks like they got some nice money to keep their mouths shut. I won't be sure about that until I have a chance to read a little further, but it seems to be what's here.

"Speaking of minor leaguers, here are a couple of boxes labeled 'Minors.' Huh. These are just file folders with what look to be last names on them. Allenberry. Cadiz. Here's a baseball name for you. Harry Horner Huepnagel. Really old file. Had to be a catcher. They are clearly in alphabetical order, and I never heard of any of these guys. Let's look in one or two . . . Here, take a couple . . . Interesting. This one looks like a dossier of some sort. There are a couple of police incident reports and, hold on, some surveillance reports. It looks like somebody was having this guy followed."

"This one is kind of the same," Liz said, perusing another file. "What are these?"

Adam thought a moment. "You know, a lot of these files are not that ancient, and the fact that I never heard of any of these players in the majors makes me think somebody was identifying and tracking minor leaguers who would cause big problems if they ever made it to The Show. And they must have used the information in some way—threatened the players, warned off the teams, who knows? Basically, this is a blacklist."

"Is that legal?" she asked.

"You got me. But it's easy to see why they wouldn't want that information out there."

They closed up the two boxes of player files and set them aside. Adam turned to the next box. "This one is labeled 'Test Results.'"

"Are they making players take the SATs or something?" Liz wondered wryly.

"Don't know till we look," replied Adam. "Let's see what this is . . . Looks like a bunch of data of some sort . . . Oh. According to the headers on these printouts, these are the results of compression tests and drag coefficients on baseballs. I guess they must test them every year. Makes sense . . . Now that's interesting. There are some differences year to year on some of these.

"You know, there's been a lot of talk over the years about the leagues juicing the baseballs. Way back around 1920 or so, the baseball was redesigned and made harder or more resilient. I think they changed the core from cork to rubber, and then they changed the kind of yarn they used to wrap it. Baseball nuts refer to the years before that as the Deadball Era. Then all of a sudden, things changed, and they were talking about the 'jackrabbit' ball and the Live-Ball Era. Maybe Babe Ruth had something to do with that. In any event, there was a big change, and ever since then there have been a lot more home runs. Around 1949 and 1950, I read, there was a big jump in the number of home runs being hit, and the ball was just being hit so hard in general there was talk about putting a protective screen in front of the mound, kind of like what they use for batting practice. Casey Stengel actually wanted to rename the game from baseball to 'helium-ball.' Or so he claimed. With Casey, you never knew.

"They've done other stuff to help the batters over the years—moving the fences in, shrinking the strike zone, moving the pitcher's mound further out and flattening it some. I guess they like lots of offense in the game more than they like good pitching or defense. In the 1960s, baseball even acknowledged they were trying out a livelier ball, though they said they dropped the idea. And I saw somewhere that there's been a lot of renewed suspicion about the clubs trying to add offensive power in recent years to help them out at the gate. So, what I'm looking at here are data that seem to support that suspicion. You know, in 2018, MLB actually bought Rawlings, the company that makes the balls. Lots of people saw that as proof of a conspiracy. Then in 2021, they even admitted publicly they had *softened* the ball to *cut down* on home runs. I guess some people are never satisfied.

"That same year, I think it was, right in the middle of the season, the commissioner decided to crack down on pitchers loading up the baseballs with stuff that made them sticky so they could spin the balls better. Pitchers have been loading up the ball with spit or various kinds of junk literally forever. It's been one of the worst-kept secrets of the game, which is kind of ironic, given where we are. Anyway, the commissioner got the umpires to start checking pitchers two or three times every game. A couple of the pitchers actually started to undress on the mound in a kind of protest. But then they wised up and made the argument that putting sticky junk on the ball was a safety issue—it let them control their pitches better so batters wouldn't get beaned by accident. In other words, the only way to play the game safely was by breaking the rules consistently. But . . . Hold on . . .

"Look at this last folder. These are . . . wow . . . These are letters of instruction from the commissioner's office to the company telling them what design changes will be required in the baseballs, and these go way back . . . way back. Long before 2018. Here's one from 1949, a couple from 1968. And this looks like internal notes about reasons to get more control over Rawlings by buying them out. That might explain . . . I remember a news story back in 2021. It never got much play for some reason. But the story was that during that season, Major League Baseball had actually used two different baseballs—one lively and one dead—and had sent them around to different teams for different series. Almost sounded to me like they might have been trying to fix the results or something, and if it happened, at the very least it could have impacted some team's fortunes or various players' stats. That's money to those guys, especially anybody due to be a free agent after that year. I'm going to need to read this more closely later. It's pretty clear why this one would be locked away. But let's move on.

"Let's see what's in . . . 'Steever.' This one looks like it goes back a long way, too." Adam took a few minutes to sift his way through the piles of paper in the box. "Wow. Another interesting little story. Back in the fifties and sixties, from what I can see. I think that's before there was any sort of contract between baseball and the players, but apparently they had some salary disputes that got referred to some form of arbitration. Steever was some kind of lawyer or something, and he seems to have been a popular arbitrator, at least with the owners. It looks like they might have split the difference with him when he ruled in their favor. Or maybe he was the guy who ratted out somebody else. Radio DJs were getting Payola from the record companies back then to play certain records, so why not? Again, I can't be sure until I can read all this stuff.

"Let's see what's in this pile," Adam said, turning to a bundled collection of folders, the topmost of which bore the label "Collins Investigation." He removed the binding and began sorting through the folders, of which there appeared to be eight or ten. "Apparently," he said to Liz, "there must have been a series of robberies of ticket proceeds at some of the ballparks back in the . . . looks like mostly in the early seventies, or around then. I don't remember ever hearing about that, but obviously it was enough of a concern that they hired some investigator to look into it. Might be something interesting in there to come back to as well." He re-tied the bundle of files and set it back on the shelf.

"That leaves . . . X.O. Luna, whoever that was." Adam opened the box bearing that label, glanced inside, and quickly closed it.

"What?" asked Liz.

"There's a bunch of photos on the top."

"So?"

"They're not baseball card photos."

"Come on, Adam. What's in the box?"

"I don't know. But right on top are a lot of these photos. Women, mostly. Fairly young women. Very young women. In very suggestive poses. And I saw one or two pictures of guys in baseball hats and not much else. Could have been players, though I can't say without looking more closely. But they had their bats in their hands, if you know what I mean."

"Oh, God. Was somebody trafficking to the players?"

"I hope not. But I guess we'll find out soon enough. You know, on the one hand, I can't wait to get into these boxes. There are probably enough things here to write about from now until we're paying college tuition.

"On the other hand, I am beginning to understand why these guys in this secret society, or whatever it is, have been trying to bury all of this material and keep it buried. True, they are covering up what looks to have been some pretty nasty, and probably some illegal, business. But, at the same time, if someone were to dump all of these files into today's media and cultural environment, it would be an unmitigated disaster for professional baseball. Can you imagine the social media hashtags? I need to think about this."

He did not recognize the voice on the other end of the phone, but he knew well for whom it spoke.

"Jim Prevost here. I work for the Senator. I gather that you are cooperating with him in setting up this hearing that's coming up. He asked me to express his continuing appreciation for that. It's citizens like you who are so necessary to our work advancing the public interest."

"Happy to be of help, Mr. Prevost," he managed to say, hoping that he sounded, if not sincere, at least not as angry as he felt.

"The Senator wanted me to keep you informed of our progress, and to let you know that we are adding some additional firepower to the hearing. We are adding a panel with some well-known former players, maybe an agent, perhaps a journalist or two, though they tend to be pretty shy about taking positions on issues. Or at least they used to be. I guess we'll see. In any event, we are hoping for lots of coverage on TV, and we are going to stream the hearing on the Senate website as well."

"Great. That's just great."

"The Senator also wanted me to ask whether you were making progress on some matters the two of you had discussed. I'm not privy to what those might have been, so please don't say anything I shouldn't hear. But I do need to ask about your progress."

"Yes, I know what that is about. Please tell him that we are hard at work on both of the issues that concerned him, and I hope to have something to report soon. But tell him that these things do take some time."

"I will certainly convey that message for you. And I really look forward to meeting you at the hearing."

With that, they ended the call.

"Think he got the message?" the Senator asked, though he had, of course, been listening in on the call.

"I do," replied CI. "Yes, sir, I do."

"Ms. Fairchild," began the visitor as he entered her office. He was an older man, graying, with old-fashioned eyeglasses and a serious expression. Seeing her condition as she rose to greet him, he amended, "Is it still Ms. Fairchild?"

"Yes. And you are?" Liz had her suspicions.

"I am an old acquaintance of your late father. And before I go on, please do accept my condolences. I did not know him well, but I knew him well enough to respect him."

"Thank you. That's very kind."

He got down to business. "This might end up being a rather . . . awkward conversation. Or perhaps not. We don't know each other, but I would like to ask you to agree before we begin to keep whatever is said in this room in confidence. I assure you it is nothing bad. The matter I want to discuss is simply very, very sensitive, and known to only a few people, of whom your father was one. In my humble opinion, it would honor his memory if we could proceed on that basis."

Liz could guess by this point where this conversation was going but worked hard not to let that show. In fact, she was interested to see exactly how this fellow across her desk was going to handle it. She tilted her head and held her tongue, which her visitor apparently took as an affirmation.

He chose "History" for $400. "Many years ago," he began, "back in the 1930s, a small group of private collectors was formed to preserve some, ah, important national artifacts. Those were the Depression years, and the men who formed this group feared that political or economic instability might put these priceless objects at risk."

Liz decided she was going to enjoy this.

"The group was set up in such a way that new members would be recruited to that mission as older ones passed on or stepped away. I sit here today as one of their successors. And because of the nature and significance of these items that were being preserved, several security precautions were adopted. Some codes and things you don't need to worry about, for example. But one of these procedures does relate to you, or at least did relate to your family. Are you with me so far?"

"Oh, yes. This is fascinating. But I get the sense we are just getting to the good part."

"Indeed. This original group decided they needed a place well off the beaten path in which to, ah, deposit their treasures, and for whatever reason, and who can say what that was, they settled on Cooperstown. They also needed someone to guard the materials, or really, to control access to them so that only members of the group or their representatives might be permitted to see them. And, for reasons again shrouded in history, but probably because of some network of personal contacts, they settled on your great-grandfather, Jake Fairchild, to be that person.

"Jake was approached, perhaps very much like I am approaching you, and a deal was struck. Jake would agree to be the point of access, the keeper of the keys—figuratively speaking, of course—and further, he agreed to accept responsibility on behalf of the Fairchild family to pass that responsibility from father to oldest son, pretty much in perpetuity. In exchange, and this is very important, these wealthy and influential men undertook to help Jake establish this very firm, A. Holt Greenstick, and to guarantee that the firm would prosper, meaning of course, that the Fairchild family would prosper, through the difficult Depression years and well into the future. Certain capital funds were invested, including those to construct this building, and certain large contracts were issued that would never be subject to review. As I said, these were very influential men."

He had been watching her face for tells the entire time, but had seen none. So he was taken by surprise by her question.

"So, are you Lot Lizard, First Fan, or Straight Arrow?"

"Ah!" he exclaimed, not sure whether he should feel relieved of a burden just lifted or concerned about one just added. He smiled. "How much do you know?"

She paused briefly to study the path forward, then took up the question.

"Actually, my father never told me anything about any of this. You know I had an older brother, right? And I suspect Dad may have brought him into this little arrangement of yours, but I can't be sure. Seems likely. But Eddie was killed overseas in the military, so whatever he knew died with him. I will say that just a few days before Dad's stroke, he told me he had something important to discuss. Maybe he knew how little time he had, maybe not. I can't say."

Liz paused to wipe away a tear.

"Anyway, he died a couple of days later. Just dropped dead on the spot. And we never had that talk. So I don't really know what it was going to be about. At that point, there were some other family members in the area, but I was the obvious one to take care of all those things you have to take care of when someone passes. And I buried myself in all of that for a while. But we also had to keep the business running, and that fell on me as well. It was a pretty stressful time."

"I can only imagine," he offered with a sympathy she took as genuine.

"You're right about one thing, by the way. This is an old office full of old furniture in an old building. I did some painting and decorating just recently, but honestly, it's lipstick on a pig. The place was just full of old junk. I mean, it was chaos. So, once I felt like I had a handle on the big stuff, and that took a good while, I got down to cleaning out the small stuff. And when I was doing that, I pulled one of these desk drawers here out all the way, and it turned out there had been a false back. Behind it, I found an envelope and a set of keys. The keys were kind of odd, really big and they looked pretty old. As for the envelope, there wasn't a lot in it—some kind of logbook with dates and funny names on it, and a small slip of paper full of gibberish. Not much to go on. But when you started in with your story before, well, I took a guess that one of the weird names was probably you."

He smiled again. "Please allow me to introduce myself. I am Lot Lizard. I wish I could be less . . . circumspect, but that is simply the way these things have been handled for generations now. I apologize."

"Well, I guess I can't call you Liz for short, since that name's taken. Mr. Lizard would be an option, I suppose. But I'll just call you Lot, if that's okay."

That broke the tension that had been building slowly for the past few minutes. The man smiled and nodded his assent.

"Liz," he said, picking up the new informality between the two of them. "Do you know what the keys are for?"

"Doors?"

"Yes, I guess I deserved that. But what I meant was, do you know which doors? Where they are?"

Liz was deciding on the fly just how open she should be with this man. Not very, she decided. At least not yet. "Well, I confess, I have been very curious about that. But like I said, my dad didn't tell me anything at all. And they do seem way too big to fit any of the locks on regular doors."

He missed the nuance of her statement, a classic nondenial denial if ever there was one.

"Liz, I can help you with that. But before I do, we need to have a serious little business talk. My colleagues and I find ourselves in a bit of an awkward spot, because the plan that was in place to control access to our . . . let's call it an archive . . . to our archive has simply fallen apart. It seems to have ended inadvertently when your father passed. And we would very much like to renew it with you for some time into the future. We would like to leave our treasures in place, and for you to serve as our gatekeeper. This would require complete discretion on your part, but otherwise the duties are small and infrequent. In exchange, we are fully prepared to honor the other side of the original deal, and to continue supporting your landscaping business. If that is agreeable, and all I require is your word because your family has acted nothing but honorably for many years, then I will gladly explain some things to you about how this works."

"I'm open to that, I guess, though this is all a bit overwhelming. You're not asking me to do anything illegal, are you?"

"No, ma'am. Nothing illegal. But something very important. Very important."

"Okay, what's the deal?"

Again, he missed the nuance, in this instance the commitment not made. He was a smart man in such matters, usually, but perhaps not on his customary guard because he was dealing with a woman.

"The keys," he began, "lead to a series of doors. You will be their keeper, and nothing more. You must never ever use the keys, but only hand them to one of the members of our little group or one of our emissaries, and allow them to open the first door. Then you must reclaim the keys from that person as they depart, and keep them safe until the next time you are visited."

"But how do I know when someone is authorized to get into this door?"

"That is what the logbook you found is for. It goes back to the beginning of our little enterprise, and at any given moment, there will be four people who can receive the keys, the three members of the group and one designated intermediary. Everyone has a personal code name, and you will be advised whenever one of the names changes. You are to keep a record of that information, basically a roster, and a record of every time someone borrows the keys. Don't keep too many specifics, just code names and years. Do you understand?"

"Yes, but it seems to me there can be a gap where I do not have the name, er, the codename for someone who shows up and demands the keys."

"Right. Do you still have that other piece of paper, I think you called it a small slip or some such? Do you have that?"

"Yes, I just stuck everything back in the envelope."

"Good. What that really is, is a kind of backup system. It came out of the challenges that sentries used to use in the military back when this thing was started up. Whoever shows up, under any and all circumstances, should recite the first line to you. It's meaningless, I know. But it has to be said precisely. Then you reply with the second line, then the two of you repeat the process with the last two lines. At that point, you hand over the keys and show them the door."

"Okay. Now about that door."

"That's—"

"No," she interrupted. "I never finished answering your question before. About the keys. It's true, they do not fit any of the regular doors around here. But there is one they do fit, or one of them does."

Lot Lizard caught his breath, a feeling that was now coming with increasing regularity.

"There was another envelope my dad left in that same drawer. In it was a list of events that he seemed to think matched up with the dates in your envelope, or at least some of them. There at the end, he'd been doing some research online. Don't know why. Maybe he recognized somebody, maybe you, but I can't say. Anyway, all of these events had to do with the history of baseball—mainly scandals or other bad news. Remember that I did not know anything about any of this. So it was all very mysterious, especially the part about the keys. I looked and looked, but like I said, they didn't seem to fit any of the locks I found. But then, when I was having the office painted, I found the secret door." She pointed over her shoulder. "I assume you know about that."

"Yes." This was getting worse by the second. "Tell me you didn't open the door."

"That door, and the next door, and the next door."

He waited for her to admit to having breached the safe, but she didn't say any more.

"And I take it you know what's down there."

"I do."

"Oh, dear. That complicates things more than a little. You are privy to information that almost no one in the world has seen. And it's information that, if it fell into the wrong hands, could destroy professional baseball, maybe forever. Liz, please tell me that yours are not the wrong hands."

"Lot, I have no interest in destroying the game of baseball. Honestly, I couldn't care less. It's not on my radar. And at this point, I am not even sure exactly what's down there in your archive. I mean, I know there's a lot of it and it's not good, but I haven't been sitting down there and reading every word in all those boxes. I do have a business to run."

"Thank God," said Lot Lizard, grasping at any available straw, and yet again overlooking the nuance in her remark.

"It seems, then, as if we have a bargain, although you are probably the first Fairchild in more than a century to know its full form and implications. Thank you. And I know you are busy, so I will let you get back to work. And let me say, I find you a remarkable woman, and I am much relieved."

As he stood to leave, she stood to shake his proffered hand. That jogged his memory.

"Oh, yes. One more thing. There is still the matter of a line of succession for your family. We'll have to talk that through a bit. But I can't help but notice that you are expecting. When's the happy event?"

"A few months yet. My boyfriend and I are working through a lot of details in the meantime, as you can imagine."

"Boy or girl?"

"Boy. We just found out a short time ago."

"And who's the lucky fellow? Who's the daddy, if you don't mind my asking."

"He lives down in the City. His name is Adam. Adam Wallace." The room was silent for a moment.

"Adam Wallace, the writer?" he asked.

"Yes, that's my guy. You've heard of him?"

Lot Lizard sat back down.

Stealing Home

Slowly the squares on the large video display filled with the faces of the principal owners of the thirty clubs. Within five minutes of the announced start time of the session, everyone was present or represented by a fully empowered proxy. The commissioner unmuted his microphone.

"Ladies and gentlemen, thank you for making the time on short notice for this extraordinary meeting. I am about to share with you some information and notice of a course of action. I do so after extensive consultation with, and with the full concurrence of, your Executive Council.

"Before I begin, let me say that this is an item of business that, for purposes of both discussion and security, we would normally consider only in a closed, in-person gathering. Time and other circumstances render that impossible. However, know that I have taken every possible step to assure the security of this video conference, and I have, in hand, written statements from each of you certifying that no other person is in the room with you or has any other form of access to this feed and that you will not be recording. A violation of that agreement will result in your immediate expulsion from the Game.

"I intend to proceed as follows. I will make a statement summarizing the matters before us. I will then invoke the following governing authorities: First, the authority granted to the Commissioner under Article Two, Section Three of the Major League Constitution, to which all of you are signatories, to act as required in the best interests of Baseball. Second, the specification in Article Two, Section Four that, notwithstanding any other limitations, the Commissioner is empowered to act, and I quote, 'on any matter that involves the integrity of, or public confidence in, the national game of Baseball.' Third, the right of the Executive Council as stated in Article Three, Section Two, Paragraph C, and again I will quote, 'to exercise full power and authority over all other matters pertaining to the Major League Clubs,' and it goes on a bit.

"At that point, we will allocate not more than five minutes to any of you who cares to comment. Following these comments, we will vote on a single, unified proposal as recommended by the Executive Council. Portions of this proposal are required under our Constitution to receive a written vote. Accordingly, we will ask that you submit your vote by email within a designated five-minute period, including your full name and the electronic designator assigned to your team. Counsel advises that this will meet the constitutional requirement. We will then announce the result and proceed accordingly."

The commissioner paused for a sip of water.

"Let me begin. Two days ago, I received a communication from a trusted friend of the game. He was, in effect, passing along a message from the Chair of the Senate Select Committee on Sports and Antitrust. In sum, the Senator was advising us that a subcommittee has scheduled for the week after next the first of what may be a series of hearings on aspects of Baseball as a business, including, specifically, the antitrust exemption. We are informed that the full committee has an interest in this matter and believes there is ample evidence to eliminate the exemption. The Senator also referenced in passing, albeit with a demurral, which I think in the circumstances we can take as an implied threat, the potential for some form of RICO action against the Game. It seems likely I will receive a subpoena to participate in one or more of these hearings, as may some of you.

"We are also informed that the subcommittee has an extensive file of particulars regarding certain unsavory events in the history, including the very recent history, of our game. Many of these are known to the public, but those of you who have served on the Executive Committee over the years know that there have been certain other occurrences that have been successfully held in confidence. Incidentally, in your comments later, please do *not* reference any such matters specifically. Further, the Senator has asked that we be informed that it is these very matters which will be the subject of the initial hearing. His point, clearly, is that our game, our personal reputations, and our collective fortunes are in immediate jeopardy. Our own attorneys advise that we take this possibility seriously. I need not tell you how fragile our standing with our fan base is at the present moment. In effect, the Senator appears to be using that vulnerability to maximize his leverage.

"That brings me to the question: What does he really want? Does he really want to destroy the game, or is there some other agenda at work? As it happens, the Senator has left no doubt as to the answer to that question. The Senator wants to be Commissioner of Baseball, and he wants to be granted a one-percent share of each of your clubs. If we agree, and if certain other conditions not involving ourselves are met, he will terminate the Senate's inquiry."

It was a good thing the other thirty microphones were muted. Still, the commissioner could read the faces of some of his colleagues, and some of the lips as well.

"As soon as I received these demands, I convened a meeting of the Executive Committee, and as you can imagine, a vigorous discussion ensued. I assure you that we weighed every possible response, including some that no doubt match what you are feeling right now. At the end of the day, however, we were left with our constitutional obligation to protect the best interests of Baseball. And, given the delicate situation of our public standing today, the likelihood that the Senator has the resources and the ability to do further damage to our interests, and our historic vulnerability on the antitrust front, not to mention other areas of potential legal liability that might be revealed through a public inquiry, we have determined that we have no choice but to accede to his demands.

"We reached the unanimous conclusion that, onerous as his demands may be, they pale by comparison to the financial damage that will be done, not only to the Game, but to each of your organizations as a result of the revelations that might emerge from the threatened Senate hearings. An estimated multiple of ten to twenty times is not unreasonable, meaning that the known cost here could be only five to ten percent of the cost of standing pat and declining the Senator's, ah, suggestion. Is it extortion? Yes. There is no doubt of that. Yet it may make considerable financial sense to yield. Those of you who have studied our history will know that this will not be the first time we have danced with the devil in service to a greater good.

"Accordingly, pending your vote to accept the plan of action I am about to set forth, I intend to step aside as commissioner in order to expedite a transition to new leadership. I have immensely enjoyed leading this organization, and I value my association with each and every one of you. Whatever our disagreements, I have always tried to be a worthy steward of the Game. In that same spirit, I now believe I must stand aside.

"As for the demand for partial ownership, the Executive Council considered several mechanisms to effect that, and concluded that the best and fairest would be to establish a special 'Ownership Interest Account' in the commissioner's office similar to the Major League Central Fund but comprising shares of each club rather than monetary contributions. Recognizing that it will take more than a few days to effect the necessary agreements and transfers at the club level, and also recognizing the need to assure that each club participates, with your assent, we will propose to the Senator a ninety-day period for completion of this process, after which, as a condition of his employment, he will be entitled to transfer the holdings of the Ownership Interest Account to his own personal account. Because he would be the commissioner at that time, with full authority over disposition of this account but also because he is surely cognizant of the complications involved in thirty separate transactions within separate and distinct leadership structures, we are optimistic that he will accept this counterproposal.

"Knowing that the Senator is unmarried and has no close family, our negotiating team will work to incorporate a rescission clause in the terms of employment to provide that, upon his passing, the Senator's ownership interest in each of the thirty clubs is to revert to the owners at that time in a manner to be determined by each organization. In other words, we will try to structure this as a temporary arrangement that will terminate upon the Senator's passing. That would mean that, in the long run, there is no enduring cost of this dilution of control to the ownership of the respective clubs. We cannot predict the outcome of that effort, but we are, again, optimistic.

"Those of you who are both managing and controlling partners in your clubs will have the easiest path here. The remainder of you, and I know there are many, will have to carry this action within your respective ownership groups, and, I hasten to add, you will need to do so without making any reference to the reasons for doing so. If we were to agree to the Senator's terms and then leak the rationale ourselves, we would suffer the most adverse consequences of *both* worlds. So please just say that the action is required due to exigent circumstances and for the good of the Game.

"Here, then, is the proposal for your consideration. 'Be it Resolved that Major League Baseball will (1) accept my resignation as Commissioner; (2) name the Senator as the new Commissioner of Baseball; (3) create within the Office of the Commissioner an Ownership Interest Fund to be capitalized by each club within ninety days with shares amounting to one percent of that club's total ownership interest; (4) distribute to the Commissioner at the end of the ninety-day period the full balance of shares within the Ownership Interest Fund as a deferred employment incentive; and (5) attempt to incorporate in any agreement with the new Commissioner such forms of mitigation and limitation as we are able to achieve.'

"Using the previously stated authorities, I now submit this proposal for a vote. We'll open the floor for discussion, subject to the five-minute rule. If you wish to speak, please indicate on the sidebar as usual and wait to be recognized."

One of the advantages of chairing a remote meeting like this one, the commissioner knew, was the ability of the Chair to control the flow of discussion through the ordering of his recognition of speakers. And in this instance, he knew with certainty where eight of the owners stood—the eight who constituted the Executive Committee. To get things started in the right direction, he recognized first one, then a second, of these individuals whom he knew to be generally respected by their peers and articulate in stating a case. Both had been forewarned, and both did their jobs well. By the time he opened the discussion more broadly, the wind that had blown through the larger group when they first learned of the problem at hand had dropped to a relatively gentle breeze, and in the end, only a handful of the other owners chose to express themselves.

"Seeing no further requests for time, I would welcome a call of the question." This was also prearranged and easily accomplished. "Ladies and gentlemen, you have five minutes to cast your votes by email. You are, as we like to say in happier circumstances, on the clock. I strongly urge you to cast an affirmative vote."

At almost the same moment, another, much smaller, video conference was getting underway. Three framed faces filled the screens. This time, however, the vessels in question seemed to be coffee mugs rather than crystalware.

"Gentlemen," said the organizer, "our tradition. I give you the GameKeepers." All three participants raised their beverages in silent accord.

"I wanted to get back to you on the actions I have taken following our last meeting. I thought this video conference would suffice, but if either of you so desires, we can get together in person once again.

"I went up to Cooperstown and met with the Fairchild woman. Her name is Elizabeth—she goes by Liz—and I found her both charming and engaging. She was also rather coy, which may serve us well in the future. But it turns out that her father had not, in fact, brought her into the loop on our affairs, though he may well have intended to do so at a dinner meeting that he did not, alas, live to attend. In the interim, however, Ms. Fairchild found our keys, our logbook, and a note with our coded exchange. In due course, and apparently inadvertently, she also found the doorway. Here is where it gets complicated.

"Not knowing of her family's commitment, she used the keys and found the archive. She did spend some time with the materials, enough to become generally familiar with their nature, but I do not believe she took the time to study them in depth, nor do I think she has a particular interest in the subject matter. Having all three keys, she obviously would have also discovered the vault door, but I have no reason to believe she figured out the combination or opened that particular door—or even that she tried to do so.

"After those revelations, she and I had a very candid conversation, during which she expressed a willingness to continue our relationship, though obviously there will be some details to work out since she, unlike any of her forbears, has some sense of what she is guarding.

"There is another complication. Ms. Fairchild is, ah, with child, which, under the circumstances, would seem to be advantageous for us as it points toward a resumption of our continuity plan. However, the father, by coincidence, is one Adam Wallace, the same fellow who wrote that book about the Cobb-Mathewson papers. Mr. Wallace, it turns out, is also aware of the archive and its contents. Ms. Fairchild and I had a very forthright conversation about the issues of confidentiality and generational change. She understands, I think, her own responsibilities and promised to have a heart-to-heart discussion with Wallace about whether and how they would deal with this matter going forward. I expect to hear back from her after they do that, but I really am optimistic, and I think for now that we should proceed on that basis."

He paused to give time for discussion but saw that both of his companions, though evidently glum, were nodding their assent. So he continued.

"I have also given considerable thought to how we might best handle the Senator. He may very well know something about what is in our collection of papers. Some things he probably knows with some degree of certainty. I would, for example, put the most recent auction acquisition in that category, because we know he has spoken of it with the Marbury House people as well as with our friends at the Hall of Fame. And, of course, there is the Wallace book. So, chances are he has a fairly detailed knowledge of that material, excluding, of course, those items we added to the file from our own collection. There is little point in making any effort to mask that material, and doing so could be consequentially counterproductive.

"Then there are things he may know, may think he knows, or may have heard some reference to—in other words, areas where his knowledge is uncertain. For example, he made specific reference to Luna, though he cannot know for sure that we have materials on such a matter, or what those materials might be. We can, with hopefully minimal risk, simply deny that we possess any such records.

"And finally, there are parts of the archive of which he is almost certainly totally ignorant. We cannot be certain what specific information is in any of these categories, but we can make educated guesses.

"One thing we can be pretty sure he does not know about is the location of the archive, our system of access, our coded exchanges, and our keeper of the keys. He has never made any reference to any of that information, either directly or indirectly. We can assume, safely I judge, that he must take for granted, therefore, that we simply keep these materials under lock and key in some typical secure location and that we access them directly.

"With that in mind, I suggest that we follow a two-track strategy. On the first track, we should retain our membership as it is now—the three of us—and keep in place all of the practices and safeguards we and our predecessors have always used. We will retain the physical archive in Cooperstown and keep the most sensitive materials there, just as we have for many years. I will simply inform Tres of the change in management at the Fairchild end, and we'll go on as always.

"On the second track, we should form a sort of shadow organization with a different name, say, The Baseball Stewardship Council, into which we will admit the Senator. I know one of you has already expressed a strong antipathy to working with the Senator, and that is a perfect opportunity to create what appears to be a vacancy that makes way for the Senator to join. I am reasonably sure he'll buy that. In fact, that particular resignation"—he glanced at the camera with a slight smile, which was returned on one-third of his screen—"will probably add credibility to the proposal. We will move a few items from Cooperstown into a different storage facility, but primarily those items we think he already knows about or that represent little real contemporary threat to the game. Those items will constitute what he will, hopefully, believe to be our entire collection. In the basement of my office building, there is a secure storage area that should serve this purpose nicely. There may be other items that he suspects we hold, but we can simply deny that and suggest that some wealthy private collector or other may have them.

"With this in mind, after my conversation with Ms. Fairchild, I rented a small truck and went back to the archive. I removed a small number of files, two from the vault, including those obtained through the last auction, which he knows about, and those in the Steever file, which he alluded to having heard about as a rumor and which are, at this point in time, relatively harmless, and the remainder from the general collection. Um, I took the Black Sox because, at this point, the confidential material would be of minimal interest except to historians—that damage was done long ago—and the Dutch Leonard file because some fellow wrote a book about that a couple of years ago. I took the Beer Night file. Those guys are mostly all dead now anyway, and I figured our friend would enjoy the read. Plus two of the drug cases that were mostly public. Those files are now stored in the basement here.

"If this arrangement works for you, gentlemen, I will proceed to implement the remaining steps. We'll need to reconvene once I have had a further conversation with our new key master, er, mistress, but that is not urgent for now. Your thoughts?"

Straight Arrow was the first to respond. "I always knew you were a cagy bastard, but this is sheer brilliance. I only hope I can keep a straight face in dealing with that son-of-a-bitch!"

"Fortunately, I won't have to do that," said First Fan. "This is elegant. Make it happen."

Every so often, especially when he was puzzling out some new argument or plot for his writing, Adam would turn off his cell phone and decouple from the grid for a few hours, walk over to Central Park, and lose himself in his thoughts as he rambled more or less aimlessly. He would eventually find himself at his favorite coffee bar for a restorative jolt of caffeine, then return home to his computer to try to capture the surge of ideas in his head. This time, with visions of archived files swimming in his head, he was all but overwhelmed by the potentialities.

When he turned the cell phone on once again, he noticed the icon for a voicemail. Dialing through, he heard this message.

"Adam! Please call me! We need to talk!"

The tenor of Liz's voice sent a chill down his spine. He brought up her number and pushed "Dial."

———

The voice on the other end of the line was not friendly.

"You and your colleagues appear to believe that I am not serious about what I said, and that you can simply run out the clock on me. I assure you, that is a mistaken belief. Continue as you are, and all will come to grief."

"I assure you, Senator, that we—they—are doing no such thing. These are complex matters and they take time to resolve. I can tell you that the teams have held a meeting and reached a decision. I am not a part of that process, as you know, but I must assume that their position has been conveyed to you, or will be shortly. If that matter is resolved to your satisfaction, I am sure the remainder of the agenda can be addressed successfully as well."

"In other words, you and your little cabal are not doing a damn thing until you have to."

"Senator, I did not say that."

"Listen. In two days, I *will* convene a hearing of the subcommittee, and I *will* be sure to include some very revealing testimony. After that, you can expect a rising crescendo of bad news week after week, then a shift to a review of the antitrust exemption with some very high-profile witnesses, followed by a recommendation to the full committee. And if that does not make the point, why, we'll just move on to looking at racketeering. You and your friends do not want to mess with me."

"Believe me, Senator, everyone understands the stakes here, and everyone takes them, and you, quite seriously. There is a great deal of interest in resolving this amicably."

"Listen, I neither know nor care about 'amicable.' I know what I want, and I intend to get it. Or I intend to exercise my legislative responsibility to protect the American people from the misdeeds of the miscreants who run and profit from this unduly privileged enterprise. You are on notice. Good day, sir."

———

Casey at the Bat
Ernest Lawrence Thayer

The outlook wasn't brilliant for the Mudville nine that day;
the score stood four to two, with but one inning more to play.
And then when Cooney died at first, and Barrows did the same,
a sickly silence fell upon the patrons of the game.

A straggling few got up to go in deep despair. The rest
clung to that hope which springs eternal in the human breast;
they thought, if only Casey could get but a whack at that—
they'd put up even money, now, with Casey at the bat.

But Flynn preceded Casey, as did also Jimmy Blake,
and the former was a lulu and the latter was a cake,
so upon that stricken multitude grim melancholy sat,
for there seemed but little chance of Casey's getting to the bat.

But Flynn let drive a single, to the wonderment of all,
and Blake, the much despised, tore the cover off the ball;
and when the dust had lifted, and the men saw what had occurred,
there was Jimmy safe at second and Flynn a-hugging third.

Then from five thousand throats and more there rose a lusty yell;
it rumbled through the valley, it rattled in the dell;
it knocked upon the mountain and recoiled upon the flat,
for Casey, mighty Casey, was advancing to the bat.

There was ease in Casey's manner as he stepped into his place;
there was pride in Casey's bearing and a smile on Casey's face.
And when, responding to the cheers, he lightly doffed his hat,
no stranger in the crowd could doubt 'twas Casey at the bat.

Ten thousand eyes were on him as he rubbed his hands with dirt;
five thousand tongues applauded when he wiped them on his shirt.
Then while the writhing pitcher ground the ball into his hip,
defiance gleamed in Casey's eye, a sneer curled Casey's lip.

And now the leather-covered sphere came hurtling through the air,
and Casey stood a-watching it in haughty grandeur there.
Close by the sturdy batsman the ball unheeded sped—
"That ain't my style," said Casey. "Strike one," the umpire said.

From the benches, black with people, there went up a muffled roar,
like the beating of the storm-waves on a stern and distant shore.
"Kill him! Kill the umpire!" shouted someone on the stand;
and it's likely they'd have killed him had not Casey raised his hand.

With a smile of Christian charity great Casey's visage shone;
he stilled the rising tumult; he bade the game go on;
he signaled to the pitcher, and once more the spheroid flew;
but Casey still ignored it, and the umpire said: "Strike two."

"Fraud!" cried the maddened thousands, and Echo answered fraud;
but one scornful look from Casey and the audience was awed.
They saw his face grow stern and cold, they saw his muscles strain,
and they knew that Casey wouldn't let that ball go by again.

The sneer is gone from Casey's lip, his teeth are clenched in hate;
he pounds with cruel violence his bat upon the plate.
And now the pitcher holds the ball, and now he lets it go,
and now the air is shattered by the force of Casey's blow.

Oh, somewhere in this favored land the sun is shining bright;
the band is playing somewhere, and somewhere hearts are light,
and somewhere men are laughing, and somewhere children shout;
but there is no joy in Mudville—mighty Casey has struck out.

—————

"The Committee will come to order. The witnesses will be sworn."

Following these preliminaries, the Chair took control of the proceedings. This was easy because he was, in fact, the only senator present, this being a Friday, when senators typically were in their home states, and his colleagues had been assured that nothing of significance would occur. Such grandstanding events were a commonplace of Congress, and potential bit players generally appreciated being given fair warning in advance so that they might put their own time to more productive use.

"This is a joint hearing of the Subcommittee on Baseball Affairs and the Subcommittee on Investigations of the Senate Select Committee on Sports and Antitrust. This hearing is being conducted under the investigative authorization dated March 1 of this year. The hearing will be arranged in panels. Witnesses will be afforded an opportunity to offer brief introductory statements, after which time questioning will commence.

"Our first panel today comprises representatives of the New York auction company, Marbury House. Mr. Tomhoff, Mr. Marchant, welcome. Is either of you gentlemen accompanied by counsel?"

"Mr. Chairman." A man seated in the first row directly behind the witness table rose to speak. "I am Philip Houston, attorney for Marbury House Auctioneers. I am here today, representing both of these witnesses. And I ask that the record show that both Mr. Tomhoff and Mr. Marchant are here today voluntarily."

"Thank you, Mr. Houston. Let the record so indicate. Now, Mr. Tomhoff, would you identify yourself for the record, please, and make any opening statement you might wish?"

"Thank you, ah, Mr. Chairman. My name is Maxwell K. Tomhoff, and I am the Auction Master for Marbury House Auctioneers. In that capacity, I am a senior executive in the sales department, and I also conduct certain of the more important sales during the year. My understanding is that my colleague and I are present today to provide whatever information we each have regarding some specific items that were sold at auction in 2021.

"In the auction business, we often combine several items with common elements into groupings we term 'lots.' The items we are referencing today were identified at sale as 'Lot 21-143B7' and included two World War I-era military documents, several letters bearing signatures of well-known athletes and others, and some manuscript pages and several handwritten notebooks that had belonged to a prominent sports journalist of the 1930s. There was vigorous bidding, and the sale ended with a strike price of $7.8 million, not including the buyer's commission. I will do my best to answer the committee's questions regarding this sale."

"Thank you, Mr. Tomhoff. And now, Mr. Marchant, if you would identify yourself for the record and then feel free to make any statement you have prepared."

"Thank you, Mr. Chairman," Frederick said with a nervous quaver in his voice. He was more obvious than Max as he read from the script

Philly-Hugh had prepared for him. "I am Frederick Marchant, and I am Director of Acquisitions for Marbury House. I am responsible for meeting with prospective sellers and for acquiring on consignment the merchandise that we later sell at our auctions. It was I who acquired the items that would later be included in Lot 21-143B7.

"I also work closely with our in-house team to coordinate the evaluation of objects and their provenance before they are brought forward for sale to the public. In the business, we refer to this as the process of conducting due diligence. We routinely seek outside verification of the authenticity of items, and we do our best to assure that the seller has the legal right to act in that capacity. In the case of Lot 21-143B7, our due diligence included such steps as consulting with baseball historians at the Hall of Fame and elsewhere, with military historians, and with experts in such factors as inks and papers. We also confirmed the identities of the sellers. In addition, because the items in question were what we would term 'barn finds,' which is to say, they came with no written chain of custody, we contracted with a firm to search all available records to determine if they had ever been reported missing or stolen. They had not. Mr. Chairman, I will do my best to answer your questions."

"Thank you, Mr. Marchant. Mr. Tomhoff, let me begin the questioning with you. One thing you did not mention in your opening statement was the name of the purchaser of this particular collection of items. We are all curious about who would spend that kind of money to buy some old baseball papers."

"Mr. Chairman, the purchaser wished to remain anonymous."

"Does that mean you know who the buyer was and are protecting his or her identity? Or does it mean that you actually have no idea who purchased those things?"

"Senator, I, that is to say, we at Marbury House, do not know the name of the purchaser. The purchaser wished to act anonymously."

"And is that unusual, Mr. Tomhoff?"

"Senator, it is not as unusual as you might think, especially in high-dollar bidding like this. People have many reasons for remaining anonymous. Some are simply averse to publicity. Some have concerns that the security of the goods they acquire at auction might be compromised if their identity were known. Some may actually be bidding on behalf of some unnamed third party. As I said, sir, many reasons."

"And would those reasons include hiding one's identity to mask the laundering of ill-gotten gains by converting, say, offshore cash to valuable objects that then might be re-sold at a later date?"

"I suppose that could happen."

"And Marbury House doesn't care about that?"

"Senator, we accept responsibility for the goods we sell at auction, and we make sure to the extent possible that a purchaser has the ability to conclude the transaction."

"That they have the money to do the deal."

"Yes, sir. Exactly."

"And how do you do that?"

"Senator, above a certain threshold, which I believe is $50,000, we ask prospective purchasers to provide proof of funds, much in the way that a realtor might ask that before selling a property."

"And did you do that with this purchaser?"

Philip Houston tapped Max on the shoulder before he could respond, and whispered in his ear.

"No, sir, we did not."

"And why is that? I mean, by the time you figured in the buyer's commission, this person was spending close to ten million dollars. Surely that's more than $50,000. Why didn't you ask for their bona fides?"

"Senator, we already knew this purchaser from previous auctions, and we were confident in the purchaser's ability to pay."

"You knew this purchaser. By name?"

"No, sir, they were anonymous in every instance. But we had their banking information on file."

"So you are saying that this buyer, this anonymous buyer, had been something of a regular customer?"

"Well, not in the sense of being a frequent purchaser, Senator. But the purchaser was known to us."

"All right, let's explore that for a moment. And let's just take the last . . . ten years. The last ten years. How many purchases has Mr. or Ms. Anonymous made during that time? More than ten?"

"I would have to check the records, sir, but I think not more than ten."

"Five?"

Houston again leaned in and offered some advice.

"It's only a guess, Senator, but I would say perhaps three times in the last ten years. We could certainly find out and share that information with the committee."

"Excellent. Would you do that, please? Say, by the end of next week? And while you are at it, would you be good enough to go back as far as your records of dealings with this particular purchaser permit? Thank you. Now, with respect to the three recent purchases you know of, were they all of baseball memorabilia, sports memorabilia more generally, or other sorts of objects altogether, like, say, fine art?"

"Senator, I believe that all were of baseball memorabilia."

"And were these generally things like, say, baseball cards or autographs, or perhaps game-used jerseys, the sort of thing that most baseball collectors seem to covet?"

"To the best of my recollection, Senator, and again we can confirm all of this from our records, but to the best of my recollection, no. This collector appeared to have an interest in more complex records of events in baseball history."

"So they weren't collecting record-book kinds of things or sentimental mementos so much as files of information about various events that have occurred in the course of baseball history. Is that your testimony?"

"Yes, Senator."

"Now let me ask you to remember as much as you can, and tell me in some detail what was in those files."

Immediately upon asking the question, the Senator held up his hand for the witness to delay his response. An aide, who had been standing behind him and to the side waiting for just this signal, stepped forward and handed him a slip of paper. The Senator made a great show of reading the contents of the note.

"Mr. Tomhoff, Mr. Marchant. I must beg your indulgence. But an urgent matter of Senate business has just arisen, and I'm afraid I must attend to it. The committee stands in recess for twenty minutes." And he tapped his gavel.

Half an hour or so passed slowly.

"What do you think, CI? Have we let them stew long enough?"

"Boss, one more degree of heat and I think you'd have them at full boil."

"They deserve it, the sons of bitches. They had a lot of damn gall trying to bargain with me. You can bet your ass they've been watching the hearing. Let's give them another minute or two to wonder what was in the note. We ought to be through here in a half hour or so. Got plans for the weekend?"

"I was thinking I might head out to my place on the Eastern Shore and do a little fishing. I know you think I'm crazy, but for some reason cleaning fish guts relaxes me. And you?"

"It kind of depends. If these guys screw with me, I think I will spend the weekend with my buddy Jack Daniels and see if we can come up with a good way to screw them back. If they fall in line, and I think they will after what we just got on the record, then I might just take a run up to Cooperstown and wander through the Hall of Fame. Kind of like checking out the back forty, if you know what I mean."

"I loved the way you slipped in the money laundering reference, and you got the auction people to agree to a deep search of their records."

"Yeah. Well, best to strike while the iron is hot. Let's return the call to the commissioner first, then the other one."

CI dialed a number. "The Senator is returning the commissioner's call."

A new voice came on the line. "Senator, thank you for returning my call. Needless to say, we have been watching the hearing."

That was the equivalent of a bend of the knee to the power, and it came without prompting. The Senator knew right at that moment that he had won.

"Listen, I saw this so-called counteroffer of yours, and it's a no-go. I'll give your people thirty days, not ninety, to get their act together, and I won't sign anything until they do. And until I sign something, I am still a very powerful United States Senator with a very prickly burr under my saddle. Do I make myself clear?"

"Yes, sir. Yes, you do. And I can tell you that we will accept your terms."

"Excellent. And, I must say, very wise. I will expect a formal offer letter bearing your signature and stating the terms of our agreement on my desk, at least as an email attachment, within thirty minutes."

"It will be there. And may I say—" The line went dead.

"Let's get the other call done."

"Is he available? The Senator is returning his call."

Lot Lizard came on the line. "Senator."

"You probably know, or you shortly will, that you are now speaking to the soon-to-be Commissioner of Baseball."

"So that portion of your demand has been satisfied?"

"It has. Have you been watching the hearing?" He respected the man for forcing him to ask, though he knew the answer.

"I've caught a few minutes of it, mainly the formalities. I was pulled away for some business. How's it going?"

"You know damn well how it's going. The only thing yet to be determined is whether I let that pompous auctioneer fellow answer the next question and the next and the next. You really don't want that to happen."

"You're correct. We really do not want that to happen. I can tell you that our little group has met, and we have agreed to bring you on as a member. We have a standing rule that there will be no more than three of us at any given time, so to make room for you, one of the current members will drop out."

"Not you. You've got balls, and you know everything there is to know about this arrangement and about what, exactly, you guys have been protecting all these years. Until I can get into all of that, I need you to stick around. After that, we'll talk about it."

"No, Senator," he replied, the bile rising in his throat. He did not like being treated this way. Did not like it at all. And, he thought to himself, the Senator might have just made his first mistake. "It won't be me. One of my colleagues has graciously volunteered to yield his position."

"I can guess which one. Didn't want to sully his good name by being associated with me, I'd wager. What a wuss. Now, as I understand it, this is all sort of an informal thing, and I can see that we ought not to do this in writing. So you give me your word. And so help me, if you lie to me and this doesn't happen, you will be one miserable bastard for the rest of your short life. Do I make myself clear?"

"You do, Senator. But that's quite unnecessary. You have my word that we will follow through on this commitment."

"Very well. You can expect to hear from me."

As he hung up the phone, CI pointed to a newly arrived email from the Office of the Commissioner of Baseball. It seemed that the commissioner had not needed anything like half an hour to draft his letter. It was probably ready to go before the two men had spoken.

The recess had lasted for more than twice as long as expected, but then a few staffers drifted back into the hearing room and word was dispatched to the witnesses and their attorney. They returned to their places, reporters and technicians resumed their positions beside and behind the several video cameras, and those spectators who had taken advantage of the unexpected break to stretch their legs found themselves scrambling to fill the seats at the back of the room that had been vacated by those whose legs did not require stretching and who had used the opportunity to improve their vantage points.

Finally, the Senator entered the room. Without resuming his seat, he picked up his gavel, ticked it on the purpose-made wooden block, and announced, "This hearing is indefinitely adjourned, subject to the call of the Chair." Then he turned and departed.

In the stunned silence that followed, Max and Frederick turned to Philly-Hugh with expressions that said, in effect, "What just happened?" He simply spread his hands wide and commented, "Guys, welcome to the wondrous world of the United States Senate. Buy you some lunch?"

"Jason?"

"Yeah."

"Hey, it's Adam. It's been a long time. How the hell are you?"

"I'm good, I'm good. But I was starting to think you'd fallen off the end of the Earth. Everything okay?"

"Okay? Yeah, I guess you could say everything is okay. But a lot has happened since we had lunch a few months ago. You remember Liz?"

"The woman we went on that snipe hunt with? Yeah, sure. Why? You seeing her now?"

"You could say that. You probably don't remember, but when you left us to head back to the farm, you made some passing remark about us being a pair of lovebirds."

"Did I? Didn't mean anything by it."

"Well, funny thing about that. We have been pretty much together since that very day. In fact, we are planning to get married next month up in Cooperstown, and we really want you to be there. I need a Best Man. Think you can make it? We can make the date work for you."

"Are you kidding? That's terrific! Congratulations, old man! I'll come, but only if I get to kiss the bride."

Adam laughed, as did Liz, who was listening on the speakerphone.

"Yeah, you can kiss the bride, as long as you keep your hands to yourself. But be warned. You may have to lean in a bit. Liz is expecting a little Fairchild-Wallace before too long."

"No kidding?! Adam Wallace, a father? And at your advanced age? Boy or girl?"

"Boy. Adam Wallace, Jr."

"Wait a minute! I never agreed to that!"

"Hey, Liz, that you? This is great news. All of it. I can't wait to see you guys to celebrate. Just let me know when you set the date. And save me a cigar!"

"Count on it, buddy."

"Hey, Adam. As long as I have you, one more thing. I have to say I've been wondering. Did you guys ever find that secret door? Did you find Jocko's papers?"

There was a telling pause in the conversation.

"Whoever fights monsters should see to it that in the process he does not become a monster."

—Friedrich Nietzsche
Beyond Good and Evil, Aphorism 146

The Box Score

Acknowledgments

I want to thank Al Arrighi, Barry Mednick, and Michael A. Rice, all members of the Society for American Baseball Research, for sharing their thoughts on off-field heroes and villains of the game. This was particularly helpful in developing profiles for certain characters in this book. I am grateful as well to Jeff Blaugrund, who subjected himself to pre-final drafts of the book and helped make it better, and to Jim Brandon for helping to light a path forward. And thanks as well to fellow SABR member Tom Steich for sharing his personal memories of Ten Cent Beer Night and the subsequent melee on The Mall, a Cleveland public park near what was then Municipal Stadium.

Thanks once again to publisher Lawrence Knorr, my fabulous editor Sarah Peachey, divine designer Crystal Devine, and the rest of the crew at Sunbury Press. It is always nice to work with true professionals.

In the prequel to this volume, I thanked my wife Amy for her forbearance as I wrote yet another book. This time, though, I think she was secretly pleased to have me fully occupied and out of her hair during the months of the COVID-19 lockdown when this one was written. I am, nonetheless, appreciative.

Notes

Pg.	Note

3   The quote from Lyndon Johnson is reported in Lawrence W. Serewicz, *America at the Brink of Empire: Rusk, Kissinger, and the Vietnam War.* Baton Rouge: LSU Press, 2007, p. 31.

13   "even managed a few treats"—All of these products were available at the time. See https://www.thedailymeal.com/eat/oldest-snack-foods/ slide-5, found online August 26, 2021.

13   "an interesting couple of weeks"—This portion of the story draws on a map of the order of battle on November 11, 1918, the date of the Armistice, specifically Map 57 from the Tasker Howard Bliss collection of World War I maps in the Library of Congress, found online July 1, 2020 at https://www.loc.gov/resource/g5701s.ct004277/?r=0.353,0.534,0.434,0.378,0.

16   "thought it might come back any time"—Manheim, pp. 214-220.

19   "the AEF's part of something bigger"—AEF is a reference to the American Expeditionary Forces, the US component of the Allied Forces. The AEF was under the command of General John J. Pershing; Generals Hunter Liggett and Robert L. Bullard commanded I Corps and II Corps, respectively, which controlled two sectors along the main front at the time of the final Meuse-Argonne Offensive that led to the Armistice. See Faulkner, passim.

23   "keep the game on the up-and-up"—For a discussion of the systematic campaign waged by baseball insiders to control Babe Ruth, see Wehrle.

32   "Abner Doubleday on this very spot"—See the discussion of 1930s-era construction at Doubleday Field found online July 1, 2020 at https://www.doubleday-field.com/about-2/history/ construction-through-the-wpa-era/.

64   "various teams had attained major league status"—See https://en.wikipedia.org/wiki/Timeline_of_Major_League_Baseball, found online July 1, 2020.

64   "in his documentary film series on the game"—See https://www.pbs.org/ken-burns/baseball/timeline/, found online July 1, 2020.

64   "Then something called Timetoast.com"—See https://www.timetoast.com/time lines/history-of-baseball--7, found online July 19, 2021.

64   "a site called Timelines.ws"—See https://timelines.ws/subjects/Baseball.HTML, found online July 1, 2020.

64   "Scandals in Baseball History"—See Tylicki.

74 "beer played a part in the riot"—There is a very thorough discussion of this event found online July 1, 2020 at https://en.wikipedia.org/wiki/Ten_Cent_Beer_Night.

80 "and were therefore exempt"—Nathanson, passim, argues that Holmes did not exempt baseball from the law, per se, so much as conclude that the law simply did not apply to a collection of essentially local activities.

80 "it will have to be the Congress that does it"—See Grow for a detailed historical and legal analysis of this issue.

93 "The vault was all but empty"—For an overview of this "event," see https://en.wikipedia.org/wiki/The_Mystery_of_Al_Capone%27s_ Vaults, found online July 1, 2020.

96 "especially at night"—See the Department of State travel advisory found online July 1, 2020, at https://travel.state.gov/content/travel/en/traveladvisories/travel advisories/the-bahamas-travel-advisory.html.

99 "dirty execs and political slush funds"—See the very thorough overview of this scandal found online July 1, 2020, at https://en.wikipedia.org/wiki/Panama_Papers.

102 "then they'd NDA it"—An NDA is a non-disclosure agreement, a contract that binds whoever signs it not to reveal to anyone the information specified in the agreement.

111 "That was the real start of free agency"—See https://en.wikipedia.org/wiki/Curt_Flood, found online July 1, 2020.

112 "a PR disaster for the sport"—These incidents are described in https://en.wikipedia.org/wiki/1994–95_Major_League_Baseball_strike, found online July 1, 2020.

116 "a baseball crime in broad daylight"—For a typical commentary on views of the game in 2020, see Boswell.

121 "salt and pepper tossed in for good measure"—The bean soup tradition in the Senate traces back to the early 1900s. The list of ingredients here is actually an amalgam of two competing recipes, one historic and one contemporary. These recipes found online July 1, 2020, at https://www.senate.gov/reference/reference_item/bean_soup.htm.

131 "banning all Cuban products from the United States"—Salinger offers a first-person account.

149 "every manufacturer seems to apply the rules differently"—The variations are summarized at https://hoogerhydesafe.com/resources/combination-lock-dialing-procedures/, found online July 1, 2020.

156 "ten billion in annual revenues"—These data were found online July 1, 2020, at https://www.statista.com/statistics/193637/franchise-value-of-major-league-baseball-teams-in-2010/.

161 "compete against Harding in some big meet"—See the account of these events found online July 1, 2020, at https://en.wikipedia.org/wiki/ Tonya_Harding.

161 "spring training and a few early games"—See https://en.wikipedia.org/wiki/1994–95_Major_League_Baseball_strike, found online July 1, 2020.

162 "the baseball was redesigned"—See https://en.wikipedia.org/wiki/ Dead-ball_era; and https://en.wikipedia.org/wiki/Live-ball_era; found online September 6, 2020.

162 "around 1949 and 1950"—See Posnanski.

163 "there's been a lot of renewed suspicion"—For a summary of the most recent "juiced ball theory," see https://en.wikipedia.org/wiki/Juiced_ball_theory, found online September 6, 2020.

163 "I remember a news story"—Bradford, William Davis. "Major League Baseball secretly used two different types of baseballs last season," *Business Insider*, November 2021, found online January 15, 2022, at https://www.businessinsider.com/mlb-used-two-different-balls-in-2021-2021-11.

175 "our standing with our fan base"—For a sense of this standing circa 2020, see Boswell, passim, and Dougherty, passim.

Sources Consulted

Berg, Ted, et al. "The 100 most powerful people in MLB," *USA Today*, April 8, 2017, found online July 1, 2020 at https://www.usatoday. com/story/sports/mlb/2017/04/08/mlb-100-most-powerful-people/100172102/.

Bigelow, Michael E. "A Short History of Army Intelligence," *Military Intelligence* PB 34-12-3, July-September, 2012, pp. 1–59.

Boswell, Thomas. "Don't let MLB owners cry poor. They can afford to do what's right for baseball," *Washington Post*, June 15, 2020, found online at https://www.washingtonpost.com/sports/2020/06/15/dontlet-mlb-owners-cry-poor-they-can-afford-do-whats-right-baseball/.

Dougherty, Jesse. "Since Game 7 of the World Series, it has been all downhill for baseball," *Washington Post*, June 27, 2020, found online July 1, 2020 at https://www.washingtonpost.com/sports/2020/06/26/since-game-7-world-series-its-been-all-downhill-baseball/.

Chafets, Zev. *Cooperstown Confidential: Heroes, Rogues, and the Inside Story of the Baseball Hall of Fame*. New York: Bloomsbury, 2009.

Faulkner, Richard S. *The U.S. Army Campaigns of World War I: Meuse-Argonne, 26 September-11 November 1918*. Washington, DC: Center of Military History, United States Army, 2018, found online August 27, 2021, at https://history.army.mil/html/books/077/77-8/cmhPub_77-8.pdf.

Grow, Nathaniel. "Baseball's Antitrust exemption: A Primer," FanGraphs, June 4, 2015, found online July 1, 2020 at https://blogs.fangraphs.com/baseballs-antitrust-exemption-a-primer/.

Kahanowitz, Ian S. *Baseball Gods in Scandal: Ty Cobb, Tris Speaker, and the Dutch Leonard Affair*. South Orange, NJ: Summer Game Books, 2019.

Major League Baseball. *Constitution*. 2005. Found online July 1, 2020 at https://ip-mall.law.unh.edu/sites/default/files/hosted_resources/SportsEntLaw_Institute/League%20Constitutions%20&%20Bylaws/MLConsititutionJune2005Update.pdf.

Manheim, Jarol B. *Deja Vu: American Political Problems in Historical Perspective*. New York: St. Martin's Press, 1976.

Nathanson, Mitchell. "Who Exempted Baseball, Anyway? The Curious Development of the Antitrust Exemption That Never Was," *Journal of Sports and Entertainment Law* 4 (2013), pp. 1–50.

Pessah, Jon. *The Game: Inside the Secret World of Major League Baseball's Power Brokers.* New York: Little, Brown, 2015.

Posnanski, "Juiced Baseballs: A History," *JoeBlogs*, July 23, 2019, found online September 6, 2020, at https://joeposnanski.substack.com/p/ juiced-baseballs-a-history.

Reinsdorf, Jonathan M., "The Powers of the Commissioner in Baseball," *Marquette Sports Law Review* 7:1, Article 6, found online July 1, 2020 at https://scholarship. law.marquette.edu/cgi/viewcontent.cgi?article=1171&context=sportslaw.

Salinger, Pierre. "Great Moments: Kennedy, Cuba, Cigars," *Cigar Aficionado* 1, Autumn 1992, found online July 1, 2020 at https://www.cigaraficionado.com/article/ great-moments-kennedy-cuba-and-cigars-7840.

Thayer, Earnest Lawrence. "Casey at the Bat," originally published in the *The Daily Examiner*, San Francisco, California, June 3, 1888.

Tylicki, Dan. "MLB History: 20 Most Shocking Scandals in Baseball History," BleacherReport.com, November 18, 2011, found online July 1, 2020 at https://bleach-erreport.com/articles/941589-20-most-shocking-scandals-in-baseball-history.

Waller, Douglas. *Lincoln's Spies: Their Secret War to Save a Nation.* New York: Simon & Schuster, 2019.

Weber, Nicholas Fox. *The Clarks of Cooperstown: Their Singer Sewing Machine Fortune, Their Great and Influential Art Collections, Their Forty-Year Feud.* New York: Alfred A. Knopf, 2007.

Wehrle, Edmund F. *Breaking Babe Ruth: Baseball's Campaign Against Its Biggest Star.* Columbia: University of Missouri Press, 2018.

About the Author

J.B. Manheim is Professor Emeritus at The George Washington University, where he developed the world's first degree-granting program in political communication and was later founding director of the School of Media & Public Affairs. In 1995 he was named Professor of the Year for the District of Columbia. He learned his love of baseball watching Dizzy Dean broadcast the Game of the Week and huddling with his grandfather for warmth on July nights at The Mistake By The Lake, AKA, Cleveland Municipal Stadium, and renewed it when the National Pastime finally returned to the Nation's Capital. Manheim brings to life his expertise in propaganda and strategic communication through his fictional stories of baseball behind the scenes. His writing will lead you to question whether what you think you know about the history of the game and about the powers who control it is real, or whether it's just a carefully nurtured product of lies, deceptions, misdirection, and propaganda. JB Manheim is a member of the Society for American Baseball Research and the Internet Baseball Writers Association of America.

www.ingramcontent.com/pod-product-compliance
Lightning Source LLC
Chambersburg PA
CBHW012207030726
47494CB00023B/2555